The Fly Boys in London

The Fly Boys in London
A novel

Stanley Morgan

Hart-Davis, MacGibbon   London

Granada Publishing Limited
First published in Great Britain 1975 by
Hart-Davis, MacGibbon Ltd
Frogmore, St Albans, Hertfordshire AL2 2NF and
3 Upper James Street, London W1R 4BP

ISBN 0 246 10896 7

Printed in Great Britain by
Richard Clay (The Chaucer Press) Ltd
Bungay, Suffolk

For Desmond Elliott

Who helped so much to get THE FLY BOYS off the ground

I

To Leonard Mousehole, milkman, the heinous screech of low-flying jets was as familiar a sound as the inane out-pourings of pop music that emanated from the tiny tinny tranny dangling from his rear-view mirror. Leonard's milk round encompassed the sprawling and breathtakingly unlovely Golden Vale housing estate situated on the eastern-most perimeter of the town of Reading, which lies deep in the heart of British Berkshire and directly beneath the flight-path of American air-traffic descending rapidly for London's Heathrow Airport.

So familiar, indeed, was the earth-trembling roar of these monsters that it barely intruded upon Leonard's concentration as he went about his milkman's tasks, collecting bottles from his electric van and delivering them on the run to four hundred and eighteen Golden Vale doorsteps.

And yet, at ten o'clock that clear and beautiful July morning, with not a single recalcitrant cloud despoiling the virgin perfection of a cobalt sky, something about the Goliath that thundered overhead attracted Leonard's attention, caused him, as he stepped from his van with a fully loaded milk-crate, to look up, miss his footing ... and drop the lot.

The crash of shattering glass brought Miss Mabel Sewet, retired school mistress and professional know-all, scurrying down the path of number 216, hands a-flutter at the sight of Leonard hopping around on one foot in a sea of milk and glass, mouth and eyes popping at the thing that hung above him in the sky.

7

'Mister Mousehole...!' she cried concernedly, fearing for her Sunday rice pudding. 'Whatever happened?'

'L ... look at it!' he gasped, pointing aloft and almost falling over. 'Did you ever see anything *like* it, Miss Sewet?'

Mabel, accustomed as he to the roar of jets, threw a puzzled glance skywards, took a second or two to absorb the phenomenum that over-shadowed Reading at a mere five thousand feet, and joined Leonard in a startled gasp.

And who could blame them?

Who, no matter how accustomed to the sight and sound of roof-level jets, would not have reacted thus to a Boeing 707 painted bright nipple-pink, its under-wings decorated in pink-and-white candy stripes, engine cowlings twinkling with a coating of mother-of-pearl sequins and its entire underbelly afire with the slogan 'GLAMOUR AIRLINES LOVE YOU' in startling day-glo puce?

'Glamour ... Airlines ... Love ... You,' read Miss Sewet, in hushed, disbelieving tones. 'Hideous ... quite hideous,' she sniffed. 'American, of course!'

'Is that right?' replied Leonard. 'Well, I thought I knew every airline flying but I've never heard of Glamour Airlines.'

'You *haven't*?' she retorted scathingly. 'Don't you read the papers, Mister Mousehole?'

'Only the sports page, Miss Sewet. Was there something about them in the papers, then?'

'Something! Only every day last week. You couldn't open any of them without reading about their round-the-world mystery promotion flight and seeing pictures of the crew in their *ridiculous* uniforms.'

Leonard frowned. 'Oh...? What about their uniforms?'

As the startling 707 slipped out of sight over the rooftops, Miss Sewet clucked her tongue in disapproval and turned to him. 'They are silver lamé, Mister Mousehole ... with pink lapels and that slogan "Glamour Airlines Love You" embroidered across the shoulders!'

Leonard gaped. 'No kiddin'! But ... not the men's uniforms, surely?'

'It's the men's I'm talking about! The two stewardesses wear dis*gusting* see-through plastic skirts that show their ...

their bikini briefs!'

Leonard's eyes popped. 'No *kiddin'*! Holy ... but ... what's it all about?'

'It's *about* the launching of a new airline,' she replied huffily. 'American style, naturally. According to the papers, a Colonel Berskin won a bankrupt airline in a poker game – but didn't realize it was bankrupt until after he'd won it. Being a man who apparently cannot accept failure, he renamed it Glamour Airlines and is advertising its existence round the world with this one aeroplane, called, ridiculously, "*Glamour Puss*". There are apparently only fifty passengers aboard, including several show business celebrities, and it's flying right round the world attracting publicity – the gimmick being that no one aboard knows where they're going next – not even the crew!'

'Get away!' laughed Leonard, wringing out his sock. 'But ... how do they know where to fly to?'

'They are instructed *en route* – from the ground,' sniffed Miss Sewet. 'Really quite childish, the whole thing.'

'Mm,' said Leonard uncertainly. 'But at least they're getting the publicity. You've got to give that to the Yanks, Miss Sewet – they certainly know how to advertise. Well, I'd better get this mess cleared up, I'm going to be late.'

But Leonard's mind was only partly on the devastation at his feet. The other part was occupied with lurid thoughts of air stewardesses dressed in see-through skirts and bikini briefs.

'They, er, staying long in London, then, Miss Sewet?' he asked nonchalantly, shuffling broken glass into the gutter.

'Nobody knew they were even *coming* to London, Mister Mousehole. Clever, I suppose,' she allowed grudgingly. 'They've got the whole world agog wondering where they'll be landing next. But I wouldn't think they can be staying long – not if they've got to go right round the world in one week. And according to the papers they've got press receptions and banquets to attend ... but no doubt you'll know all about it within the hour, it's bound to be on radio and TV. Believe me – by the time that thing takes off again, we'll all be sick to death of Glamour Airlines.'

'Mm,' went Leonard, his mind now totally occupied with

9

how soon he could finish his round and get into town for a squint at the airstews in see-through skirts that showed their knickers.

But let us now leave Leonard Mousehole to his seamy thoughts and elevate our own to a loftier level – to around five thousand feet, and investigate the goings-on in the cockpit of Boeing 707 *Glamour Puss*.

Here we discover a team of four dedicated flyers, hunched over their controls and instruments in deadly concentration as they prepare for that most exacting of in-flight sequences – the final approach to landing.

Positioned in the front seat and to the left – the driver – Captain Rossiter, on whose silver-lamé-ed shoulders lies the awesome burden of bringing safely to earth more than a hundred tons of screaming machinery and its belly-load of human cargo.

Captain Alfred Rossiter – known more familiarly throughout the trade as 'Cock-up' Rossiter ever since that fateful night three years earlier when he had managed, in fog, to land at the wrong airport in Miami and, while attempting to park his 707 in unfamiliar surroundings, had sheared the entire tail section off a dozing DC8.

Captain Cock-up Rossiter, a short, stocky, prematurely grey-haired American of thirty-eight, whose interest in breeding rabbits is exceeded only by his total disenchantment (to say nothing of loathing) for this entire cockamamie round-the-world promotion tour with special emphasis on the ludicrous uniform he is obliged to wear.

Bitter indeed had been the words that passed between Rossiter and Colonel Godfrey Berskin during the preparation for this flight – and had it not been for the existence of a certain tape recording, now firmly in Berskin's possession, which exposed an attempt by Rossiter to obtain money from his own crew in return for permission to participate in this seven-day junket, Rossiter would not only have advised Berskin where to stuff his detested silver-lamé uniforms but would have voluntarily helped them up there.

Needless to say, then, that our gallant captain has not been

10

in the best of humours since his ignominious departure from Kennedy Airport, New York, the previous evening, nor is he likely to regain much of his natural, earthy charm throughout this entire seven-day mystery flight, resenting the whole bloody fool idea as he does. Though we *can* be certain that, with a goodly portion of his mind constantly on the tape recording in Berskin's safe, he will do his utmost to ensure the success of the venture and preserve Berskin's continued goodwill.

So much, then, for the captain.

Seated to his immediate right – the co-driver – First Officer Paul Rogers, nicknamed 'Ramjet' – a dark, curly-haired, All-American Don Juan who bears no less than a passing resemblance to a youthful Victor Mature, a characteristic which never ceases to delight him, particularly during the interminable hours he spends before his private mirror, perfecting the arched Mature brow and the sultry Mature leer. Practice which, it must be admitted, pays him amorous dividends that would not have disconsoled the great screen lover himself, even in his cornucopian heyday.

Now to the seat directly behind the captain. At the tiny navigation console, a tall, splendidly elegant blond Englishman watches the approach on Heathrow with pleasurable anticipation. For London, to James De Courcey Crighton-Padgett, is home.

Soho, Knightsbridge, Park Lane – these are 'Lord' Jim's territories, his kingdom, and in these familiar surroundings much game, he knows, is in the offing.

As an absolute minimum he can count on the adulation of at least six former girl-friends, who, primed by the welter of advance publicity, would surely be waiting for his touchdown – and up – eager to give their all. But then a mere six of the more beautiful and accommodating birds in London would be nothing compared to the veritable deluge of femininity who would soon be clawing to climb on the publicity band-wagon, – their arms linked with silver-lamé as the TV cameras turned and the Press photo-flashed and scribbled.

By heaven, mused James, this was going to be a stop-over to remember. Never would the little darlings be so numerous and

11

willing. The problem would be sorting out the best for the sinfully short time he'd be in London. What a dreadful shame he wouldn't be able to favour them all. Still ... he sent a glance to Ramjet Rogers, his close chum and fellow lecher, and his grin deepened, knowing he could more than rely on Ramjet's helping hand. And not only Ramjet's ...

He now transferred his gaze directly across the narrow cockpit to the fourth member of the crew who sat ultra-attentive to the vast array of dials on his engineer's console, the hard muscles of his superbly developed body bulging and twanging beneath his silver-lamé uniform as he twiddled a knob or flicked a switch, knowing that in big Bush McKenzie he had a second voracious ally only too willing to help accommodate any over-abundance of pulchritude.

But in that direction Morton 'Bush' McKenzie, gentle Australian giant and thorough-going muscle-nut, had his own campaign already formulated, a campaign embracing the earliest possible seduction of Miss Patricia Pell, the lithe blonde journalist and dedicated body-builder seated less than fifty feet behind him in the cabin of *Glamour Puss*, the groundwork for which early union having already been laid (largely by Miss Pell herself) just before take-off from Kennedy.

Yes, reflected Bush, his eye running automatically over the vast array of dials on the console, twenty push-ups to a clean-and-jerk she's mine before midnight ... and with gams like hers it's got to be unbelievable.

At that moment, interrupting his reverie, the wry, blatantly taunting voice of the London Airways traffic director crackled in his earphones, addressing Rossiter.

'A very good morning to you, captain. London Airways welcomes *Glamour Puss* to London. Be assured a *very* warm reception awaits you at Heathrow – including a saucer of milk.'

Cock-up scowled, shifted the butt of his cheroot to the corner of his mouth with a deft roll of his tongue and replied, 'Zat so? Thanks a lot, London Airways ... and while you're on would you like our speed and heading before we hit Southend-on-Sea or don't you bother with such trivialities in this part of the world?'

Ramjet Rogers sniggered but cut it short as Rossiter glared at him.

'*Certainly*, we bother, captain,' replied London Airways. 'It's the least we can do for our visitors. May we have your speed and heading, please?'

'Three three zero – estimating Woodley at five thousand,' growled Rossiter.

'Roger, *Glamour Puss*. Reduce your speed to two three zero over Woodley. Stay at five thousand for descent to four thousand over Ockham. Report crossing Woodley.'

'Two three zero over Woodley – descend to four thousand at Ockham. Report crossing Woodley,' repeated Rossiter, then snapped off his mike and jerked a glance at Ramjet. 'Bunch a goddam clowns down there. Can't they just bring us in without all the jokes?'

Ramjet grinned, tickled by Rossiter's permanent cantankerous scowl. 'You'll have to get used to it, Cock-up, it's going to be the same everywhere we land. We're famous!'

'Horseballs,' muttered Rossiter. 'And can the "Cock-up", Rogers – in public I'm "Captain".'

'Certainly, Cock-up.'

'Well, chaps,' exclaimed Lord Jim, rubbing lascivious hands, 'we're almost there. And a nice warm welcome awaits us. By the sound of things, I'd advise you to stand by for the time of your lives.'

'Already in gear,' grinned Ramjet.

'Once knew a bird who came from Golders Green,' cut in Bush McKenzie, with a wistful shake of the head. 'Finest pair of pectorals I've ever laid ...'

'All right, all right,' growled Rossiter, 'belay the filth for later. I realize it comes as an irritating intrusion into more worthy preoccupation, but might I rudely remind you bums that we're on finals and ...'

'Ooh!' Ramjet gave a start and jerked upright in his seat. 'Er ... we're crossing Woodley now, Skip.'

'Thank you very much, Number One, nice of you to take the trouble.' Rossiter snapped on his mike button. 'London Airways, this is ...' through compressed lips he indicated their correct numerical identification, '... Four Two Seven ...

13

crossing Woodley.'

'Roger ... *Glamour Puss*.' A hint of a smile. 'Report crossing Ockham.'

'Report crossing Ockham ... Four Two Seven,' acknowledged Rossiter, and released the button. 'Smartass!'

Now he buzzed the cabin. A momentary delay, then a peremptory knock and the door opened, admitting the angelic features of Chief Steward Michael 'Sugar' Sweetman, flushed with concern. Even above the roar of the engines and the air conditioning Rossiter could plainly hear the noise coming from the cabin. He swung round and frowned at Sweetman, attempted to peer past him into the plane.

'Jeezus, Sweetman, they still at it?'

Sugar gave a disgusted tut and rolled his eyes despairingly. '*At* it! Harder than ever! My God, you've no *idea* what we're having to put up with back here. They've been boozing solidly since we left Kennedy. The only sober one is the parrot and he's had a few. Senator Chortle is chasing Babs up and down the aisle ... Delicious O'Hara is in the latter stages of a striptease ... and Lush M ... I mean, Vincent Martino has collapsed across the bar. It's *chaos* in here!'

'I can hear it, Sweetman!' shouted Rossiter. 'Well, tell that goddam group to stop playin' and get everybody battened down, we're on finals! We'll be touching down in ten minutes!'

'Huh, fat chance of getting *them* seated ...'

'*Do* it, Sweetman – or you'll be singing castrato next leg out!'

'Ooh ...!'

Sweetman slammed the door and spun round, dispiritedly surveying the tableau of unbridled jollity erupting before him. Fifty of them ... twenty members of the American press, twenty members of the public, a doctor, a French chef, and eight celebrities – all dedicated to drinking everything in sight and squeezing the maximum self-enjoyment out of every second of the seven-day-free-for-all.

There was Gloria Fullbrush, imperious movie queen and professional trouble-maker, detested by everyone on board, with the possible exception of the three muscular studs she'd

14

brought along for her personal comfort ... Delicious O'Hara, the sultry strip queen, now down to her bra and pants and a couple of lunch menus ... Senator Sam Chortle, free-loading barrel of pomp and dedicated lecher ... Lush Martino, one-time crooner and full-time alcoholic who *never* knew where he was ... Craven Snipe, snide gossip columnist and all-round louse, destined to be assassinated before the tour was much older ... and then there was the group – The Skull and Cross Bones – four long-haired idiots dressed in pirate gear, led by the skeletal, orange-haired Shag McGee who wore a live, eye-patched parrot named Marlon on his head as a publicity gim-mick ...

My God, groaned Sugar, deafened by the racket, his sensi-tive nerves already in shreds – and this was only the first day!

A female shriek from the forward galley sent him hurrying to investigate. Flinging back the curtain he discovered his pneumatic airstew Babs 'Boobs' Buchanan fighting for her vir-tue (long since abandoned) with a very jolly Karl Makepiece, a pork butcher from Idaho, who had one hand up her see-through skirt and the other poised for a plunge down her plateau-like cleavage.

'*Mister* Makepiece ...!' exclaimed Sugar. 'Put my assistant down this instant, if you please!'

Makepiece turned, grinned, stewed to the gills. 'Oh, hi, there, Sugar ... jus' havin' a friendly li'l chat with Miss B ...'

'Out!' commanded Sugar. 'Take your seat and belt up – we're coming in to land.'

'Yiiipppeee!' laughed Makepiece. 'Well, toodle-oo, Boobs, baby, see yuh later!'

As he exited, weaving, Sugar turned to her with concern. 'You all right, angel? Ooh, *honestly*, the way people change when they get a few drinks in them. *That* little squirt ...!'

'He makes the fourteenth,' sniffed Babs, adjusting her skirt and resettling her melons. 'They're all going berserk!'

'Look, love, we're coming in to land – we've *got* to get these imbeciles strapped in. Where's Wilma?'

Wilma Fluck, blonde and equally pneumatic second stew-ardess, was at that moment doing an obligatory tango and

15

heading inexorably towards the rear toilets in Senator Sam Chortle's determined grasp.

'I don't know,' squeaked Boobs. 'I've had my own problems.'

'Find her. Get them seated, for Godsake, or Rossiter will disembowel me.'

He strode out into the cabin. 'Ladies and gentlemen...!' he bellowed. 'Ladies and ... oh, this is ridiculous.' Turning, he forced his way through the crowd to a tiny stage on which The Skull and Cross Bones were making an horrific din with 'Cringe', one of their own compositions based on an old New Guinean eye-gouging chant.

'Hey...!' Sugar thumped Shag McGee between the shoulder blades, almost dislodging the parrot who let out a terrified screech.

McGee shot round, wincing as Marlon's talons bit deep. 'Watcha do that for, man?'

'Because I want you to shut up, that's why!' yelled Sugar. 'We're coming in to land – so get seated and belt up!'

'Oh.'

McGee turned to his two guitarists – Sydney on lead, Frankie on bass – and slit his throat with his finger. They slithered to a halt but Stanley, the drummer, head down and oblivious to everything, kept going, hammering the skins murderously.

'Hey, Stanley...!' shouted McGee.

No reaction.

'Staaaan ... leeeeyyy!'

Still nothing.

McGee gave the nod to Frankie on bass who levered a half-eaten apple out of his trouser pocket and hurled it at Stanley's head with all his strength.

'Owww!' Stanley stopped and looked up. 'Hey, watcha do that for?'

'We've stopped,' said McGee.

'Oh.'

'Secure those instruments and get in your seats!' snapped Sugar. 'Come on, now – move!'

He about-turned, pushed into the crowded aisle, ordering

everyone to sit down and fasten their seat-belts with a determination bordering on the brutal, a necessity previously unheard of in all his days as Air Steward, and underlining (if more emphasis was needed beyond the evidence of one's eyes!) just how far removed from a normal trans-Atlantic flight was this ... this unmitigated orgy.

'Senator ... *Senator* ... will you *please* release Miss Fluck this instant and take your seat, we're coming in to land!'

'Splendid ... splendid!' boomed Chortle, his arms locked about the nubile Fluck. 'Well, you jurst go right ahead an' set her down, son, you have mah full permission. Honey, you do the dangdest tango.'

'Senator ... please ...' she pleaded, straining to extricate herself. 'You have to sit down!'

'Well, all rightee, but on one condition – that you sit right beside me and comfort me. Old Sam gits kinda nervous in these thangs – particularly at landin' time.'

Wilma cast a woeful glance at Sugar.

'Do it ... do it! Just get him seated.'

Sugar pushed on, reached the cluttered bar and attacked the crowd around it. 'Now, come on, everybody *must* sit down, we're landing any minute now ... Miss O'Hara – will you *please* put your clothes on and ... oh, *God*, I shall go mad ... *mad*! Now, please, I insist you sit *down* ...!'

Reluctantly, boisterously, they moved away, revealing Lush Martino, smashed to the hair-line, weavily attempting to add a ninth glass to a lop-sided tower of eight.

'*Mi*ster Martino ...'

'Ssssh! Quiet, old buddy, this is a *ver* .. y tricky operation. Have to get ten up there before ...'

'Mister Martino, you *must* sit down – this very instant! We're about to land!'

Slowly, with the delayed reaction of the absolutely shickered, Martino removed his eye from the tower of glasses and levelled it, bemusedly, at Sugar. 'Land ...? Howja mean "land". Land where, old buddy?'

Sugar sighed. 'In *London*. Now, for heaven's sake ...'

'London!' frowned Martino. 'Now, what the heck'm I doin' in London.' He peered about him in myopic confusion. 'Say

17

... what joint is this, anyhow ...?'

'Oh, my God ... Mister Martino, you're on a jet ... Glamour Airlines, don't you remem ...'

Craasshh.

Over went the glasses. 'The hell I am,' grinned Martino. 'Y'know, that makes me feel a whole lot better. This room kinda had me worried, movin' around like that ...'

'Mister Martino ... will you *please* sit down, we're coming in to *land*!'

'Sure thing ... just one more li'l drinkie ...' He threw the remnants of the first drink that fell to hand down his throat, picked up another, and weaved away down the aisle to fall into the seat already occupied by lady-journalist Miss Billy Jo Labinovitch.

With a bone-weary sigh Sugar surveyed the cabin, saw that everyone was now, unbelievably, seated, then turned and hurried down the aisle to the cockpit intercom.

'Yeah?' Rossiter responded.

'Everyone battened down, captain – and, so help me, I'd give a year's pay to keep them like this for the next seven days.'

'You an' me both, Sweetman ...'

'Lush Martino doesn't even know he's on a plane! He thinks he's in a bar somewhere!'

'Funny you should say that, Sweetman ... I keep gettin' the same impression. 'Kay, get strapped in, we're going down.'

The voice of London Approach broke into Rossiter's conversation, a voice this time devoid of levity. 'Four Two Seven ... this is London Approach. You're closing on Centre Line from the left. Continue heading two ... eight ... zero. Check your wheels are down and locked.'

'Four Two Seven ... wheels down and locked,' replied Rossiter, grateful for the absence of wisecracks. 'Heading two ... eight ... zero.'

'Roger, Four Two Seven ... you are now on Centre Line – eight miles from touchdown.'

Eight miles, mused Ramjet Rogers with excitement. Wonder what sort of reception Old Man Berskin has lined up for us? Bound to be maximum press and TV coverage, he'd make sure of that. Hell, in an hour or two we'll be famous all over Britain and Europe. He imagined himself posing for the cameras, his Glamour cap tilted to a rakish, Mature angle, saw himself at the receptions, the parties, surrounded by splendid-looking women, all yearning to be favoured with a nod, a word, a caress ... by heaven, he was going to make the most of this opportunity ...

'Three miles from touchdown...' intoned London Approach. 'Maintain your glidepath, you are on Centre Line ... clear to land Runway Two Eight Right. Surface wind one ... one ... zero at twelve knots. Coming down nicely, Four Two Seven. Two miles from touchdown...'

Only two more miles, thought James Crighton-Padgett. How wonderful to see dear old London again. Wonder how much free time we'll have? Probably very little, Berskin would see to that. He'll have every damn minute crammed with press interviews, TV interviews, receptions – but ... he smiled to himself ... they'd have to be allowed to go to bed some time. And then ...

'Reduce your airspeed to one ... three ... zero, Four Two Seven. You are right on Centre Line. One mile from touchdown...'

Well, we're blinkin' here, sighed Bush McKenzie, bubbling with pleasurable anticipation. And what, I wonder, will this little stop-over bring? A lot of bloody time-wasting interviews, that was certain, but after the day's work was done ... well, Miss Pell, darlin', what d'you say to a half-hour workout and a quick rub-down...? You know, that's exactly what I thought you'd say ...

'You are coming up to touchdown, Four Two Seven. It's all yours, now, captain. Happy landings and a pleasant stay. Talkdown complete ... and out.'

'Thank you, London Approach.'

Moments later the huge pink sprawl of *Glamour Puss* thundered over the buildings bordering Runway Two Eight Right and with a crumpy squeal settled its weight on British concrete.

And Operation Glamour had begun.

2

'External power,' droned Rossiter.

'Checked ... and on,' responded Bush McKenzie.

'Essential power ...'

'On external.'

'Number Three engine ...'

'Is ... off.'

'Beacon ... all engines stopped.'

'Off,' replied Ramjet Rogers.

'Battery ...'

Having brought *Glamour Puss* to a faultless halt at the Aviobridge passenger jetty of Channel Six, Pier One, Terminal Three, Cock-up Rossiter was now engaged in the final Leaving Aircraft Check with his co-pilot and engineer, a must for all pilots who prefer to find their aeroplane in much the same position when they finally return to it.

'Chocks,' Rossiter continued, addressing Ground.

'In position.'

'Brakes ... off. PSU fan ...'

'As required,' responded McKenzie, impatient to finish the routine check and get out there into the excitement.

'Crew oxygen ...'

'Off,' they all chorused.

'Radios, radar, and Doppler ...'

'Off,' replied Ramjet, swinging in his seat to grin at Lord Jim.

'Leaving Aircraft Check...'

'Com ... plete!' grinned McKenzie.

Rossiter expelled a relieved sigh and fell back into his seat. 'Now what, skip?' Ramjet enquired eagerly.

'Now, how in hell do *I* know? For all I know about this tour that crazy Berskin might have ordered an immediate refuel and take-off for Honolulu!'

A rap on the cockpit door cut him short. The door opened, admitted a riot of noise and the flustered features of Sugar Sweetman. 'Finished the check, captain?'

'Yeh, what is it, Sweetman?'

With a furtive glance behind him, he slipped into the cockpit, closing the door. 'Captain ... you are not going to be*lieve* this ...'

'Oho, you are *wrong*, Sweetman ... I am prepared to believe *anything* connected with this lunatic operation. What is it now – no, don't tell me, let me guess ... Senator Chortle has just exploded all over the cabin ... Delicious O'Hara is streaking stark naked down Runway Ten Right ... and Lush Martino is sittin' on the tail singing "Swanee" ... right?'

'No, no ...' tutted Sugar. 'It's got nothing to do with that lot – it's *him* ... Thing ... he's right outside, waiting to see you.'

Rossiter sighed, patience stretched to the limit. 'Who *Thing*, Sweetman ...?'

'Our courier! The bloke who's organizing everything in London! And, my *God*, you should see it – green velvet suit ... wide-brimmed fedora hat ... and a handbag.'

Rossiter shot round. '*Hand*bag!'

'Well ... sort of shoulder-bag – you know, the sort that hangs down here on a strap. Quite chic, I suppose ... tooled brown leather with a little fringe running along the ...'

'Oh, my God,' groaned Rossiter. 'And he's organized everything.'

'Everything ... transportation ... the press receptions ... the lot.'

'I, er, take it you don't somehow altogether approve of him, Sweetman.'

'Huh! Swept up the stairs like Tittifalah and without so

much as a by-your-leave started ordering *my* passengers about ... "get your hand-luggage together" ... "be prepared to disembark in three minutes" ... "have your passports ready". Too damn pushy by far...'

Rossiter threw a glance at Ramjet and sighed wearily. 'Is this or is it not all I need? My cabin crew hates our courier and our courier carries a handbag! Rogers ... would it be OK with you if I made you captain for forty-eight hours while I flake out in here? OK, Sweetman, show him in and let's get it over with. Christallmighty ... green velvet!'

'*And* a lace shirt with bits sticking out of his cuffs...'

'Get him, Sweetman.'

Sweetman exited, muttering.

'Disaster ... I can taste it,' remarked Rossiter. 'Strong as garlic. Two bits to a ball a chalk we...'

The door flew open and in he strode, a pale, slender creature of indeterminate age but in fact knocking forty, the brim of his bottle-green fedora hiding all but a glimpse of longish ginger hair and his pallid, freckled, almost translucent features.

'Captain...' he gushed, fluttering ginger lashes and extending a bony, freckled hand. 'Arnold Bottum – at your service.'

Rossiter, unable to stand, remained seated, but took the proffered hand, regretting it instantly. It reminded him of a raw haddock.

'Bottom...? Did I hear right?'

'By way of introduction' ... continued Arnold, diving into his handbag ... 'my card.'

Flamboyantly he passed the gold-trimmed pasteboard to Rossiter who looked at it and read aloud, 'Arnold Bottum PR Limited ... oh, you spell it with a "u" ...'

Arnold coughed.

'... Public Relations Grandmaster and Promoter Extraordinary.' Rossiter slid a glance at Ramjet. 'Well, now, gentlemen, it sounds as though our fears were quite unfounded. With this sort of billing how can the project possibly fail?'

'Fail!' Arnold's mouth dropped open. 'My *dear* captain, what talk is this! Immodest though it may sound, you can rest assured that you and the Glamour promotion project now safely lie in the most able PR hands in the whole of Great

Britain! Indeed, do you suppose for one moment that Colonel Berskin would have arranged it otherwise?'

Rossiter pursed his lip thoughtfully. 'No, I guess he wouldn't at that. So – Berskin has hired you to look after the whole show, hm?'

'Everything. And looked after it certainly is – down to the last *tiny* detail ... transportation, accommodation, press coverage, entertainment...' Arnold swung his handbag in front of him and fished out a set of stapled, typewritten sheets. 'I've prepared a complete itinerary for you, starting as of this moment and providing minute-by-minute details of where you will be and what you'll be doing until your departure at 16.00 hours tomorrow.'

'Oh, 16.00 hours, hm...' muttered Rossiter, taking the itinerary and running an eye over it. 'Today, Sunday ... 11.00 hours – press reception in VIP Lounge, Heathrow ... 11.30 hours – embark transportation for Hilton Hotel, Park Lane...'

'The Hilton!' exclaimed Lord Jim. 'Whizzo – rather partial to the old Hilton, brings back happy memories. Once met a TWA airstew there who...'

Rossiter flattened him with a glare. 'Crighton-Padgett ... shut up. Apart from any other consideration we don't have time to listen to the details of your lurid conquests ... come to think of it, according to this schedule we don't even have time to go to the can! Jesus, Bottum, you've really got us leapin' around ... 12.30 – arrive hotel ... 12.35 – another press reception ... 13.00 – banquet lunch with more press coverage ... 15.00 hours – visit the BBC TV studios ... 17.00 hours – visit to the Independent TV studios ... 19.00 hours – back to the hotel for a wash and brush-up ... 20.00 hours – banquet dinner at the Cinnamon Rooms, Knightsbridge – dinner expected to last until 24.00 hours...'

'What you might call a rather full day,' observed Ramjet, gnawed by sudden apprehension that he might not have time to fit in even *one* clamouring lovely.

'And night,' added James, attacked by precisely the same premonition.

'Ha!' laughed Rossiter, 'you guys ain't heard nuthin' yet.

Tomorrow is a real lulu! Breakfast is at ... 7.30 hours ...'

'Seven-thirty!' expostulated Ramjet.

'Positively obscene,' scowled James.

'Bleedin' ridiculous,' added Bush.

'8.30 hours – embark transportation for Hyde Park Corner...'

'Hyde Park Corner?' frowned James. 'What on earth for?'

'Photographic session,' cut in Arnold. 'Colonel Berskin wishes the project to be identified with the essence of London.'

'... 9.00 hours – outside Buckingham Palace...' continued Rossiter.

'Outside?' queried James. 'You mean you haven't arranged shots with the Queen, Bottum?'

Arnold sniffed. 'We did try, but she's at Sandringham.'

'How thoughtless,' observed Rossiter. '9.30 – Mall ... 10.00 hours – Houses of Parliament ... 10.30 hours – Fleet Street ... 11.00 hours – Trafalgar Square ... 11.30 hours – Piccadilly Circus ... and back to the hotel for lunch at 12.00. Embark transportation to Heathrow at 14.00 hours ... take-off 16.00 hours. And very nice, too, Bottum, nice tight schedule, if ever I saw one,' yawned Rossiter. 'Should be an absolute ball.'

'Why, thank you, captain,' beamed Arnold. 'I can assure you it assures us the maximum press, radio, and TV coverage, and all-round publicity possible. Not a *single* moment of your precious time will be wasted, I promise you.'

'Oh, I believe you,' nodded Rossiter. 'Fine ... fine schedule. There's just ... one teensy-weensy drawback that I can think of ... one *tiny* fly in the proverbial ointment that might *just* blow your lovely tight schedule to hell and gone ...'

Arnold's beam died. He compressed his paper-thin lips determinedly, ready for battle. 'Oh ...? And what, pray, might that be?'

Rossiter nodded towards the door. 'James – open it.'

James did so.

The cacophony rampaged into the cockpit, forcing Rossiter to shout. '*That*, Mister Bottum, is your fly – fifty jazzed-up freeloaders hell-bent on havin' themselves a ball! If you can get them to even *listen* to this schedule – never mind stick to it

– you should change your name to Jesus and make a fortune round the clubs!'

Arnold gaped, affronted. 'B .. but they *must*! I mean ... they *must*!'

Rossiter waved a hand towards the mayhem. 'Go tell them they must, Bottum. I've babied them for the last eight hours – from here on they're all yours.'

'But ... you're the captain! They *have* to do what you tell them! I mean, Colonel Berskin assured me ...'

'With all due respect, Bottum, Colonel Berskin is a cunt! He thinks he can buy people like he buys supermarkets – which, while he's paying them – he probably can. But not that bunch. He's promised them a Glamorous seven-day round-the-world wing-ding with no expense spared and just happened to pick the fifty people in the whole of the USA most likely to take ridiculous advantage of the offer. But don't take my word for it – look at them!'

Almost tentatively, Arnold turned and looked down the great length of the plane and blanched at the holocaust rocking it, then turned on Rossiter in desperation. 'Captain ... you must *do* something! Now! Please! Our schedule begins in ...' a panicky glance at his diamanté wrist-watch, '... thirteen minutes precisely. The press are waiting in the VIP Lounge at this very minute! We must get them over there! Can't you use your PA system to quieten them down ...?'

Rossiter shrugged. 'I can try, Bottum ...' He turned in his seat, unhooked the microphone, and blew into it. 'Ladies and gentlemen, this is the captain speaking ...'

Ramjet grinned. 'You sure the PA's on, Skip?'

'Sure, it's on. Can't you tell by the sudden respectful silence?' He cleared his throat. 'Er, ladies and gentlemen, this is Captain Rossiter ... could we please have silence for a minute ...'

Everyone in the cockpit leaned to the door to see what effect the announcement was having.

'Ladies and *gentlemen* ...!' Rossiter now shouted. 'Could we *please* have ... ladies and gentlemen ... F'CRISSAKE – STOP THAT GODDAM RACKET!'

Silence – broken only by an anonymous female giggle from

the forward galley and a stupendous belch from Lush Martino draped once more across the bar.

'Thank you,' snarled Rossiter. 'Now, it's nice t'see you folks having a great time – heck, that's what this tour is all about – but now and again I'm afraid a little promotion business is going to have to interfere with the picnic and I'd be most obliged if at those times you'd try and co-operate with the management and give us your undivided attention...'

'Hear hear!' agreed Martino, waving a boneless hand. 'How 'bout three cheers for the captain ... hip hip ...'

Rossiter annihilated the threat with a deafening cough. 'Thank you – but save it for later. Right now I have on board the man who is responsible for our schedule while we're here in London. He has lined up for us a very full itinerary of press interviews, photographic tours, and banquets' ... buzz of excitement ... '*none* of which we're going to make unless we keep rigidly to his schedule and help him all we can ... by being *punctual* ... and enthusiastic. So, it's all up to you, folks. Everything is up to you – and I do mean the success or failure of the entire promotion campaign. So – here we go. I'm going to hand over control right now to our London courier who, until we take off again at four o'clock tomorrow afternoon, is for all purposes your captain. Ladies and gentlemen ... a warm welcome for your London courier ... Mister ... Arnold ... Bottum!'

Stunned silence.

A delighted Arnold accepted the microphone from Rossiter, brought it to his mouth, took a deep preparatory breath ... and in the next moment was floored by a thunderclap of derisive laughter. Everyone in the cabin collapsed, fell about. Waves of ridicule roared down the aisle and into the cockpit, swamping Arnold who staggered back, mouth working like a spilled goldfish.

'OHHH ...! NO ...! OHHH ...!' Stupified with indignation he rounded on Rossiter. 'Stop them! Stop them! How *dare* they! Well, *really*, I've never been so ...'

'Shut that door!' yelled Rossiter.

The door slammed, shutting off the noise.

26

'W-e-l-l!' gasped Arnold, white with rage. 'I have *never* been so insulted...'

'I know, I know,' sighed Rossiter. 'But, then, you've never had to deal with a bunch like this before. They're excited, Bottum – wound up tight – and they've also been on the gravy for eight hours. Now, my advice is relax ... let them have their laugh – then go out there and show 'em who's boss.'

'I've a jolly good mind,' retorted Arnold, hitching up his handbag, 'to abandon this project right now! *I* can't help being called Bottum...'

'No,' agreed Rossiter, fighting to contain his own laughter, aware that Rogers, McKenzie, and Crighton-Padgett were doing the same. 'No, you can't,' he said, thinking what a berk Arnold was for using the name in business. He held out his hand for the microphone. Arnold surrendered it petulantly.

' 'Kay, ladies and gentlemen ... now that we've all had a good chuckle, how about settling down and giving me some of that co-operation I just asked for...'

He nodded to James who opened the door, revealing the inmates not in the least contrite but a little more receptive.

'Now, that's much better. OK, here we go again ... I am handing you over to Mister Arnold...' he paused, defying them to laugh and winning. '... To Mister Arnold Bottum, who will instruct us regarding disembarkation. Mister Bottum...'

Shaking with indignation, Arnold accepted the microphone and said aloofly, 'There are at least *thirty* members of the British press waiting for us in the VIP Lounge – and have been waiting for nearly an hour. Please collect your hand-luggage *immediately* and follow me through to the Lounge as quietly ... and sedately as possible. Thank you.'

He turned abruptly and thrust the microphone at Rossiter. 'I shall wait no longer, captain. I have *my* reputation to maintain with the press. It is now up to your cabin crew to get these people off the aeroplane as fast as they can. I'm going.'

And turning on his three-inch heels he went.

Rossiter watched him disappear through the cockpit door then murmured disconsolately, 'Know what I think, men...?'

'Yes,' they chorused.

'You're damn right. This tour was cursed from the start. Well, come on, let's get these bums into the VIP Lounge before Arnold has a nervous breakdown. I've gotta feeling that guy ain't gonna last till teatime.'

3

In a spirit of carnival exuberance, shepherded by a flustered Sugar Sweetman and flanked by his dizzy assistants Wilma Fluck and Boobs Buchanan, the motley assembly tumbled from the plane and straggled in the wake of Captain Rossiter and his crew, who in turn sauntered with a certain aimlessness behind Arnold Bottum, still stiff with pique and determined to let everyone know it.

'Arnold's really got his knickers twisted,' observed Lord Jim, nodding at Bottum who was striding ahead, handbag clamped aggressively to his side.

'Well, serves him right,' muttered Rossiter. 'If you go into business with a name like Bottum you expect to be laughed at – unless you're runnin' a Gay Club or something.'

'Once knew a bloke in Sydney named Scrotum,' observed McKenzie, exercising his biceps on the trot with a bit of dynamic tension. 'Made a fortune with that name.'

'Oh . . . how?' asked Ramjet, genuinely interested.

'Went into business making carrying bags for bowling balls.'

'No kidding?'

'No, straight up. But by the same token, I also knew a fella in Adelaide named Dick who had really bad luck with his name.'

'How come?' enquired Ramjet.

McKenzie grinned. 'He got run over by a truck.'

Ramjet sneered.

'How do you think the press will react, Skip?' asked James, observing that they were getting close to the lounge.

Rossiter humphed. 'I think they'll take one look at these uniforms, Crighton-Padgett, and fall down laughin'.'

'I really can't agree,' said Ramjet, adding another five degrees starboard angle to his cap. 'I personally find these creations altogether...'

'Fetching?' suggested James.

'The very word. Dammit, Cock-up, they're cut to perfection. A trifle flamboyant, perhaps – but there's no denying Binky Everard's masterly scissor work.'

'That so,' scowled Rossiter. 'Then we'll have to content ourselves with permanently differing opinion, Rogers – I think you look a cunt.'

'Skip...!' pouted Ramjet.

'Take it easy, it ain't personal. I think I look an even bigger cunt – I'm the captain!'

'The object of the exercise'... put in Lord Jim, stung by Rossiter's remark in light of the high opinion he held of his own immaculate appearance... 'is to attract attention...'

'Ho, we'll do that all right, Crighton-Padgett – as surely as two dogs screwin' in church. Yeh ... and maybe the analogy ain't so inappropriate at that. I know *exactly* what you three rams have got in mind.'

Ramjet opened his mouth to object but caught the eye of the other two and changed it to a grin. 'Well, hell, Skip, as you said – there've got to be *some* damn perks in all this.'

Several yards to the rear, Delicious O'Hara, exotically swathed in a voluminous white ostrich-feather boa and very little else, was discussing much the same subject with acidic gossip columnist, Craven Snipe, himself a vision of exotic sartoriality in black suit, black velour fedora (its brim raised on one side only), and swirling red silk-lined opera cape – his invariable attention-seeking garb. In addition he sported a gold-knobbed, ebony evening cane and completed the affected ensemble with a foot-long ebony cigarette holder.

'Well, Craven, baby,' Delicious growled sexily, her only manner of speech, 'watcha think of the uniforms?'

Craven released a smile, an expression closely resembling the lip-twist of a cornered wolf. '*U*niforms, darling? Oh! you mean those ambulatory bill-hoardings. They come as no surprise, O'Hara. Anything less preposterous, tasteless, and intrinsically weird from Godfrey Berskin, a man whose gluttony for wealth is only exceeded by the enormity of his ill-breeding, would have quite shattered my faith in human nature. But ...' he sighed, 'no doubt they will more than adequately serve the purpose intended.'

'Yuh reckon we'll pull the press, huh?'

'Indubitably. There is not the slightest doubt that by tomorrow morning – given that the Queen doesn't steal the front page by abdicating – we shall be splashed over the British tabloids as graphically as footprints on a ceiling.'

'Hey, I like that,' grinned Delicious, giving him a nudge.

Snipe shrugged modestly. 'A simple enough turn of phrase, O'Hara.'

'I didn't mean the purple prose, Snipe – I meant the publicity. I reckon this tour could open up all sortsa possibilities for a girl like me. I reckon by tomorra night I could be phonin' my agent with news of some pretty breath-takin' offers.'

'I have not the slightest doubt ...' he replied snidely, stung by her dismissal of his artistry, 'that you will get the offers you justly deserve, O'Hara.'

She shot a look at him, eyes narrowed. 'You know, Snipe ... I have the distinct feelin' you were just rude to me.'

He smiled icily, 'Heaven forbid, dear lady. *That* I would save for my column.'

And simultaneously ...

'Mister Martino, *please* get up ... come on, put your arm round my shoulder ...'

'I'm fine, Sugar, old buddy ... it's this damn movin' sidewalk.'

'Mister Martino, we're not *on* a moving sidewalk. Now, do get up, the press is waiting.'

Lush wobbled to his feet. 'Press? What press? Who press?'

'The *press* press! Now, *please* make an effort to walk straight. If the press see you ... well, you know ...'

31

Martino straightened, comically affronted. 'Sweetman, are you suggesting I'm slewed ... stewed ...'

'No, of course not ...'

Martino chuckled. 'Then you must be, too. I'm squiffed to the gills and fully intend to remain so throughout the entirety of this ... whatever it is we're doin'. But have no fear, Sweetman ... when the need arises ... has Martino ever, to your knowledge, ever let the side down ...?'

'Well ...' Sugar hesitated, remembering Lush falling off the stage at the inaugural Ball.

'Yuh're damn right he has,' agreed Martino, nodding like his neck was broken. 'Here, have a mouthful of bourbon ... Christ, it's empty. Sweetman, would you happen to have a shot somewhere about your person?'

'Mister Martino,' groaned Sugar. 'We're getting left behind ...!'

'Then we will run and catch up, old Sugar.'

They broke into a lop-sided trot, covering all of ten yards before Lush fell down again.

The buzz of expectant chatter ceased abruptly as Arnold Bottum, pausing in the doorway to collect himself, crossed the threshold of the VIP Lounge and paused dramatically, beamed triumphantly at the gratifyingly large assembly, and announced: 'Ladies and gentlemen of the press ... it is my pleasure and privilege to present, for the first time on British soil, the crew and honoured guests of *Glamour Puss* ... the unique and *ultra*-newsworthy emissary of that most recent and exciting addition to the international jet scene ... *Glamour Airlines*! Ladies and gentlemen ... it's *Glamour* time!'

On that note of high triumph he spun round, arm extended – and came face-to-face with a twenty-stone cleaning lady, complete with bucket and mop.

The press erupted in laughter.

'Aaaahhhh!' gasped Arnold, clutching his throat. Good God, what was *happening* to him! Twice in one day! Furiously he beckoned to Rossiter, still twenty yards away and moving with all the urgency of a man about to be shot.

'Come on, come on, for heaven's sake ...!'

32

As they drew to him, Arnold cleared his throat, composed himself, and again turned to the press, despising their derisive laughter. 'Well, we'll try again! Ladies and gentlemen of the press ... this time it really *is* the crew and honoured guests of ... *Glamour* ... *Airlines*!'

In Rossiter strolled, acknowledging the considerable applause with the merest nod, knowing that in the next breath the applause would give way to hoots of laughter as the reality of their uniforms struck home.

It did.

'My God, it's Gilbert and Sullivan!' called someone.

'Two tubs and a fourpenny cornet!'

The disciplined assembly broke, surged forward, swamped the in-pouring guests with a barrage of camera flashes and a torrent of questions.

'Captain Rossiter – please! Dan Taylor of *Aviation Today*. Would you please tell me what you think of your uniforms?'

'Sure.'

Taylor waited.

'Well, captain ...?'

'That's it.'

'But you've said nothing.'

'And that's what I think of the uniforms.'

'Well, hello, there ...'

Ramjet turned, his heart quickening and his brow arching maturely to the caress of the mink-soft female welcome, the sight of her causing a quick intake of breath and an immediate abandonment of all other plans.

'Well, hello yourself, Miss, er ...'

She was young and very lovely, tall, slender, and chic in a green trouser suit and saucy matching cap perched on golden-red hair. Sultry amber eyes regarded him playfully, promising fun. 'Now, you've just *got* to be Paul Rogers ...'

He laughed and offered a mocking salute, sixth-sensing that all he had hoped for on the tour was happening before his very eyes. 'At your service, ma'm. But how did you know?'

'Well ... the press release described you as tall, dark, and very handsome. You just *had* to be you.'

'How ... *very* kind.'

She might also have added that every press outlet in the country had received a veritable avalanche of photographs from Berskin Promotions, New York, but did not. She knew her fish – and how to catch him.

'Annabel Bear...' she smiled, extending her firm, tanned hand. *'Woman's View.'*

'Enchanted,' he gulped, taking it, thrilling to its warmth. Annabel bare, he reflected – what an incredible thought. 'What can I conceivably do for you, Miss Bear?'

Smilingly: 'Well, my magazine is essentially interested in the ... *maleness* ... of the Glamour operation – and they hardly come more male than you, Mister Rogers.'

'Well, thank you,' he effused, almost embarrassed by the compliment. 'But how can I possibly help you? Name it and it's yours.'

'You're very kind, but ... well, the essence of my work is ... *intimacy*. My thousands of female readers will be interested in the *intimate* you, you understand...'

'Oh, certainly. The, er, *intimate* me, yes, of course.'

'But...' she sighed, glancing about her at the boisterous crowd, 'this hardly seems the time or the place to...'

He held up his hand. 'Miss Bear, say no more...'

A relieved smile. 'Oh, you *do* understand.'

'Overwhelmingly.'

'But ... where?'

'Yes, a problem. We're on a devilish tight schedule...'

'I know.'

'From here we go straight to the Hilton for another press reception, then lunch, then out to the TV studios, then dinner until midnight...'

Glumly: 'I know, I know – I've read your schedule ... and tomorrow's just as full. That really only leaves...'

They looked into each other's eyes, Ramjet's heart exploding as he read her unspoken conclusion.

'Yes,' he whispered. 'That only leaves ... tonight.'

'After the dinner.'

He nodded. 'Yes ... after the dinner. Will you ... come to the Hilton?'

She shook her head. 'No, too noisy. The place will be milling with people ... and I couldn't possibly come to your room.'

Ramjet's hopes faded. 'You couldn't, hm?'

'But ...' a devilish smile, 'you could come to mine.'

Ramjet's hopes soared. 'Why ... yes.'

'I'm staying at a small ... unpretentious hotel in Soho – The Phoenix, it's very inconspicuous. And it does have a rear fire-escape.'

'It does?'

'Huh huh – leads down into a quiet back street. I thought ... if you took a cab from the Hilton after the dinner and ...'

'Yes?'

'Well, I've booked a room on the first floor – at the rear. I could be watching for you and ...'

'Go on.'

'No one would see you enter or leave ...'

'Not a soul.'

'Your uniform is *so* conspicuous ...'

'Fearfully.'

'I wouldn't want to embarrass you ...'

'How *very* kind.'

'You won't be disappointed in the result, I promise. It will be a *very* satisfying exclusive.'

'I, herm, I haven't the slightest doubt.'

'Say ... one o'clock, then?'

'How miserably the time will pass.'

Warmly: 'For me, too, Paul.'

He smiled at her, relaxed, secure in the certainty of the evening. 'Tell me ... why me?'

A mocking smile. 'You mean you really don't know? Are you trying to tell me you don't *know* you're the handsomest man in the Glamour crew ... and that every woman in London would give *anything* to be in my position right now?'

He grinned at her. 'Well ...'

'Of course you know it.'

'Now, wait on – what about my chum Jim Crighton-Padgett? He's a very handsome fella – suave, sophisticated. Looks pr-e-t-t-y devastating in his uniform ...'

'Well, yes ...' she agreed, with an uncertainty that delighted

Ramjet. 'But I won and chose you.'

'I see . . .' His brows knit. 'Hm?'

She laughed contritely. 'I'm afraid I'm guilty of a little subterfuge . . .'

'Oh?'

'Look . . . I hope you won't be annoyed . . .'

A reassuring grin. 'Now, how could I possibly be annoyed with anything you did?'

'You're very gallant.'

'Tell me about it.'

'Well . . . for a start you must realize that an exclusive interview with a member of the Glamour crew – particularly with you, McKenzie, or Crighton-Padgett – constitutes one of the scoops of the year among women's magazines?'

'Is that a fact? Well, well . . .'

'And when we discovered that all the women's mags were scheduled for interview at the Hilton, we . . .'

'Er, hang on – who's "we"?'

'I'm just coming to that. Anyway, we . . . sort of jumped the gun and arranged through . . . certain friends . . . to get to you first, out here at the airport . . .'

Ramjet's eyes crinkled. 'How very enterprising of you. You deserve to win. But I'll ask again – who's "we"?'

'A girl-friend – well, really a competitor – she writes for *Tomorrow's Girl*. And right now . . .' a mischevious smile, 'she is putting the same proposition to your handsome, debonair side-kick – James Crighton-Padgett.'

Ramjet spun round, peered over the crowd and found Jim on the far side of the room, deep in it with a gorgeous, raven-haired, vaguely Oriental girl dressed in cool blue silk. He laughed, tickled to death. 'Well, whadya know! Now, isn't she something!'

'Oh . . . you're sorry I won first choice.'

He shot back to her, appalled. 'Good heavens, no. Not on your life. No, ma'm, you are absolutely perfect.'

A relieved smile. 'I'm very glad. But you're right – she is something.'

'Is she Chinese? She looks kind of . . .'

Annabel shook her head. 'No, she's Sumatran. Her name is

36

Delphinia Hart, her father is American.'

'And all heart, I'd say,' he grinned. 'She seems to have poor old Jim in a bit of a mess. So – you two naughty girls pulled a fast one on your sister-journalists, huh?'

'Do you blame us?'

'Not in the least. As I said – very enterprising. But ... how is she going to arrange things with Jim?'

Again the mischievous smile. 'In precisely the same way. Delphinia and I have each booked a room ... same hotel ... same floor ... in fact, next door to one another.'

Ramjet laughed aloud. 'By heaven, Annabel...'

'I do hope you won't think us ... *too* forward. But an exclusive interview is *so* important to us.'

'Oh, I do understand – absolutely,' he replied, thinking – James, old chum, we're in! Not ten minutes ashore and it's happening – and with two of the sexiest-looking foregone conclusions we've clapped eyes on in a long time.

Incredible, thought James C–P simultaneously, finding it hard to believe it was happening so quickly *and* with such an adorable piece of grumble as the heavenly smelling creature standing before him.

'Must I wait until one tomorrow morning?' he pleaded. 'Dear Miss Hart, you have created for me a very real dilemma.'

'How is that?' she smiled, blinding him with snow white teeth and wafting him with long, dark lashes.

'Very simple – how can I possibly give my undivided attention to dutiful interviews when the thought of seeing you again fills my fevered mind?'

She giggled. 'You *do* exaggerate, James.'

'You think so?' He clutched his heart dramatically. 'Delphinia, you have positively harpooned me with your loveliness. I have an ache, a fierce throbbing right here which only being alone with you can soothe.'

James had a fierce throbbing all right, but it wasn't in his chest. He had not encountered a bird he fancied so much on sight in years. The smell of her ... the voluptuous cuddliness of her. His fingers tingled for her flesh.

'But,' he continued, dejectedly, 'wait I will if wait I must.'

'You ... don't think badly of us – of Annabel and me – for doing this?'

With a boyish grin he glanced across the room to where Ramjet was pouring it into the ravishing red-head, his Mature brow so arched it had disappeared into his hair-line, then shook his head reassuringly. 'Delphinia, how on earth could we think anything but the most ... charitable thoughts about girls like you? On the contrary, I'm sure I speak for Ramjet when I say we applaud your enterprise ... and your thoughtfulness. Fancy renting a couple of quiet hotel rooms to save us embarrassment with our uniforms.'

'James...' she all but whispered, 'I'd better let you go. The other females are beginning to eye me suspiciously.'

'What other females?' he enquired gallantly.

'You are sweet. Until one o'clock, then?' She offered her hand.

'Until one,' he sighed, taking it, thrilling to its warmth. 'Adieu, Princess.'

And then, with a final, lingering smile, she was gone.

By the Rigid Rod of St. Rude, thought James, if this daft tour ain't looking up a treat. Ramjet, old son – we're in! Looking across the room he espied his penial pal about to be similarly deserted by the adorable Annabel and decided on a sly sidle over to compare notes, but at that moment was intercepted by a lady of house-like proportions who fetched him up sharp by stepping in front of him.

'*Mister* Crighton-Padgett ... Marjorie Minns from *Needles and Pins* ... mind if we discuss the cut of your jib?'

And simultaneously ...

'Senator Chortle, sir, may I have a word with you?'

'Certainly, son, certainly,' Chortle responded, touching a match to a foot-long Havanna and momentarily losing sight of his interviewer in the ensuing smog. 'Hello, you still there?'

'Yes, S .. Senator,' coughed the interviewer, a pale, pimply lad named Twigg. 'May I ask you, sir ...' cough, '... whether you intend, during your visit, to study...' cough cough, '... the current socio-political impasse...' cough, '...

38

which as the whole world knows ...' cough, '... is stultifying stolid industrio-managerial unification ... a .. and ...' cough cough, 'usurping the essential cohesion concomitant with ... with ... Senator, will you excuse me, please, I believe I'm going to be sick...'

'Certainly, my boy ... nice talkin to yuh.'

While meanwhile ...

'Hello, there!'

Shag McGee turned, almost dislodging the parrot from his head. 'Hi, man.'

'Stylus McKnee from *Snap, Crackle, and Pop*. Could you answer a few questions for our avid readers?'

'Sure. Here – give Marlon a peanut.'

Stylus dug into the bag and handed one to the drummer.

'That's Stanley,' explained McGee. 'Marlon is the parrot.'

'Oh.'

Marlon cocked his head at the proffered peanut then dived for it, taking McKnee's forefinger instead.

'Yooowww!'

'He got your finger?' enquired Shag.

'Like a vice, man!'

'Stanley ... Marlon's got this guy's finger.'

'Mm?' Stanley looked up from his comic. 'Oh.'

Withdrawing a drumstick from his pirate's boot, he thumped Marlon on the head and he let go.

'That thing's dangerous,' complained McKnee, sucking his finger. 'You oughta put a muzzle on it.'

'Nah, he's just short-sighted on account of the patch. What were the questions, man?'

'Er ... you doin' any gigs during your stop-over?'

'Sure – at the banquet tonight.'

'Any of your own stuff?'

'All our own stuff. We don't play nobody else's.'

'Why's that?'

'We can't read it.'

'I see. Is it true that parrot stands there on your head all the time you're playin'?'

'No, sometimes he falls off.'

'How long has the group bin together?'

'Er...' Shag frowned and scratched his head. 'Hey, Stanley ... how long we bin together?'

'What's today?' asked Stanley.

Shag shook his head and the parrot slid down his neck.

'Hey, Sydney...' called Stanley.

Sydney stopped picking his nose and looked up, finger poised. 'Yeh?'

'What's today?'

Sydney shrugged. 'St. Valentines?'

'That's in January, man.'

'Easter?'

'Ya dumb bugger...'

'Ask Frankie,' suggested Shag, reseating Marlon.

'Hey, Frankie...'

The bass guitarist opened his eyes. 'Yeah?'

'What's today?'

Frankie's bovine brows knit in consternation. 'To*day*? Erm...'

'Forget it.'

Frankie shrugged. 'OK' and went back to sleep.

'Any more questions?' McGee asked McKnee. 'Anythin' at all, we don't mind.'

'Yeh,' scowled McKnee. 'Anybody gotta plaster? My finger's bleeding.'

Arnold Bottum glanced anxiously at his diamanté watch and gave a start. 'Er ... ladies and gentlemen...'

No one took the slightest notice of him so he climbed on a chair. 'Ladies and gentlemen ...! Look, I know our schedule allowed for a thirty minute interview here, but as we were late getting in I'm afraid I'll have to cut this a trifle short...'

A groan from the press.

'I know, I know, I'm very sorry, but if we don't get back on our schedule now we're going to be late at every point throughout the day. So if the crew and guests of Glamour Airways would kindly follow me, we will proceed out of the terminal to the awaiting transport. Members of the press ... thank you *very* much for attending. Do, by all means, stay

with us as we leave the terminal if you haven't got all you want
... but, crew and guests, this way *if* you please...'

With a gay hop he jumped down from the chair, got his
handbag caught in the struts, tripped over it, and fell on the
floor.

'Aaaaggghhh!' he raged, looking up to find Lush Martino
standing over him, weaving like a bullrush in a breeze.

'Aha...! A drinkin' man!'

'Mister Martino, I am *not* drunk! I .. s . slipped!'

'S-u-r-e, yuh did,' Martino grinned. 'Say, you wouldn't
happen t'have a little snort on you, would yuh?'

'No, I would not!' Arnold struggled to his feet, extricated
his handbag, and stormed from the room.

'I tell you,' Rossiter remarked to Bush McKenzie, 'that guy
ain't going to last. He has the look of a fella teetering on the
lip of a nervous breakdown. One thing, though – he won't go
over lonely. I'll be right behind him.'

As the assembly raggedly excited, Lord Jim and Ramjet
converged at speed, grinning like a couple of two-dicked dogs.

'James, old chum, I do not b*elieve* it!'

'Force yourself – it happened.'

'But ... she's so beautiful!'

'Mine, too – simply radiates Eastern promise. Ramjet, it's
uncanny – precisely as we called it.'

Ramjet regarded him archly. 'But then – why not?'

'A couple of *very* smart girls – got in fast before the opposition.'

'Well ... if it's a Rogers' exclusive Miss Annabel Bear
wants – that's precisely what she'll get.'

'Hear, hear – I concur absolutely. One o'clock at the
Phoenix. Delphinia, dear Hart, your hour is close at hand.
Whooppee!'

Exit our heroes, cocooned in joy, little realizing, poor
fools, what anguish lay ahead.

4

For Arnold Bottum, fresh trouble erupted as the procession straggled through the glass doors of Number Three Building and came upon their mode of transportation parked waiting at the kerb.

At first sight of the huge pink-and-candy striped, single-decker bus, its be-sequined fenders and hub-caps, and the slogan 'Glamour Airlines Love You' emblazoned along its side in hideous day-glo puce, Miss Gloriana Fullbrush, celebrated actress and professional scene-stealer, of whom we have so far heard blessedly little, felt it high time she made her presence felt and did so with a shriek of protest so loud it frightened forty seagulls off the roof and pushed Arnold three feet nearer the verge of his nervous breakdown.

'NO!'

Arnold fell against the bus and clutched his brow. 'Oh, my God, what *now*!'

'That ... is what now!' she bellowed, levelling a quivering finger at the offending vehicle. 'That ... monument to Berskinian vulgarity! Young man, do you realize who I *am*?'

'Y ... yes, Miss Fullbrush, of c .. course ...'

'And you expect *me* to ride into London on *that*!'

Arnold, pale and trembling in the face of so unexpected and volcanic an onslaught, opened his mouth and managed a pathetic, hoarsely croaked, 'Well ... yes!' And then the full impact of her terrible, and utterly contrived, fury hit him.

One particular piece of advice Gloriana had taken to heart while clawing her way up the theatrical ladder was contained in the old Thespian adage 'Never let them forget you're on stage!'

Well, she'd been 'on stage' in London for almost twenty minutes and felt it time everyone was reminded of it. And so, ensuring through the corner of her eye that she had the shocked attention of every journalist in the gathering, she cut loose at Arnold with a barrage of invective that buckled his knees and simultaneously sent the press into a frenzy of delight. At last things were livening up!

Pop ... flashed the cameras. Scribble went the pencils.

'I'll tell you this just once, Bottum ... Gloriana Fullbrush will not set *foot* in that ... Philistine contraption! So get your tight little ass outta here, little man – and get me a limousine! And not just *any* limousine! I want a Rolls-Royce! A *white* Rolls-Royce! A white Rolls-Royce *convertible*! I want the hood down so my public can see me! God in heaven, I'm a *star*, you silly boy ... and I demand to be *treated* like a star!'

'B .. but, Miss Fullbrush,' wailed Arnold, close to tears. '... the schedule ...!'

'*Fuck* the schedule!' she roared, rounding on the press. 'That's F-U-C-K ... get it down! Without Fullbrush there *is* no schedule!'

'But the *press* ... we'll be late!' cried Arnold, searching the crowd for a sympathetic eye but finding every single one trained on the quivering Fullbrush.

'The press *adores* to be kept waiting,' she retorted, re-enacting a line from one of her films. 'For Fullbrush they will wait forever!'

All good ego-staring stuff which, as the initial shock of her outburst subsided, began giving other notables in the crowd cause for narcissistic reflection.

By God, mused Senator Chortle, bracing his shoulders, the bitch has somethin'. Is this any way for a United States senator to enter the city of London – aboard a bus! Chortle, you're slipping! She's stolen your thunder! Stap me is she hasn't pulled off one of the scene-steals of the tour!

A glance about him saw similar conclusions reflected in the

43

green-eyed, grim and gritted expressions of Delicious O'Hara and Craven Snipe, and, sensing that they, too, were about to pounce, he thrust his bulk into first gear and bulled through to the front, defying every member of the press not to notice him.

'Now, see heyah, young fella ... it appears to me that your briefin' as to the importance of certain personages aboard this Glamour flight has bin singularly inadequate – t'say nuthin' of downright negligent...'

Gloriana speared him with a glare. 'Keep the hell out of this, Chortle! Go find your own soap-box!'

He half-turned to her with a twisted smile, keeping his profile to the cameras. 'Now, Gloriana, honey, have a care...' he murmured, his rumble rich in threat. 'Ah don't suppose that *too* many members of the press know your real name is ... Gladys Makewater.'

She gasped, the hiss of a cornered cobra. 'You ... slimy toad!'

'All's fayah in politics an' publicity, my dear,' he chuckled, returning his rostrum wrath to the cameras. 'But it seems ta me that Colonel Godfrey Berskin, chairman an' founder of this imaginative new enterprise, would at this moment clutch his heart in horror if'n he knew that his London representative wus deemin' to defile th' dignity of the Senate of th' United States of Amurica by askin' one of *its* representatives to ride inta the city of London aboard a common or garden bus – t'say nuthin' of this heyah *partic'lar* vehicle...'

Arnold's orbs bulged. How could this be happening to him! He had fought tooth-and-nail against enormous opposition for the highly lucrative and immensely prestigious Glamour account and had supervised every facet of the campaign personally, assiduously ... had seen to it that the colour scheme for the bus was *exactly* as his instructions from New York had decreed ... and that *all* his instructions about everything were executed to the letter. How could things be going so wrong! How could these *awful* people refuse to get on his bus! Dammit, it was no more gaudy than the jet in which they were flying round the world!

'*Sen*ator...' he begged, pleaded, whined. '*Please* ...

44

Chortle silenced him with a hand. 'No, siree! Where Ah come from we believe in th' dignity of man bein' paramount above all thangs ... and Ah jurst can't find it in my heart to offend the principals Ah hold deyah back home by complyin' with your less than dignified request to board this harlot buss ...'

'Gets you right here, doesn't he?' drawled Rossiter, indicating his armpit. 'Did you ever hear such a car-load of crap?'

Ramjet grinned and shook his head. 'I tell you, Skip, I think Berskin is a hell of a sight smarter than we gave him credit for. I reckon he knew all along that Fullbrush and Chortle would pull something like this. They're going to make more column-inches than even *he* envisaged.'

'And not only them,' Bush McKenzie chipped in. 'Here comes the delicious O'Hara with her tuppenceworth – with Craven Snipe in hot pursuit. You going to have a go, Skip? I reckon as captain you deserve a white Rolls convertible. Me ...? Well, being a reasonable sort of fellow, I'll settle for a gold Merc with stereo and TV ...'

The voluptuous O'Hara was indeed about to put in her tuppenceworth. Slinging the ostrich boa determinedly about her naked shoulders, she barged to the front and assailed Arnold with a sneer that drained away the last teaspoonful of blood left in his cheeks and had him begging for death.

'Now, see here, Shorty – anythin' this dame gets, O'Hara gets, un'erstand? Nobody's upstagin' *this* chicken, now or any other time. I'm not so damned crazy about this tit-pink creation myself an' though I don't normally go outta my way to see Fullbrush's point of view I gotta admit this time she's gotta case. A white Rolls convoitable will go nicely with my outfit – so how's about hustlin' around an' gettin' us three or four.'

'The .. three or f .. *four*!' gasped Arnold, eyes like ping-pong balls.

'Well, sure, sugar – yuh don't surely expect me ta ride with *her*, do yah?'

'Oh, my God,' choked Arnold, clutching his stomach. 'I think I'm going to be sick.'

'After – first, go get the Rolls.'

'But ... f .. from *where*?'

Delicious shrugged, allowing the boa to slide from her bosom as she caught sight of a photographer lining up on her. 'How in hell do I know? Go phone the car-hire ...' she broke off to smile sultrily as the camera flashed, '... people.'

'I ... I ...' croaked Arnold, beginning to slide sideways along the bus, looking as though he was about to turn and flee, never to be seen again.

'Er ... one moment more, young man!' The imperious, cultured drawl of Craven Snipe ensnared Arnold's stricken attention. 'My name is Snipe. Unaccustomed to travelling in candy-striped and sequined monstrosities as these several ... celebrated personages ... claim to be, and as vociferously as they have presented their arguments in favour of a more dignified form of transport, I assure you that unless I am similarly transported to London, I will return to New York on the next available scheduled flight and *demolish* the entire Glamour campaign in my column tomorrow morning. I have only to apply the adjective "asinine" to Glamour Airlines to bring the silly charade crumbling around Berskin's ears – and *then* God help you, Mister Bottum. So, pop along, there's a good chap, and order the limousines.'

It was at this point that Lush Martino, happily unaware of the furor around him, was suddenly stricken by a certain physical need, and, seeing before him the face he vaguely remembered as representing some kind of local authority, took a lurch forward with the intention of button-holing Arnold with a friendly request.

'Say, now, young fella .. I ...'

For Arnold, that did it. Throwing his hands in the air, he let out a wail, 'All right ... all right, I'll get you a Rolls! I'll get *them* a Rolls! I'll get *everybody* a Rolls! My *God*, to think I gave up Baxter's Burst-Proof Toilet Paper for this!' And then he fled towards the terminal.

Lush Martino blinked uncomprehendingly at the disappearing madman and turned to Rossiter. 'Now, what got into *him*? Did I say I wan'ed a Rolls? Did anybody hear me say I wan'ed Rolls? *I* don't want no Rolls. All I wan'ed was a li'l drink. Anybody know where a guy can get a drink round here?'

46

One of the press men travelling with the group sauntered up secretively to Rossiter. 'Al Brady, captain – Wisconsin Star. Do you see this kind of hooha happenin' everywhere we stop?'

Rossiter gave a rueful smile. 'You complaining, Mister Brady?'

'No, siree, I am not. It makes great copy.'

Rossiter nodded. 'Sure it does – just so long as you guys don't forget to report the result.'

'Result? How d'you mean, captain?'

'That Glamour Airlines *did* supply the Rolls convertibles.'

Brady's brows rose. 'You reckon he'll get them?'

'I know he will. Bottum has got his reputation on the line with this tour – and so has Colonel Berskin. I'd appreciate it if you fellas would remember who's picking up the tab on this – and why you're here at all. Have fun – but don't lose sight of the object of the exercise, hm? The temperamental shenanigans of these theatrical buffoons might make good copy, but we're here to promote Glamour, not satisfy their egos.'

'Well, yes ... sure,' replied Brady, flattened by the unexpected rebuke, his impression having been of Rossiter's disenchantment with the operation and of his readiness to condone all critical dirt. 'Sure, I'll remember that.'

Rossiter nodded tersely. 'Pass the word. I don't care how you spell it as long as it comes out *success*.'

As Brady disappeared to confer with his peers, Lord Jim sidled close and murmured, 'Why, captain, what touching loyalty. Who would have guessed that beneath that hard-bitten old exterior beats the heart of a true-blue company man.'

'Up yours, Crighton-Padgett,' scowled Rossiter, re-lighting his stogey and contemplating for the umpteenth time the tape in Berskin's possession. If he, as captain, let this schmozzle get out of hand, allowed Glamour Airlines to become a laughing stock around the world, he had no doubt whose head would roll on their return to New York. And though breeding rabbits offered considerably more aesthetic delight than shoving a nipple-pink 707 round the skies, its monetary reward was monumentally less.

Thus calculating, he felt it time to step in and ensure his continuing employment with a few choice directives to the characters making all the fuss.

'Miss Fullbrush ...'

Gloriana turned, pinch-nosed, and examined him. 'Now, which one are you – the steward? I must say you all look alike in that ridiculous outfit.'

Rossiter's jaw clanged shut on his cigar. 'No need to be offensive, ma'm, I'm the captain an' you know it. If you have any trouble remembering the face, just count the stripes ... one ... two ... three ... four. Any time you see four stripes, that'll be me – the captain.'

'Captain maybe, but *certainly* no gentleman. A gentleman would remove the cigar from his mouth when addressing a lady.'

'Maybe I will – when I meet one.'

Gloriana's eyes flared. 'How *dare* you speak to me like that ...!'

'Oh, I dare pretty easily. As the captain of this operation I'm responsible for its success – and there just ain't going to *be* any if you and a few others ...' he glanced brazenly at those responsible for the current hiatus, '... are going to stand on your precious dignity every five minutes and demand special treatment!'

'I'm a star!' she cried. 'I deserve special treatment!'

'Then take it up with Berskin tonight by phone!'

'Oho, I most *certainly* will!'

'OK – but don't take it out of this poor guy, Bottum! With a name like that, he's got enough problems. Hell, we haven't bin landed more than an hour and the guy's on the skids for a nervous breakdown already. Berskin sent him a schedule and he's tryin' his best to stick to it – or was up until five minutes ago. Right now I reckon he's hangin' himself in the toilets! If there's anything in the schedule you don't like, go along with it and complain afterwards.'

'And *who* ...' she demanded, 'the hell are *you* to tell Full-brush what to do!'

Delicious O'Hara, sensing the sympathy of the crowd – meaning the sympathy of the press – veering in Rossiter's direction and that moment offering another column-inch or two to any champion of Rossiter's cause, sauntered into the

48

fray, boa twirling aggressively and hips swinging like a pendulum.

'Ain't the guy just told you, Fullbrush – he's the captain, is who – an' he's right. Poisonally, honey, I regret makin' a hooha about the Rolls, but this bitch kinda got me steamed up ...'

Pop! went a flash bulb.

'This way, Miss O'Hara ... atta girl.'

Delicious wreathed a variety of smiles to the flurry of flashes, then abandoned them and rounded again on her archenemy. 'Still, I guess makin' a howl about somethin' every step of the tour is the only way you're gonna *pull* any press, hey, Gloriana.'

Gloriana's lip curled demoniacally. 'You ... loose-mouthed slut!'

Mah God, Chortle, blinked Senator Sam, what *is* becomin' of yuh? This big-tit baggage has just stole *anuther* scene from yuh!

'A-herm, ladies ... ladies,' he gushed, interposing his bulk between them and the cameras. 'Now, lan'*sakes*, let us remember that we are *guests* in this fine country ... and Ahm sure, on reflexion, that the good captain has a ver' valid point. Ah, too, sir, am somewhat ashamed of mah recent insistance on a more befittin' mode of transport and even *more* ashamed – t'say nuthin' of downright distressed – at the thought of us keepin' all those kindly members of th' *press* ...' (here a subtle turn to the cameras with a gracious, self-effacing smile while the bulbs flashed), '... waitin' our selfish pleasure. Now, it seems to me that th' very least we could do foah our good friend Bottum is to set aside our petty personal preferences ... conceal, nay, bury any self-righteous indignation we may have felt regardin' this scheduled form of transportation ... and join t'gether in a common cause ... sharin' each joy an' overcomin' every trivial annoyance that this grand adventure may bring ... workin' in lovin' harmony with each other towards one common goal, one bright and shinin' goal, one ...'

'Aw, shut up!' rapped Gloriana.

'Say, wha's everybody standin' around for, anyway?' drawled Lush Martino. 'C'mon, now, you guys, who's hidin' the booze!'

Rossiter cleared his throat authoritatively. 'I, er, take it then that we have a majority vote in favour of getting on the bus?'

A hearty chorus. 'Yes!'

'OK, then ... Miss Fullbrush – would you be so kind as to lead the way?'

With an enraged swing of her raven mane, Gloriana entered the coach, swearing revenge on Rossiter within the hour and itching to get to the nearest trans-Atlantic telephone.

It was as Rossiter, the last to board, was about to set foot on the coach step that Arnold Bottum emerged from the terminal, pale and perspiring, and in obvious distress stumbled towards the coach, seeming not to notice until the very last moment that the crowd was no longer standing there. Pushing through the members of the press, the realization finally dawned on him and pulled him up sharp, gaping at Rossiter.

'They recanted,' explained Rossiter.

'But ... they can't! I mean, they can't! I've ... just scoured London for four white Rolls-Royces ... found them locally ... promised them the *earth* ... they'll be here any minute!'

Rossiter shrugged. 'Cancel them.'

'But how did you ...?'

Rossiter glanced into the bus. 'I appealed to their better natures. They took some finding but I finally made it – with the help of the press.'

'But they can't! They *must* ride in the Rolls-Royces – I've reshaped the whole arrival!'

'Try and make them. They're now on a democracy kick. Nothing on *earth* would persuade them to ride in anything so ostentatious as a white Rolls convertible ...' he grinned, '... *or* retract the posture witnessed by the press.'

Arnold's face crumpled. 'Oh, no ... it's a dream ...'

'Now, don't cry, Bottum.'

'I'm going mad! What will become of me!'

'Just take it easy, it's not your fault.'

'But the Rolls-Royces ...!'

Rossiter gave the matter the once-over. 'OK – we still use them. They will travel in line – ahead of the coach, a kind of Glamorous vanguard?'

'But ... carrying who?'

Rossiter grinned. 'One of the few perks of bein' a captain, Bottum, is that I can at least shove my crew around.' Swinging up into the bus he commanded: 'Rogers, Crighton-Padgett, McKenzie, Sweetman, Buchanan, and Fluck ... downstairs – on the double!'

Twenty minutes later a startling motorcade emerged from the access tunnel running beneath Runway Ten Left and joined the main A4 road to London.

In the lead, as befits a captain, Cock-up Rossiter reclined in the rear seat of the open-topped Rolls momentarily at peace with the world. How pleasant the summer sun upon his face, the scent of aviation kerosene in his nostrils. And how gratifying the waves and whoops from the populace on either hand. By heaven, the Fullbrush bitch was right, he grudgingly admitted. There is simply nothing like a white Rolls-Royce (and even more nothing like *four* white Rolls-Royces) for catching the eye.

Could there be a single person out there not instantly impressed by this procession and immediately converted to flying the Glamour way? And who gives a stuff, thought Rossiter, lighting a fresh cigar. I'm just so dadblasted glad to get this bunch of nuts outta my hair for half an hour, I wouldn't care if I was riding a fork-lift truck.

A sentiment certainly not shared by the duo of suave sophistication languishing in the upholstery of the limousine behind.

With caps jauntily raked and smiles of disembowelling charm fixed on their faces, they bowed and waved to left and right, regally accepting the horn-toots, waves, and cheers of the spectators as no more than their due reward for outstanding attractiveness.

'Don't know about you, James,' declared Ramjet, Victor Maturing a splendid-looking girl clean off her bicycle, 'but I am overwhelmed by the rightness of this moment. It never occurred to me, until I climbed into this sumptuous chariot, just what was missing from my life. Suddenly it all fell into place. I *belong*, James, I *belong*.'

51

'*Et moi,* old thing. Not that this, of course, is the first time I've ridden in a Rolls, but it has been quite a time.' He smiled, wistfully. 'Once developed a ... certain attachment for a lovely creature who owned a Corniche – as well as a sumptuous pad in Eaton Square. Splendid cars for a spot of spontaneous seduction – bags of fore and aft leg room.'

'Must have been hard to abandon a find like that,' commented Ramjet, devastating six females in a bus queue with a smile and a salute.

'Oh, I had help – from two sources, actually. From both barrels of her husband's shotgun.'

Ramjet laughed, then sighed. 'How perfect this would be if only *they* were with us.'

'I know, I was just thinking of them. Pity they couldn't have ridden along. I must say Delphinia transcends even my wildest expectations. She really is a knockout.'

'Yes,' nodded Ramjet, sliding more comfortably into his seat and grinning lasciviously. 'I must admit my priapic hopes didn't extend *too* much further than the adorable Annabel, either.'

'What a *bore* this schedule is, old chum. Hell, there's hardly time for a pee between events, let alone anything else. I think we ought to have a word with Cock-up about it, for the future. Dammit, there's got to be *some* personal pleasure in all this.'

Ramjet's grin embedded itself in his countenance. 'Oh, there will be, James – like at one a.m. tomorrow morning for instance.'

James responded with a pandemian leer, the harbinger of gross and vile intent.

While directly behind ...

'How're you feeling, angel, any better?' Sugar enquired solicitously, addressing the still-pale and somewhat-trembling Arnold.

'Yes, a little,' Arnold replied faintly. 'I think the breeze is doing me good.'

'Ooh, you did look poorly back there, I felt ever so sorry for you. I wanted to say something to that madam, I can tell you, but I thought it might only make matters worse for you. Great black hag ... thinks because she's made half-a-dozen *very* bad films she's Raquel Welch. Been like that ever since the tour started ... Steward, get me this ... and Steward, get me that. I know what I'd like to give her – a boot out of the door at thirty thousand feet. Making my life a misery. Still – you don't want to hear about my worries, God *knows* you've got enough of your own, poor lamb.'

'Sorry I took the rotten job on,' moaned Arnold. 'I never *dreamed* it would be like this. Berskin made it sound so ... so exciting, so glamorous. Launching a brand new airline with a round-the-world mystery flight, I mean, the idea's absolutely *splendid*. Right, Arnold, I thought – here's a chance to make a big name for yourself. Sugar, you have no *idea* the work I've put into this in the past few weeks ...'

'I have, pet, I have. It can't have been easy. And then to meet up with the likes of Fullbrush and Chortle ... raving egomaniacs, they are. But never mind, you've done a wonderful job so far. Berskin can be nothing but pleased.'

Arnold sighed disconsolately. 'I'm not too sure. If that Fullbrush woman gets on the phone to him and starts complaining ...'

'Now, don't upset yourself,' Sugar commiserated, patting Arnold's knee. 'As it turned out she might have done you a big favour. I must say this parade of Rolls looks *very* impressive. We're attracting *so* much attention ... ooh, I say, what *lovely* material. I meant to tell you how *very* chic I thought your outfit was.'

'Oh, d'you like it?' asked Arnold, brightening.

'*Adore* the hat – and the lace shirt. The moment I saw you I thought to myself now *that* is class. Wherever did you get them?'

'Well,' enthused Arnold, recovering fast, 'do you know Chelsea at all?'

'Intimately!'

'Well, there's this new boutique in the Kings Road called "Frills 'n Thrills" ... in*credible* line in Italian lace underpants ...'

'No ...!'

And bringing up the rear ...

'Wilma, isn't this just yummy!' squeaked Boobs Buchanan, squirming in her seat and waving aloft to a scaffoldful of bricklayers wolf-whistling the two near-naked lovelies in the back of the fourth open Rolls.

'Just ... divine,' sighed Wilma. 'Gee, I've wanted to ride in a white Rolls convertible all my life. Kinda gives you goose-bumps, doesn't it?'

'Could be the breeze,' suggested Bush McKenzie who had gallantly elected to ride with the girls as protector – in case the sight of two near-naked lovelies precipitated a full-frontal attack. By way of reward he had seated himself in one of the fold-down jump-seats directly in front of them and was currently experiencing the greatest trouble keeping his eyes from their thighs, exposed as they were beneath their see-through plastic skirts. For as big a bundle as he went on Miss Patricia Pell's outstanding muscular development, there was an awful lot to be said for a pair of boobs like Babs' and a brace of veritable melons like Fluck's.

What, he pondered, as they passed beneath the Chiswick flyover, would his chances be in all *three* directions during the next seven days? The thought of executing push-ups over the recumbent forms of all three fashioned a grin of devilish intrigue on his granite features and established, there and then, his project for the week.

'A lovely day, girls,' he observed poetically, breathing deeply of the Chiswick ozone, deciding there was not a moment to lose in the preparation for his triple seduction. 'Aah, don't you smell it in the air?'

They abandoned their waving and gave a couple of sniffs.

'Exhaust fumes?' enquired Babs.

He laughed, expansively. 'No ... romance!'

'Romance?' replied Wilma, sniffing again.

'Why, certainly. Oh, come now, girls, surely you've given some thought to the romantic possibilities of this trip? Can you honestly say the prospect of a wild affair with an English lord ... or a filthy-rich Arab sheik ... or a big, bronzed Aussi life-guard hasn't crossed your naughty little minds...?'

'Huh!' went Babs, 'and who's had time! I, personally

speakin', have had my hands so full preventing Sam Chortle getting *his* hands full, I haven't had a chance to think about lords and sheiks and life-guards...' She flashed a smile, indicating a swift change of tack. 'Though now you come to mention it, I suppose it *is* a golden opportunity...'

'Diamond-studded!' agreed Bush. 'I mean, what a terrible waste – dropping down into the glamour cities of the world – maybe Paris, Rome, Cairo, Sydney, and not makin' the most of the opportunity. Look upon it as a holiday! And what is a holiday without a little romance?'

Wilma sighed dreamily. 'Gee, I sure would give *anything* to meet up with some movie producer. I'd give *anything* to get into movies...'

'Well, we'll have to see what we can do for you,' Bush enthused. 'Heck, girls, we'll be rubbin' shoulders with all sorts of TV and movie people. Wilma, we'll just have to see to it that you get full exposure.'

Her blue eyes widened gleefully. 'Oh, Bush, d'you think it's possible!'

He leaned towards her and patted her naked knee fraternally. 'Wilma, love, you just leave it to me. I shall make it a personal crusade for the duration of the trip. Look upon me as your agent, if you like.'

'Oh, Bush, that's terribly sweet of you. I'd be *ever* so grateful.'

'Think nothing of it, love. And who knows ... there may be some little thing you can do for me in return.'

'Oh, *anything*!'

Spot on, he thought, transferring his hand to Babs' naked knee. 'And for you, love ... anything that looks promising in the millionaire line I shall steer in your direction. Not, mind you, that you couldn't pull them all by yourself, but I might be able to sort of break the ice, know what I mean?'

Babs responded with a giggle that spoke volumes.

And while all this was going on...

'The *nerve* of those guys!' ragged Gloriana Fullbrush. '*I* order the Rolls and *they* ride in them! Look at them! – waving to the crowd like the goddam stars of the show!'

'Which indeed they are,' interjected Craven Snipe from the seat behind, finding solace for his own annoyance in the relegation of Gloriana Fullbrush to the front seat of a common bus. For Craven Snipe, for all his posturing, was a man of considerable aesthetic integrity who abhorred temperament supported by little talent, and as it was his confirmed opinion that Fullbrush's temperament was supported by no talent whatsoever, he, in consequence, abhorred her totally.

'Crap!' she retorted tartly. 'Berskin invited *me* on this tour to pull the press! Without me Glamour Airlines wouldn't get five lines in the Tomato Growers' Weekly!'

'A preposterous fib and you know it,' Snipe replied coolly. 'You saw how the press reacted at the airport – they made a bee-line for the crew ... and quite rightly. They *are* the stars of the show, Gloriana, whether you like it or not. You and O'Hara and Martino and Chortle are mere appendages – props to the Glamour theme. Darling, *do* realize you're not attending your own world première ... that this is Glamour's moment, not yours – and then we can all calm down and have an utterly lovely time.'

'Hear hear,' agreed Lush Martino, rolling up. 'Craven, old buddy, would you happen to have a li'l shot a somethin' on you ... bourbon, gin, sulphuric acid ...?'

'Alas, dear boy, I lack entirely and the bar is still an eternity away. However, my advice is to approach the young and hairy persons in the rear. Sharing your love of music, they may also effect an affinity with the other of your talents. Why not enquire?'

Lush peered myopically down the bus. 'You mean the guy with the parrot on his head?'

'The very same.'

'Oh, you do *see* a parrot on his head.'

'Certainly. It is his *modus operandi.*'

'Thank God, Craven ... for a moment I had the fear they were comin' on me again. Used t'see parrots all the time, mostly with two heads. Thanks, ole friend ...' He took a floaty step or two down the aisle but quickly returned. 'What d'ya say the parrot's name was again ... modus ...'

'Operandi,' smiled Snipe.

56

'Yeah ... screwy name, huh?'

With considerably difficulty he negotiated the aisle and reached the group, seated side-by-side on the rear seat.

'Hi, there, fellas!'

'Hi,' they chorused.

'You guys busy right now?'

'Yes, kinda,' said Shag McGee.

'Oh,' said Lush, understandably puzzled since the four of them appeared to be just sitting there and the parrot didn't seem all that busy either.

'Er, doin' what, exactly?' enquired Lush.

'We're composin',' explained Shag.

'Composin',' nodded the others.

'Now, that ... is interesting,' said Lush, slithering into a seat. 'Mind if I listen in?'

'No, that's OK,' said Shag.

'Bein' in the same business, I'm naturally interested.'

'Oh, you play with a group?'

Martino winced.

'What's yuh gimmick, man?' enquired Shag.

'Mm?'

'Yuh know – like Marlon, here.'

'Marlon ...?'

'The parrot, man – up here on my head.'

'His name's Marlon? Snipe told me it was ... it was...' Lush shook his head. 'The hell with it. Say, would you fellas happen to have a little tiger juice on yuh ... just a li'l somethin' to keep the membranes moist?'

'You mean ... alcohol?'

'That's the general direction, friend.'

'Stanley's gotta Coke.'

'I've gotta Coke,' said Stanley, brandishing the can.

Vincent blanched. 'No thanks – gotta watch my liver. Nuthin' else, huh?'

'No,' replied Shag.

'We've got Marlon's gin,' suggested Frankie.

'Oh, yeah!' said Shag.

'The parrot's a lush?' asked Vincent.

'No, he can hold it OK. He needs it to sleep. He don't sleep

57

so good without a shot. It's his nerves.'

'He looks kinda nervy,' agreed Martino. 'Do you think he'd mind parting with a little snort?'

Shag shrugged. 'We could chance it. Sydney ...'

Sydney stopped picking his nose. 'Yeah, Shag?'

'Give this fella a belt of Marlon's gin.'

Sydney opened his guitar case and produced a fifth of Gordons, its appearance lighting up Martino's eyes like glowing coals.

'Atta, *boy*! Hell, I never thought I'd be grateful to a parrot for a drink. Gotta lot more goin' for him than a lot of humans I know. Thanks, Marlon ...'

'Shag McGee!' screeched the parrot, cocking his head on one side and observing his gin disappearing down Martino's throat.

'Oh, boy ...' gasped Martino, lowering the bottle but making no attempt to return it. 'Say, I interrupted you fellas ... you go right ahead with your composin' and forget I'm here.'

'Oh, we're still doing it,' said Shag.

'What ... right now?'

'Sure – all the time. We never stop.'

'But ... I ain't heard anythin'.'

'That's because we do it silent. You get more uniqueness that way.'

'I'll bet.' Vincent took another deep swallow, closely watched by the parrot. 'Being a lyric man myself I'd kinda like to hear some of your stuff. What you workin' on right now?'

'An adaptation of an old Celtic haggis-stuffing chant. It's never bin done before.'

'You surprise me,' said Vincent, throwing another double down his throat. 'Mind if I hear it?'

Shag shrugged and turned to the others. 'OK – who wants the first line?'

They all looked at each other.

'OK' said Shag, 'I'll take off an' see what hatches,' He began clicking his fingers in rock beat, and, sensing what was coming, the parrot tightened its grip on Shag's head and shrieked, 'Blast off!'

'OHHH ... yellow belly bubbly gum and knickers on a string!' howled McGee.

'Father's makin' whoopee with his kinky ding-a-ling!' added Sydney.

'Carrots make yuh randy, boy, and chicory makes you sneeze!' contributed Frankie.

'If it wasn't for your shin bone, you'd be walkin' on your KNEES!' bellowed Stanley.

Chorus: 'Oooooooohhhhhh ... ooooooohhhhh ... ooooohhhh ... ooooohhhh!' they wailed, intending to continue into the second verse, but at that moment, seeing the last of his gin gurgling down Vincent's gluttonous gullet, Marlon let out another ear-splitter and took off in a towering rage, landed on Martino's head and began hacking out beakfuls of hair and spitting them on the floor.

'Yiiiikkkeee!' Martino let out a piercing shriek, took an almighty swipe at the bird with the empty bottle, missed, and socked himself a beaut. 'Ooowww! Getimoff! Getimoff! He's killin' me! Ooooooh! Oooowww! F'fucksake *do* somethin' you guys!'

Leaping from his seat he hared down the aisle, the lads after him, Stanley taking wild swipes at Marlon with his drumstick, missed once and caught Sam Chortle a biff on the ear, missed twice and knocked Craven Snipe's hat off.

'Getimoff! Getimoff!' screamed Martino, swinging his arms in a frenzy, ducking, weaving, throwing himself from side to side, finally falling full length into Gloriana's lap, whereupon the parrot, suddenly presented with a target of irresistible attraction, spat out a mouthful of Martino's hair and bit her hard on the left tit.

The awesomeness of her shriek hit Marlon like a baseball bat and with a screech almost matching her own, he took off in a flurry of flapping feathers, rose vertically to the roof and let go a load right in Martino's ear.

'They s .. say it's lucky,' said Shag McGee and Martino kicked him on the knee.

5

There was no denying that the nearer the Hilton the motor-cade got, the more cheerful Arnold Bottum became. It was there for all to see. Whatever colour they ever attained had returned to his pallid cheeks and somewhere along Kensington High he even managed a coy wave in response to a personal remark from a group of coarse soldiers.

Whether it was the consoling company of Sugar Sweetman, ever ready with a word of sympathy and a knee-pat of en-couragement, or the drive in the fresh air, or the fact that after a disastrous start they were, (due to the moderate Sunday traffic) miraculously more or less on time, even Arnold wouldn't have been able to say, but it was probably all three.

'Feeling better, aren't you?' smiled Sugar. 'Thought the drive would do you good.'

'Oh, oodles better, Sugar, thanks ever so much. I must say you've been a great help. Don't know what I'd have done without you.'

'How are we doing for time?'

'Oh, marvellously, marvellously,' he said, glancing for the three-hundredth time at his diamanté wrist-watch. 'Only about ten minutes late. 'Oh, I *do* hope there's a big press turnout. You never know, you know, right up to the last minute. They say they're coming then just don't turn up.'

'Now, don't worry, they'll be there, I just know. I have every faith in you. And they do have a very exciting story.'

'Well,' sighed Arnold, 'we'll soon know. Only another few minutes.'

Down the sun-filled canyon of Knightsbridge they drove and on to Hyde Park Corner, leaving the chic shops behind, the buildings finally giving way to the sylvan loveliness of the park, lush in its summer foliage.

A few moments more then a left turn into the park itself, into Park Lane West, a short drive up the Curzon Gate, a right turn onto Park Lane East and a quick return into the forecourt of the Hilton Hotel.

Long before the procession came to a halt, Arnold could see that his fears about the press had been needless, for clustered around the hotel entrance was a group of perhaps fifty journalists and photographers, eagerly awaiting their arrival.

As Rossiter's Rolls stopped, the pressmen broke and surged forward, deluging him with questions and photo-flashes.

Dutifully he got to his feet and posed for them, seriously, smilingly, comically, every which way, until one of them asked him to salute.

'The hell, I will, I'm no goddam doorman. OK, fellas that's enough. Go get the rest of my crew.'

'How about a group photo, captain – with the Hilton in the background?'

'OK, get them together.'

With squeals of delight Boobs and Wilma posed and preened as the flashes flared.

'This way, Babs ... say, could you bend down a little further ... holy Jeez, they're ... that's beautiful.'

'Now you, Wilma...'

'Charlie, your camera's shaking.'

'Bert, you ain't looking through this viewfinder!'

'OK, girls, now how about one sitting on the bonnet of the Rolls...?'

And so on.

For a full five minutes the crew posed in every conceivable position, Rossiter mostly scowling, Ramjet arching his brow so high he was getting a headache, James charming the lens-caps off the cameras, Bush flexing his muscles till they looked as though they'd burst, Sugar not giving a stuff, and the girls lapping it all up like a couple of thirsty spaniels.

'OK ... OK, that's enough!' Rossiter said finally. 'Don't

forget we've got some celebrities on board. Right, Arnold – let 'em out!'

Arnold signalled the bus driver who hit a switch and opened the pneumatic doors. First out was Fullbrush, madder than a scorpion that'd just sat on its own sting. Out she rushed, clasping her left breast, making a bee-line for Rossiter.

'Yuh ... silver-laméd skunk! How *dare* you keep me locked in there!'

'It was for your own benefit, Miss Full ...'

'Bollocks!'

'... brush. I wanted the crew outta the way so you could have the press all to yourself.'

'Rossiter ... you are trying your damndest to annihilate me press-wise! Well, we'll just see what Berskin has to say about it! ... like right now!' Into the hotel she swirled, smashing a photographer out of the way with a vicious chop to the head.

'Now, what got *her*?' he winced, rubbing his ear.

'My parrot,' replied Shag McGee. 'He bit her on the boob.'

'No kiddin'?' grinned Rossiter. 'Pity he ain't an eagle.'

'... and may Ah say, friends...' Senator Chortle was intoning, stetson over his heart in a posture of totally contrived humility, 'what a great personal pleasure an' privilege it is to be here in your wunerful city. Ah come as ambassador of filial friendship from mah own great land across th' sea, carryin' a whole mess o' cordial greetings from th' good folk of th' United States of Amurica to their beloved cousins in the United Kingdom, yes sirree. An' may Ah also say ...'

At that moment Lush Martino fell down the steps of the bus and put his foot inextricably through Stanley's drum, stealing the attention of the entire press as he was carried into the hotel for its removal by the resident carpenter and taking the press with him.

'Fatdangedn'fuckit!' seethed Chortle, crumpling his hat. 'That guy'll do *anything* ta hit the headlines!' He really was having a lousy press day. But, he schemed wolfishly, his mind on the TV coverage later that afternoon, the meat is yet ta come!

High above, in the gracious, spacious pink-and-white sitting room of Suite 702, a profoundly beautiful roof affording panoramic views of Hyde Park and south to Victoria Station, Miss Gloriana Fullbrush, star of stage, screen, and filthy temper, rammed a cigarette into her foot-long holder and snatched testily for the telephone, receiving the hotel operator's response instantly and courteously.

'Can I help you, Madam?'

'What kept you!' barked Gloriana.

'Madam . . . ?'

'What's happening with that New York number? I could've walked there and back by now!'

'I'm sorry for the delay, madam, but it has only been five minutes. I'll call you the moment it comes through.'

Gloriana slammed the phone into its cradle, sprang from the chair, strode across the room, snatched up her lighter, flicked it ineffectually several times then hurled the offending mechanism at the wall.

'Ge.e.r.a.l.d.!'

From the adjoining room emerged one of her three accompanying studs, an extravagantly beautiful young man of infinite indolence, clad only in an enquiring expression.

'Ready, Gloriana . . .'

'Not that, you idiot – get me a light!'

'Certainly, Gloriana.'

'And put your damn trousers on – you look like a penniless pole-vaulter!'

'Yes, Gloriana.'

He disappeared into the bedroom and re-emerged, trousered, with a book of matches.

'I'll show that bum,' seethed Gloriana, sucking the cigarette into life and blowing a furious stream of smoke at Gerald's navel. 'I'll have that Rossiter crawling on his hands and knees beggin' for *mercy* by the time I've finished with him!'

'Yes, Gloriana.'

The phone rang. She leapt to her feet, hurling Gerald aside with a thump in the chest. 'Go play with yourself – this is private!'

'Yes, Gloriana.'

She snatched up the phone. 'Yes?'

'Your call to New York, Miss Fullbrush...'

'About time ... hello...!'

A female voice, amazingly clear, announced, 'Colonel Berskin's residence ... who is calling, please?'

'Is that you, Destry? This is Gloriana Fullbrush ... is Berskin there?'

'Why, Miss Fullbrush...! How are you?'

'Never mind how I am, Destry – where's Berskin?'

'Well ... in bed, Miss Fullbrush. It's only eight a.m. here.'

'Wake him up, I want to speak to him!'

'But, Miss Fullbrush ...'

'*Get* him, Destry!'

A fraught pause. 'I'll ... see if he's asleep. Hold the line.'

Gloriana held ... and held ... and was about to hurl the phone through the window when the sleep-drugged growl of Berskin came on the line. 'That you, Fullbrush ...?'

'Sure, it's me! Now, listen here, Berskin...'

'Fullbrush! ... do you realize what *time* it is here in New York! It's eight o' goddam clock in the morning! What's goin' on over there!'

'I'm quittin' this mother-fuckin' tour is what's going on, Berskin – unless I get some respect around here! What the hell's the idea of shoving me in a tit-pink bus at London airport! And you'd better have a word with this dumb-bell captain of yours, he's gettin' above his station!'

'Rossiter? What's he bin doing?'

'Ha! What *ain't* he been doing! He hired four white Rolls-Royce convertibles for himself and the crew for the ride into London – while we were pigging it in that damn bus – is what he's been doing! The guy's gone berserk! Drunk with power! Now, you get him back down where he belongs – or I quit this minute!'

'OK ... OK! You tell him to expect a call from me at seven thirty tonight London time, I'll set him straight. Four Rolls-Royces! Holy Jeez ... anyway, apart from that, how's it going? Did you get good press at the hotel?'

'Lousy! Rossiter and his merry men hogged the lot! Nobody else could get a word in. I tell you, Berskin, this guy's developed a Hitler complex. Thinks he's King Dick over here.

Well, dick he certainly is, but he sure ain't the king. Now, you get him off my back and tell him to steer more publicity my way or I am o-u-t, y'hear?'

'I'd have t'be stone deaf not to, Fullbrush. OK, tell him seven thirty. Mighta known I couldn't trust a bunny-lover. You get right in there, Gloriana, an' do your stuff. And don't forget you're selling *Glamour*!'

With a smile like a coyote's snarl, Gloriana replaced the receiver and stood up.

'Gerald ...!'

Gerald emerged from the bedroom, once more clad in nothing but eagerness to please. 'Now, Gloriana ...?'

'Put it away, you blithering idiot. We're going to lunch.'

While in the foyer ...

'Engineer Officer Morton McKenzie ...' read the cute, dark-haired receptionist, perusing the registration card he had just completed. She looked up, flushing a little in his towering, muscular presence, thinking she'd never encountered such a handsome trio of fly boys in the three years she'd been booking in international aviation Adonises.

'You're the Australian one, aren't you?' she smiled, glancing at James and Ramjet standing a little way down the desk.

'Too right,' he grinned. 'Now, how did you know that?'

'I heard it on the radio this morning. Oh, we know all about you.' She leaned closer, beckoning him forward, and whispered, 'Which one's Lord Jim?'

Bush stabbed a finger in James's direction. 'Ugly, isn't he?'

She laughed. 'I think you're all lovely.'

'Now, isn't that nice.'

Flustered by his smile, she turned for his key and gave it to him. 'Room 614 ... it's a lovely one overlooking the park.'

'You're too kind, Miss ...'

'Adamson.'

'Miss Adamson.'

'I hope you'll have a very enjoyable stay with us.'

'If only it was longer. Talk about a flying visit ...'

'Maybe you'll be coming here a lot – when Glamour starts its regular runs.'

'I certainly hope so.'

'Yes ... so do I.'

Holy mackerel, he sighed ... if only there was more *time*. He turned towards Lord Jim, discovered that both he and Ramjet were deeply ensconced in their own flirtation with another receptionist, called, 'See you fellas later, I'm nipping up for a quick sluice,' then about-turned and collided with a girl.

'Oops!' he laughed, throwing his arms around her, instantly stirred by the feel and the smell of her. Releasing her he stepped back ... and swallowed hard. He had not been wrong. She was a knockout ... blonde, built, and utterly desirable.

'Gee, I'm ... I'm sorry,' he stuttered. 'Didn't see you there.' He coughed. 'I sure do now though.'

A nice smile, enjoying the flirtation. 'That's all right, no harm done.'

He shook his head. 'Oh, I wouldn't say that ...'

Mock consternation. 'Are you hurt somewhere?'

He nodded and clutched his heart. 'Right here. A chap doesn't run into a girl like you and emerge unscathed, you know.'

A reproving smile. 'Take a cold shower, it'll make it all better.'

She made a move to pass him and approach the desk and with a laugh he continued towards the elevators.

Dammit, why couldn't Berskin have made it a *four*-week tour! Seven days was bloody ridiculous. He decided he'd have a word with Rossiter about it, see if he couldn't get an extension ... claim crew fatigue or something.

He entered the car, grinning to himself. By heck, crew fatigue would be no lie the way things were going. The uniform was like a magnet to the little darlings. Berskin had certainly come up with a winner as far as the birds were concerned. Well, if it was like this in London, what was it going to be like if they hit Sydney!

Humming happily to himself, he rose to the sixth floor and did a little jig along the corridor, convinced that Ramjet, Jim and he should pressure Cock-up for an extension and deciding he'd approach the lads about it over lunch.

Entering room 614, he flung his overnight bag on the bed,

opened one of the windows, inhaled a huge chestful of fresh air, and studied himself in the wardrobe mirror.

'Bush, old son,' he said, flexing his biceps, triceps, pecs, and lats, 'I envisage for you a *very* interestin' time on this tour.' He tipped his cap to an outrageous angle and offered himself a flamboyant salute. 'First Officer Morton McKenzie – at your service, ma'm. If you'd care to lie down over here, I shall extol the delights of Glamour service to your complete satisfaction.'

With a laugh he flung his cap onto the bed, peeled off his jacket, removed his T-shirt and studied his fine, naked torso in the mirror. Not bad for a lad who's once been a seven-stone weakling. Mind you, he *had* only been five years old at the time.

Swaggering into the bathroom, he filled the washbasin, lathered up and hit himself in the face with three pounds of soap-suds – and then the knock sounded on the door.

'Oh, blimey ... jusht a minute!'

Towelling suds from his eyes, he opened it.

'Oh!' she laughed, 'I must have the wrong room. I was looking for Engineer Officer McKenzie not Father Christmas.'

Bush's ticker did a somersault. It was the blonde he'd bumped into in the foyer!

'Oh ...! Ah ... well, fancy meeting you again!' he blurted, thinking aye aye, now what's going on here?

She glanced quickly up and down the corridor and took a step nearer, obviously wishing to enter. 'I ... wonder if I could have a word with you?'

'Well ... sure .. certainly ... come on in.' She walked past him, bending his mind again with her perfume, and he closed the door.

Now, suddenly alone with her, in *his* room, the immediate excitement he'd felt in the foyer multiplied ten-fold. Down there their meeting had been accidental; now there was purpose to it. She'd followed him! By heaven, he'd pulled his first bird!

And *what* a bird ... eyes of cornflower blue and hair to bury your face in. A twenty-year-old filly with a naughty gleam in her eye and the equipment to back it up, standing there all loose and cuddly in a thin floral summer dress that saved you the trouble of wondering what was going on underneath. McKenzie, he conjectured, your hour has come.

'I was, er, just taking a wash,' he said ridiculously, not really knowing what he was saying and barely able to say it for the lump in his throat.

She laughed. 'What else?'

'Yes!' He gave a quick dab at the suds. 'I, er, hope I didn't do any damage downstairs. You haven't come to sue me or anything, have you?'

She shook her head, smiling at him. 'No, I haven't come to sue you. I've come to offer you a hotel service.'

His heart sank. 'You ... work here in the hotel?'

'Mm mm.'

'Oh ...'

A laugh. 'You sound disappointed.'

'Oh, no ... it's ... well, I'm just surprised – you being dressed like that. I thought you were a guest or ...' he gulped his disappointment. 'Look, d'you mind if I wash this soap off, my face is getting stiff.'

'No, I don't mind. May I talk to you while you're doing it?'

'Well, sure ... I'll leave the door open.'

He entered the bathroom and began sluicing his face, thinking, yer too good to be true, mate ... things like this just don't happen in real life. Ha! mighta known – a hotel service. They'll be on us like locusts everywhere we land.'

'My name is Cynthia Long,' she said from the doorway, her voice low, disturbingly sexy. ' "Sin" for short.'

Bush stopped sluicing, his heart skipping a beat. She was giving him the jolly old come on! He looked up at her, squinting through water, and knew from the audacious directness of her gaze that he was right.

'Sin Long, hm?' he grinned. 'I bet you get your leg pulled about that.'

'Among other things.'

Oh, blimey ...

With shaking hands he reached for the towel and straightened up, dabbed at his face and made a big thing of drying his mighty chest, saying, 'And ... what service are you selling exactly, Miss Long?'

'Sin?'

'Sin.'

'Personalized neuro-muscular and custom-applied physio-relaxator therapy.'

He laughed. 'Terrific – but what service are you selling exactly?'

'Massage, Mister McKenzie – in the privacy of your own room.'

Bush went a little dizzy. 'I ... see,' he croaked, running the towel, quite unnecessarily over his corrugated stomach muscles.

'You ... approve of massage?' she asked softly, covering his body with a slow, bold approbation, in a manner that told him her interest ran far deeper than the normal clinical interest of a professional masseuse.

'I should say I do,' he assured her. 'Never miss one after a work-out in the gym. As a matter of fact, I was wondering if I could squeeze in a bit of gym time here in London, but we're on such a tight schedule ...'

'Yes, I know. That's why I thought you might like a massage here and now – to freshen you up after your long flight. You must be *awfully* stiff.'

The double entendre brought him out in a sweat. 'I can hardly walk,' he grinned.

She gave a delightful smile, like she was working on commission. 'Then you would?'

'Sure thing. Even if I didn't need one, how could I possibly pass up the opportunity?'

'You'll feel so much better afterwards, I promise.'

'Sin, girl, I feel better already – just talkin' to you.' He threw the towel over the rail and raised his hands in surrender. 'Well, here I am. Where do you want me?'

She nodded. 'On the bed ... take your trousers off.'

'Mm?'

She laughed. 'Take your trousers off. You got shorts on, haven't you?'

'Sure.'

'So?'

'Well, it's . . .'

'. . . the first time you've been massaged by a female, hm?'

He shook his head. 'Nope – but it's the first time I've been done by a cracker like you.'

'Thank you – but try to think of me as sexless.'

'Ha!'

'Like a doctor or . . .'

'Sin, love, desist, you're wasting your time. It wouldn't matter if you were dressed like a welder, you'd still wreck a fella's blood pressure.'

She contrived a sigh. 'Officer McKenzie . . .'

'Bush.'

'Mm?'

'Bush. It's my nickname.'

'Because of your hairy chest?'

'No,' he laughed, 'because of the time I used to spend in the outback. You were going to say . . .'

'I was going to *ask* if you are ever going to remove your trousers.'

'Ah, well . . . yes, why not.'

He made a move for his flies. With a grin she turned into the bedroom. 'I'll prepare the bed.'

With shaking hands and thumping heart he dropped his trousers and stepped out of them, adjusted his Y-fronts to a semblance of modest order, and approached the door, discovering her peeling off the blanket and smoothing out the sheet.

'All set?' he asked.

She turned her head, her smile fading as her eyes covered him from head to toe then came back for another eyeful at the half-way mark. 'What a *splendid* specimen of manhood,' she whispered. 'You must spend absolutely *hours* doing it.'

'Just . . . whenever I can.'

'Such dedication.' She patted the bed. 'Come and lie down.'

He advanced into the room, inwardly a-quiver. 'Front or back first?'

'Your back. Lie face down.'

He did so while from her shoulder-bag she took a small bottle of oil, poured a drop into the palm of her hand, set the bottle down, bent towards him, and began.

Her first fleeting caress, so very gentle, sent a shudder of ecstasy rippling up his spine, bringing his hair erect, and closing his eyes with a soft moan.

She grinned, delighted with his reaction. 'Nice?'

'Ohh ... *baby* ...'

'We'll soon smoothe out all those nasty aches and pains,' she cooed, trickling her mink-soft hands up and down his backbone then up over his Samsonian shoulders, feeling him relax completely, sink deep into the mattress under her spell.

'You have a wonderful body,' she murmured approvingly, relishing its strength, its golden sheen. 'You have no idea what a pleasure it is to do this ... a rare pleasure.'

'Thank you,' he mumbled, his face in the pillow. 'I'm surprised you notice ... thought a body would just be a body in your job.'

'Oh, no! Masseuses are only human, you know – we can't help admiring a beautiful body when we ... come across it.'

'I can see your point. Matter of fact, I rather fancy the job myself ... provided I got customers like you.'

She slapped him playfully on the bottom. 'Behave yourself.'

'You're askin' an awful lot ... the things you're doing to me right now. Tell me ... do you ever get any trouble?'

'Trouble?'

'With your male clients. Do they ever get randy on you?'

With his eyes closed, he failed to see her quick, devilish smile. 'Occasionally.'

'Reckon you know how to deal with them, though, hm?'

'I reckon.'

'How do you ... oh, that's beautiful ... cope with them – a Kung Fu kick in the artichokes?'

'Something like that,' she laughed. 'It ... depends ...'

'On?'

'On the man.'

'I see. And, er, how would you cope with a bloke like me?'

'Are you ... likely to get randy?'

'You keep stroking me there and I wouldn't like to say what'll happen.'

'You mean ... here ... like this?' she chuckled, running her

71

fingers up his leg and sliding them under his shorts.

He jumped. 'Ex*actly* like that.'

'Bush ... can you move over a bit? The bed's too low, I'll have to sit down. Makes my back ache.'

He grinned. 'What you need is a good massage.'

'Are you offering?'

'Let's ... just say one good turn deserves another. How about it?'

'You just keep quiet and concentrate on being done.'

'You know, I'd say your job was a lot more dangerous than mine. I can imagine an awful lot of fellas getting some mighty fancy ideas in this position.'

'Ideas don't hurt. Anyway, it's all part of the therapy – gets the juices working.'

He chuckled. 'You can say that again.'

'Now, *that* sounds ominous. And at this point, with certain clients, I might have to revert to Plan B.'

'And what is Plan B?'

'I become aloof, ice-cold, strictly impersonal.'

He pretended a shudder. 'How terrible. Don't think I could stand that. Are you ... thinking of reverting with me?'

A small pause ... and a soft response. 'No, not with you, Bush McKenzie. This is bonus day for me. Do you realize how many millions of British women would give their eye teeth to be doing what I'm doing right now ...?'

'Ha!'

'No, I mean it. You Glamour boys have stirred up terrific excitement over here. Your pictures have been in all the papers for the past week ... and when we heard on the radio this morning that you were heading for London ... well, I reckon there're going to be a few thousand female suicides in the provinces because they can't get to see you in the flesh.'

He chuckled. 'And you really do mean "in the flesh". Well, anyway, they'll get a chance to see us on TV.'

She sighed woefully. 'A *very* poor substitute.' Then a devious chuckle. 'Oh, if only they could see me now. Ha, I do like it – a Glamour man all to myself and *really* in the flesh. What a lovely thought.'

'It's not exactly disaster for me, either. You might have

72

been a twenty-stone all-in-wrestler – the usual masseuse type. Hey ...!'

'What?'

'I want to turn over and look at you.'

'So – turn!'

He flipped over, lay with his arms behind his head, looking at her. 'Yes ... just as beautiful as I remembered.'

'Arms down, eyes closed, mouth shut,' she ordered, pouring more oil into her hand.

Now, she moved closer to him, placed her hands on his powerful chest, shivering slightly, thrilling to the majestic maleness of him and to his pullulating priapic promise. What a romp this one would be ... hard as iron, big as a bull. With pounding heart she lowered her gaze, down across the washboard plateau of his belly to the mound of imprisoned joy threatening to burst his shorts, a right old handful even in repose.

The sight of it stirred her mightily and the sudden image of her mounting him where he lay caught her breath in a tiny, indrawn gasp. Suddenly the twinge of delicious pain, the heart-cry from her loins, was too much to bear and she decided instantly on the short-cut. What the hell was the point of pretending any longer?

'Phew!' she sighed, wiping an arm across her forehead. 'Don't you think it's awfully warm in here?'

He opened an eye. 'I thought it was dead right – mind you, I'm not doing any work.'

'It's the angle of attack,' she explained. 'It's much easier on a massage table ... I'd be standing over you. It's much less of a strain.'

'Mm,' he mused, working on the problem. 'Isn't there any way you could ... you know ... maybe kneel up ... on the bed?'

'Well ... I could try.'

He inched nearer the edge of the bed, making more room for her. She knelt at his side, made a few passes, then sank back on her heels, shaking her head. 'Nope, the angle's still wrong. Maybe if I could get my knee in between yours...'

'Hm hm,' he nodded, opening his legs.

She swung her knee in, now straddling his right leg, her own excitingly parted and the flimsy dress riding high on her naked thighs.

'Ah, much better,' she smiled, leaning far forward and once again attacking his chest muscles, her splendid breasts almost totally exposed to his view.

It was all too much for him. With wildly thumping pulse, his mind addled by her perfumed closeness, her jiggling boobs, he cast all caution to the devil, grabbed her wrists and spread them wide, bringing her hard down on top of him.

She gasped. 'Hey ...!'

'I can't stand it any longer! You're driving me crazy!'

'Let me ... go! You're ruining my dress!'

'I'll buy you another ... ten!'

'The oil ... I'll get oil on it!'

'Then take it off!'

'Are you mad?'

'Yes ... for you!'

She fought valiantly. 'Bush McKenzie ... this is ... *not* part of the service!'

'Then change the service.'

'Will you ... *please* let me go!' she cried, wriggling all over him, thrilling to his stupendous hard-on. The size of it!

Suddenly she relaxed, went totally limp, simply lay upon him, delighting in the rock-like core between her legs.

'That was ... very naughty,' she panted, her cheek against his and the man-smell of him driving her cuckoo. 'Very ... deceitful, too.'

'I couldn't help myself,' he gasped, kneading her mounding buttocks in his trembling hands. 'The sight of you ... kneeling over me ... it's more than a man can stand.'

'Nevertheless, it's ... very rude to grab. At least you might have asked.'

'You'd have said no.'

'I ... might not have done.'

A stunned silence ... broken by his rumbling chuckle.

Cynthia raised her head. 'What's funny?'

A relieved laugh. 'I thought you'd yell the place down and call the management!'

'Well . . . if it hadn't been you, I would have.'

'Am I forgiven?'

She lowered her cheek again and idly twirled a curl of his chest hair around her finger. 'It . . . depends.'

'On?'

'You.'

'Oh . . .?' The lump was there again, choking him. 'How on me?'

'On . . . how well you make love to me.'

He gulped.

She moved then, withdrew from him until she was kneeling upright between his legs. For a moment she looked down at him, smoulderingly, then slowly undid the buttons of her dress and demolished him with her sudden nakedness.

She held out her arms, posing for his inspection. 'Any complaints?'

He shook his head wonderingly. 'Not a one.'

Then she fell forward and attacked his shorts, peeled them off, and stared wide-eyed at the prize she had revealed. 'My . . . God!'

He laughed. 'Any complaints?'

'Yes,' she nodded. 'I can still see him.'

And then she swallowed him.

'Ohhh . . .!' she gasped.

'What's the matter?'

'Bush, I'm coming . . .!'

'*Again?*'

'Again . . .'

'But . . . this is three times!'

'Four – but who's counting. McKenzie, you're driving me crazy . . .!'

'Wonderful.'

'Wonderful . . .? It's fantastic . . .! Ohhhh . . . oh, my God, I'm there!'

'Tally-ho!'

'OHHHH . . .!'

High above and wide astride him, she rode him in frenzy to the peak of ecstasy then collapsed upon him, breasts heaving against his sweating, oily chest, her ruptured breathing hissing in his ear. 'Oh, God ... God, that was beautiful ... oh, you big, hard, gorgeous, randy brute ... I want to stay here all day long and just do it and do it and do it ...'

'Suits me just fine,' he laughed, hugging her to him. 'If only we had more time ...'

'We have *some*, though, haven't we? You don't have to go for a while?'

'Well ... lunch *is* supposed to be at one. It's about that now.'

'Do you *have* to go?'

He sighed regretfully. 'If I don't they'll come looking for me.'

'Oh, fuck it, Bush, I *need* you ... we've only done one way! I want it dozens of ways!'

He laughed. 'You do?'

'Of course, I do ... backwards, sideways, upside down, on the floor, in the shower ... I can't let you go now ... I *won't*!'

'Baby, you know I'd rather stay here doing you than go down to some daft lunch, but ...'

'Oh ...' she groaned. 'Well, how long have we got, then?'

'Five minutes ... ten at the most.'

She nodded, determinedly. 'OK – so why are we wasting it? Let's go ...!'

'Which way?'

'Every way! Let's grab a bit of each.'

'All right. First ...?'

'Backwards!'

'Way ya go!'

She sat suddenly erect, gasping as he again took her to the hilt, then slowly raised herself from him, grimacing as he withdrew. 'Bush *McKenzie* ... that is positively indecent!'

With a laugh he rolled off the bed. She dived forward, buried her cheek in the pillow, then he was up behind her, settled himself, took careful aim ... and thrust.

'Yoooowwww!' she gasped.

'Comfy?'

'You struck bone! ... breastbone! Ohhh ... ohhhh, honey go ... GO!'

76

He went.

She tore at the pillow, clawed the mattress, moaned and groaned and yelped then suddenly it was on her, a right old ripper that soared so high and stayed up there, way at the top, sustained by Bush's pile-driver thrust.

'Stop ... stop!' she cried, tearing her hair in frenzy.

'You mean it?' he gasped.

'No ... no! Oh, God, it's too wonderful! Bush ... I want you on the floor ... crush me ... smother me ...!'

'Right ho, girl, off you come!'

She flung herself from the bed onto the thick, curly carpet, spreading herself hungrily. 'Quick ... quick!'

Down he went, all the way home.

'Oh, Bush ... Bush ... shoot me! ... fill me ...!'

'But ... what about the shower!'

'Fuck the shower! Fill me!'

Released now from all restraint he went berserk, pummelled and pumped like fury, goaded by her screaming need. And then ... a gargantuan gasp and with a whild whoop he exploded, really came apart at the seams.

'Ohhhhh ... Mc ... *Kenzie!*' she cried, collapsing beneath him.

'Hohhhhh, yourself!' he laughed, collapsing beside her.

'You ...' she shook her head. 'God you've *finished* me!'

'I'm not so flamin' lively meself.'

She chuckled delightedly. 'Boy, you really do go.'

'*I* really go! Who was it hit double figures?'

'Well, what d'you expect with that thing? Just the sight of it ...'

A rap on the door startled them. Bush raised himself on an elbow. 'Yes, who is it?'

'Your captain, McKenzie!' shouted Rossiter. 'Come on – hop to it, lunch is ready!'

'Ten minutes, hm?'

'Ten minutes nuthin'! Get your ass downstairs on the double, everyone's there!'

'OK, OK.'

'What're you doing – a few pre-lunch push-ups?'

Cynthia stifled a laugh.

77

'Yes, sort of,' grinned Bush. 'Just limbering up after the flight.'

'Well, make sure you limber down – like right now!'

'All right, you go ahead.'

Rossiter shuffled off.

Bush touched her nose affectionately, said regretfully, 'I've got to go, honey.'

'I know. Bush ... it was wonderful.'

'Crazy. Boy, I wish there was more time. Never mind, we'll be doing a regular route pretty soon and I know where to find you.'

She nodded. 'Sure ... come on, you'll be late.'

They dressed quickly and Bush saw her to the door, suddenly remembering: 'Hey, I almost forgot ...!'

'What?'

'Your fee!'

She hesitated. 'Oh ...'

'Heck, no you're a working girl. The management will be wondering what you were doing up here if you've nothing to show. How much is it?'

Regretfully. 'Well ... it's kind of pricey, I'm afraid. You know what Hiltons are like.'

'Sure, I know. How much do I owe you?'

'Bush ... it was such a pleasure I really hate to take the money ...'

'Nonsense ... we're getting well paid for the tour. Just name it.'

She sighed. 'You know, normally I don't mind charging at all, but ... Bush, I'm afraid it's twenty pounds.'

'Twe ...' He gave a cough, then a shrug. 'Well, like you said, it *is* the Hilton.'

'I really am sorry.'

'Nah, think nothing of it.' He got out his wallet and counted off the bills. 'Only got dollars, I'm afraid, but they shouldn't mind.'

'No, they won't.'

'That's, er ... well, let's call it sixty bucks – with a little something for yourself.'

'Oh, Bush, thank you.'

'No,' he grinned, 'I thank *you*. It was beautiful. I feel a new

78

man.'

She laughed. 'You do?'

'Sure – about half as strong as I was but *very* relaxed.'

She tucked the bills into her shoulder-bag, kissed him on the cheek, and opened the door. 'Have a lovely time around the world. How I envy all those girls out there.'

He groaned. 'You're joking. You've left nothing for them.'

'Good. Well, goodbye, Bush ...'

' 'Bye, Sin – and thanks for coming ... I mean ...'

'Thank you!' she laughed and was gone.

Bush closed the door, heaved a sigh, shook his head, gave her a moment longer, then left the room.

Floating along the corridor he suddenly realized he had no idea where the luncheon room was located, so he descended to the foyer and approached Miss Adamson on reception.

'Why, Officer McKenzie ...' she smiled, flusteredly.

'Hello, Miss Adamson. I seem to have lost the rest of the crew. Could you point me in the right direction?'

She did so, adding. 'I hope you found everything to your liking.'

A lop-sided grin. 'Miss Adamson, I can truthfully say I have never stayed in a more accommodating hotel. I think your room service is out of this world. I feel a completely new man after that massage.'

Her smile faded. 'Erm ... massage?'

'Sure – you know, the old rub down. Ironed out all the creases a treat.'

Her frown deepened. 'But you said ... room service.'

'Sure – you know, the girl that ... Miss Long, the girl that ... does the massaging ...' She was shaking her head. '... in the room ...?' His voice tailed away.

'But ... we don't *have* such a room service, Mister McKenzie.'

He gulped. 'You don't?'

'Indeed not. Er, what was this Miss Long like?'

'Like ...? Well, I think you saw her. I bumped into her right here ...'

Her eyes widened. 'The blonde? ... in the floral dress?'

'Yes, that's her.'

'But ...' she shook her head bewilderedly, 'she doesn't work for us. She asked me the way to the ladies' powder room.'

Buzz gaped at her. 'But ... well ... are you *sure*?'

In answer she glanced along the counter to the dark-haired girl who had booked in James and Ramjet. 'Marion ...'

She came over.

'Marion ... we don't have a massage room service, do we – a girl named Long?'

Marion flashed a bemused smile at Bush and frowned at Miss Adamson. 'Massage room service – are you kidding? We'd have the League of Decency storming the foyer before she'd finished her first client.'

Adamson turned to the perplexed McKenzie. 'What exactly did she ... say?'

'Say? Oh, just that she ... oh, it was all perfectly *respectable*, you understand. I mean, she was *very* professional ... no hanky-panky or anything. No, she just said that she was offering a massage room service and asked would I ... well, after the long night flight and all I naturally ...'

'Oh, *naturally*,' hastened Adamson, glancing with horror at her friend. 'Well, what a peculiar thing ... er, Marion, I really think we ought to tell the management. I mean, we can't have freelance masseuses wandering in off the street and ...' She turned to Bush. 'Mister McKenzie, I *do* apologize if you've been troubled by this woman ...'

'Troubled! Oh, no, not troubled, Miss Adamson. As I say, she was *very* professional and ...'

'Well, how much did she ... sort of *charge*?'

A throw-away laugh. 'Oh, hardly anything at all ... five dollars ... *very* reasonable, I thought. Well, ha! I'd better be off. They'll have finished lunch by the time I get there. I'll, er, see you later ...'

He turned away, dying for a chuckle. Well, by God, could you beat that! He'd been hustled in Honolulu, seduced in Sacramento, laid in Llandudno and now hooked in the Hilton. Sixty bucks he'd parted with, neat as ninepence. And, he reflected, as he headed across the foyer, worth every blinkin' penny of it.

Ho ho, well, now, that was one up on Ramjet and Lord Jim! And he couldn't *wait* to tell them.

6

Bush McKenzie fell asleep during lunch. One minute he was chatting away to Delicious O'Hara, seated on his right, enjoying the friendly warmth of her hand upon his thigh and wondering if there'd be anything doing in *that* direction later in the tour, and the next minute, overcome by exhaustion, his chin dropped to his chest and he was away.

O'Hara, naturally taking umbrage, hit him over the head with a stick of wet celery, waking him with such a start that he stuck his elbow in his soup and knocked his cob and butter into the velvet lap of Princess Rominova, an émigré journalist fallen on hard times and currently freelancing for such publications as the 'Embalmers and Allied Trades Monthly', seated on his left.

'Yuh bum!' raged Delicious, momentarily dropping her Mae West croon in favour of her natural Brooklyn scrawk. 'Yuh fell asleep on me! Nobody falls asleep on O'Hara – leastwise not sittin' down!'

'Sorry, love,' he apologized. 'Must be the wine.'

A plausible excuse since the wine, copiously provided by Arnold Bottum as a press enticement, was wreaking its insidious havoc up and down the vast table, to the extent that all in attendance were, at least, giggly and at most smashed to the eyeballs.

Lush Martino, as might be expected, fell firmly into the latter category, the removal of Stanley's drum from his foot constituting the reason for his current celebration. Seated between Gloriana Fullbrush and Boobs Buchanan, he had so far spent the entire meal time attempting to relate a joke to either one, or both, or neither, and had so far managed no more than the opening line.

'Say, now, lissen...' he insisted, turning on Boobs and grabbing her arm as she was about to sip her white wine, jolted it, and spilled a quarter glass down her yawning cleavage.

'Eeeeek!' she screeched. 'It's f .. freezing!'

'Here,' said Lush, fumbling for his hanky, 'let me ... OK – let you.' He shoved it down her bosom and watched weavingly as she plunged and scoured. 'Now, where was I? ... damndest joke you ever heard ... hey, Gloriana, where was I?'

Gloriana turned with a sneer. 'Where were you when, Vincent?'

He blinked at her. 'Where was I when? What a ridiculous question. What d'you mean where was I when? Doesn' make sense.' He turned back to Boobs who was ringing out the hanky into her side salad. 'Does that make sense to you, honey?'

'Oh, I'm not going to eat it.'

'Hm...?'

'I shan't eat it.'

His brows met in a confused frown. 'Honey ... did I ever tell you the one about the Martian who landed in Vegas, walked up to the first one-arm bandit he'd ever seen, and said, "Take me to Adolf"?'

'No, tell me.'

'Well, there was this ... I just told yuh!'

'About what, Mister Martino?'

'Jeezus, is *every*body pissed around here!'

While down the table ...

'Gee, I'm so *thrilled* to be able to interview you, Mister McGee, 'trilled teenage reporter Shirley Curl.

'Oh, really?' replied Shag, emptying his salad into his shirt pocket for Marlon.

'I should say so. Gee, my readers are going to be *scats* with my exclusive about you and your *yummy* group on this your

82

first visit to London.'

'Oh, really?'

'I should say so. But ... apart from the information on the press hand-out, could you possibly give me some, well, more *intimate* information about you and your *fab* group for your simply *millions* of British fans?'

'Sure,' he said, adding a little salt to the salad. 'Whatdya want to know?'

'Well ... for instance – how you live. I expect you have a *fab* pad in New York – something like the Beatles had in "Help" ... or was it "Hard Day's Night"?'

'No.'

'Oh ... which film was it then?'

'I mean, no I ain't gotta fab pad. I live in an undertaker's parlour...'

'Oh, come on.'

'... in a coffin.'

'Aw, come *on*!'

'Perfec'ly true.'

It was anything but perfec'ly true. Shag lived with his mother. But the coffin story made more press.

'In a *coffin*!' scoffed Shirley, an attractive girl with poker straight hair and a squint. 'Shag McGee, you're putting me on!'

'Nope. It's my uncle's parlour. My parents were killed in a popcorn explosion when I was three days old ... my father overloaded the machine. I was raised by my uncle who only had one room for himself, so my four brothers and me had to sleep in the coffins.'

'Way ... out!' giggled Shirley, scribbling madly on her thigh.

'What you doin' that for?' enquired Shag.

'What?'

'Writing on your leg.'

'I forgot my pad. Tell me ... how did the parrot get into the act?'

'Fortuitous, really. My uncle had a budgerigar named Alice Fay. One night it flew out of its cage and perched on my head while I was lying in my coffin. On seeing this phenonem ...

phemonem ... this strange occurrence, my younger brother, Flint, said, "Hey, wouldn't it be sumpn if you grew up to be a famous pop star an' wore a parrot on your head". And so...'

'Er, hang about, I've lost something...'

Shag made a dive under the table but Shirley stopped him. 'No, I mean in your story. You said you were only three days old when your mother died...'

'Right on.'

'So ... how can you have a younger brother?'

'Er ... ah, we was twins! He was born the day after me. Mute point, granted, but I always think of him as my younger brother.'

'Fine,' she nodded, writing now on her other leg, having filled the first. 'And what happened ... oh!'

'What's wrong?'

Wide-eyed with horror, she pointed her ball-point at the spreading patch of blood over Shag's heart. 'Y .. you're bleeding!'

He looked down. 'Nah, it's the tomato. Marlon likes tomatoes. Raw onion on rye is his favourite, but he sure digs tomatoes.'

'Raw ... onion ... on ... rye...' she wrote, the rye disappearing up her knickers. 'We'll have to try and get him some.'

'Already got some,' grinned Shag, slapping his pocket. 'Wow, that tomato's cold.'

Sam Chortle was indisputably in his element. Seated between voluptuous airstew Wilma Fluck, on his right, and nubile lady journalist, Billy Jo Labinovitch, on his left, he poured a non-ending stream of charm, wit, and bull-dust into their delicates while now and then dropping a hand to their thighs for a fatherly feel, encouraged that so far neither one had seriously objected.

What-*ho*, he thought to himself – played with tact, subtlety, and caution this could well lead to a little after-hours hanky-panky that would make this stuffing tour just the minutest bit worthwhile. And this, undoubtedly, seemed the time to strike – while the spirit of Nuits St. Georges '72 was upon them.

Thus, emboldened by four glasses of the sporting little wine himself, he made his play.

'Devilish tight, wouldn't you say mah dear,' he murmured fruitily, leaning closer to Wilma for another sly feel.

She turned to him, seemingly oblivious to his creeping encroachment on her honour. 'Who is, senator?'

'Sam,' he chided her. 'Call me Sam. Not "who", mah dear – "what". The schedule. Damned tight, wouldn't yuh say? Don't give us a *smidgin* of time to ourselves ... to do the li'l thangs ever' human heart cries out ta do ... ta take a leisurely stroll through a woodland glade ... smell th' flowers and listen ta the birds asingin' in the trees ... ta take a li'l pleasure among solid citizens in a cheerful hostelry along the dusty road ... know what Ah mean?'

'No.'

He heaved a sigh of diminishing hope. 'Ah *mean*, honeh, that it's a cryin' shame that fat cat Berskin hasn't lined up some night-life fo' us! Heck, think about it ... we go straight from here to th' TV studios, then back to th' hotel, then on ta that there dinner which lasts till midnight ... gosh a'mighty, where's th' *fun* in all this? ... tell me where in heck the *fun* is.'

'I ...'

'Heck 'n goshakes, here we all are doin' Berskin a *mighty* big favour ... advertisin' *his* airline, talkin' ta the *press*, appearin' on *TV*, an' generally breakin' *our* backs fo' his benefit – an' gettin' *nothin'* in return! Now, does that seem fayah and right ta you?'

'Well ...'

'O' course it don't an' I'm glad t'hear yuh speak your mind. Look, tell yuh what ...' he inched closer, slipped his arm round her waist, lowered his voice to a murmured growl. 'Honeh, Sam Chortle is just *not* gonna stand by an' see you girls taken advantage of, no siree. If Berskin is too danged tight-fisted ... too thoughtless to see you girls have some fun, then Sam Chortle is gonna rectify that injustice. Tell me, dear, what is your room number ...?'

'Erm ...' Wilma did not know her room number from the dish of olives she was absently demolishing, but one thing she *did* know and that was that she had absolutely no intention of being humped by this fat pig that night or any other night. And so, in order to avoid immediate unpleasantness, she selected the first number that popped into her squiffed little mind which happened to be the number of an apartment in the Bronx which she had once briefly shared with an Italian minestrone millionaire whom she'd met on the Cincinatti run, and replied, 'Eight oh six.'

'Eight ... oh ... six,' he repeated lasciviously, fixing it firmly in his mind. 'Well, now, mah dear, how would it be if old Sam kinda popped along to eight ... oh ... six tonight – say around one thirty? – armed with a coupla bottles of best bubbly – an' tried ta compensate a li'l for Berskin's dis*gus*tin' lack of hospitality?'

She gave an affected giggle and fluttered her eyelashes. 'Senator ... I think that would be just fan-tastic!' She gave a wince as his fingers dug deep.

'You betcha sweet li'l ole *bippy*, it'll be fantastic,' he chuckled. 'OK, honeh, you got yourself a date!'

Consumed with self-satisfaction, he straightened in his chair, his eye sliding greedily to the fine specimen of womanhood on his left. Well, he chortled, and why not? Nuthin' like a little reserve in th' bank to fall back on.

Biding his time, he waited until she drained her glass then plunged, seizing the bottle.

'Allow me, honeh ...'

'Why, *sen*ator,' she smiled provocatively, 'I do believe you're trying to get me shickered.'

'Now why would Sam Chortle want ta do a thang like that?'

'Possibly in the hope of seducing me,' she suggested, with startling honesty.

He gave a start, startled by her honesty. 'Why, Miss Labinovitch ...!'

'Go on,' she laughed, nudging him, 'be honest. Wouldn't you *like* to seduce me?'

'Why, I ...'

She moved closer, growled sexily. 'Wouldn't you like to come creeping along to my room tonight and make mad,

86

tempestuous love to me . . .?'

'Mah *dear*, I . . .'

'Wouldn't you just *love* to tear off all my clothes . . . and fling me naked on the bed . . . and climb on top of me . . . and . . .'

'Ssssh, my dear!' he protested, glancing about him. 'F'gosh-sakes . . .'

A taunting whisper. 'Well, wouldn't you?'

'Well . . . y . . yes, Ah *would* . . .'

Her face snapped straight. 'Well, tough luck, you randy old bastard! You couldn't get within a *mile* of my pants if you were the last man on earth! And the next time you grab my leg like that, I'll drive a fork through it – get it?'

Chortle got it.

At the same time, Captain Cock-up Rossiter, positioned centre-table in the seat of honour, was also getting it – both barrels – from Lady Penelope Sedgwick-Best, a sultry, raven-haired beauty and professional nymphomaniac, known to her more intimate friends as Slut.

Attracted by the novelty of the challenge offered, she had, on hearing of Glamour Airlines' pending arrival in London, temporarily set aside her determination to seduce every single member of a visiting French tennis team and had instead fixed her sexual sights on the entire Glamour crew, a project which, at the very least, would provide a memorable entry in her Screwy Scrapbook and a proud wall-plaque for the Games Room of Sedgwick House, and at the very most result in five delightful rumbles of which she was patently fond.

Chagrined to discover, however, the tightness of the Glam-our schedule which would, time-wise, disallow a total harvest, she had settled with true blue-blooded grit for the leader of the pack, convincing herself that, as their representative, seduction of him was in essence seduction of them all, and that its ac-complishment would, in all conscience, constitute total victory.

So determining, she had, in her inimitable fashion, set about acquiring not only an invitation to the press luncheon but also a seat next to the good captain, and was at that moment earn-estly ensconced in the mission she had set herself.

'Your first visit to London, captain?' she husked, leaning close and sending him cross-eyed with a whiff of Jean-Pierre Fontainbleau's staggering new perfume 'Rut'.

'No, ma'am,' he replied hazily, partly from 'Rut' but mostly from 'plonk'. 'Used to fly in regularly with Dewey.'

'Ah. And ... who is Dewey?'

'Dewey Airlines, ma'm – what the line was called before it became Glamour.'

'A *fascinating* story. Your Colonel Berskin sounds a thrilling sort of person to know.'

'Yeh, thrilling.'

'... bold imaginative. What an *inspired* concept – Glamour for the masses.'

'That's the word for it.'

'And what an inspired choice of crew to launch the project. I don't suppose I've ever seen such a handsome, charming, and ... well, yes – *glamorous* assembly of men in one aircrew ... Rogers, McKenzie, Crighton-Padgett – three outstanding specimens, each in his own way ... and, of course, you yourself, their leader, *dear* Captain Rossiter. How *very* striking you look in your Glamour uniform.'

The touch of her hand on his arm, her perfume, her closeness, and the outrageous sensuality of the woman rocked Rossiter to his boots, set his heart thumping and his free hand shaking so much his ice-cream slid off his spoon and plopped unheeded into his wine.

'You ... think so?' he croaked, quite astounded by this totally unexpected show of affection from such a ravishing creature.

'Indeed I *do!*' she enthused, intimately close, fingering his silver-lamé sleeve. 'You cut a very dashing figure – far more so, if I may say, than the other members of your crew.'

'Aw, come on ...' he grinned.

'No, no, I mean it! Oh, tall, bronzed, athletic they look, certainly, and they'll undoubtedly send thousands of women ga-ga on this tour – a certain *type* of woman, that is. But there are other women, dear captain – perhaps just that *little* more discerning – who search beneath the exotic exterior for the more meaningful qualities in a man ... qualities of maturity, wisdom, gentleness, and sensitivity. And for such a woman there could only be one man of real interest in your crew ... and I think you know who he is.'

'Well, I ...'

'Ah,' she sighed, 'and modest, too. Is there no *end* to your attributes, captain?'

'Well, I ...'

Tongue-tied little runt, she thought despairingly. God, have I really picked a dog after all? Have I passed up the beautiful horny Rogers, the deliciously muscular McKenzie, and the delectable Crighton-Padgett for this! Well, Rossiter, you're going to come up with a kicker whether you like it or not! Penelope is *not* wasting her goodies on any limp Leonard, project or no project!

Determination re-affirmed, she moved into second gear and attacked out of the sun on the vanity tangent.

'Captain ... does it surprise you that a woman like me finds you fascinating? I'm sure it doesn't. I'm sure that wherever you've touched down in the great wide world there has always been a discerning woman attracted by your unique and *exciting* brand of animal magnetism.'

Rossiter blinked. 'Mm?'

'Oh, come,' she smiled, 'modesty forbids, I know, but I can't be fooled. I feel it here.' She clutched her left breast, a fair old handful, delighting in the nervous sweat that broke out on Rossiter's upper lip as his eyes invaded her cleavage. 'Captain ...' she continued imploringly, 'time is short – *des*perately short – and there is so much I wanted to know about you ... the *essential* you. Not the glitter and tinsel of your public life, but the quiet, secret by-roads of your alter existence – your hopes, your dreams ... your hobbies, for instance. What sort of hobbies do you enjoy?'

'I breed rabbits.'

'Rabbits!' she exclaimed, a surprising reaction since she didn't know a Flemish Giant from a fan-tail pigeon. 'How incredible ...'

'Oh?' said Rossiter, coming alive. 'You breed them, too?'

'Well ... not exactly *breed* them, but I simply *adore* the fluffy little darlings. How many times I have determined to do something about breeding them, yet, sadly, have never actually been able to start. It was my late husband, you know ... couldn't stand them near him. He had an allergy to their fur.'

'Oh, too bad ...'

'One felt the loss,' she nodded disconsolately, 'and went on hoping that one day ... oh, captain, there is *so* much you could teach me ... if only there was more *time* ...'

'Pretty well non-existent,' he allowed. 'Soon as we've finished lunch it's out to the TV studios, then it's over to Knightsbridge for the banquet which lasts until midnight...' He sighed unhappily.

'And ... after dinner?' she probed, tentatively.

'Well, I ...'

'Captain ... I would hate to think that what I am about to suggest might be construed as immodest, but ... couldn't we ... after the dinner ... perhaps a quiet drink...?'

He cleared his constricted throat. 'Well, certainly ... that would be ... but doesn't everywhere close down ... I mean ...'

She lowered her dark lashes, modestly, yet continued to press home the attack with insidious insistence. 'Yes, I'm afraid so. Captain ... had we the time I would *dearly* love to invite you to my home this evening, but since that isn't possible, I ... would not take amiss an invitation to yours instead.'

'Mine? ... but, I ... oh.' The point went home, bringing a flush to his face. 'Well, I ...'

'I would be *most* discreet,' she whispered earnestly. 'I would be a shadow – unseen, unheard. No one would know, I promise you. Captain...' once more her fingers crept to his sleeve, 'it would mean *so* much to me. An hour, no more.'

Holy Boeing, gasped Rossiter, is this happening! Hee hee! He'd pulled a bird! Great balls of bullshine – one of the best-lookers at the table *and* a title to boot!

It was the stripes, he decided. She was one of those dames who just *had* to screw the chairman. Captain or nothing. He'd met them before. They waltzed past the minions, regardless of type, and made a bee-line for the bald-headed old coot on the rostrum. It was a kink with them, a matter of personal honour. And he'd copped one!

90

Well, OK ... why *should* Rogers and the other two flash idiots garner all the oats? As he'd pondered many times in the past month, there had to be *something* extra for the captain on this damned tour.

'Rabbits,' he sighed, wallowing in her smouldering gaze, 'is a very extensive subject, not easily covered in one hour.'

'I know,' she nodded. 'Then ... two?'

'Minimum, Lady Sedgwick-Best.'

'Please ... Penelope.'

'I'd hoped you'd say that.'

'And yours?'

'Alfred.'

'How well it suits you. And ... your room number?'

'Six two three.'

'Six two three.'

'You won't forget it?'

A smile. 'It is engraved on my heart.'

'Say ... one o'clock?'

She said, 'One o'clock.'

Held by her yearning gaze, he felt for his wine and raised it to his lips. 'To ... rabbits?'

Her smile curled his toes. 'To ... bucks and does.'

He chuckled.

They drank.

He choked.

'Corked?' she enquired.

'Ice-creamed,' he grimaced. 'What a strange way to serve it.'

7

Goaded by a twittering Arnold Bottum into a semblance of
haste, the crew and celebrity guests, all nicely squiffed,
boarded the coach unpromptly at two forty-five, leaving the
driver, a toothless Cockney named Arthur Wind, a commodi-
ous fifteen minutes to cover the half-hour journey to the BBC
TV studios in Shepherd's Bush.

So to nobody's surprise they were late.

Angered in the extreme by this unpunctuality was, among
others, Valentine Douche, a rangy, lank-haired youth of many
pimples who aspired to the exalted office of assistant to the
producer of the BBC current affairs programme 'In Town
Today', due for transmission tomorrow. For on these slender,
dandruff-spattered shoulders lay the responsibility of ensuring
that the Glamour party, duly made-up and briefed, were on
the set of Number Two studio in good order and state of
readiness dead on the stroke of three fifteen. And as it was
stroking three seventeen as the coach drew up to the reception
doors, he had, being a young man of distinct acumen, the
sneakiest suspicion they weren't going to make it.

Primed, therefore, with a concern bordering on dementia, he
cast aside all normal smiling ingratiation and thundered towards the glass door fit to be tied, hit the door one hell of a
thump with the heel of his hand, realizing too late he had
chosen to charge the one locked door in the line.

Thud. The impact of headbone on quarter plate shook the
building.

Cross-eyed with shock he staggered back, proceeded on his heels until he encountered the reception desk, came to an abrupt halt, then slowly slithered down into sitting position, still clutching his clip-board.

Mavis Proudfoot, blonde receptionist and professional hysteric, let out a shriek of horror and doubled round the desk, crouched down, got up, crouched down again, decided on the kiss of life, and was hard at it when the gang burst through the door, led by a very flustered Bottum, and came to a colliding halt.

'Well ...!' gasped Arnold, who had secretly heard things were not all sweetness and light as they were cracked up to be at the BBC. But in broad daylight!

'Wey hey!' chortled Bush McKenzie. 'Now this is what I *call* a reception. I bags next go when he's finished. In line you fellas ...'

'Well, if this goes on at the Beeb,' grinned Lord Jim, 'the mind *boggles* at what we'll come upon at the commercial place.'

Mavis Proudfoot, angered by their skittishness, rounded on them tempestuously. 'He's hurt! He ran into the door! Quick, somebody ... get help!'

At which Valentine Douche opened his eyes, frowned bewilderdly, then spotted a familiar face close to his and wreathed a stupified smile. 'Hello, Mavis, you're early.'

'My God, he's concussed! Quickly – a doctor ...!'

'Doctor?' frowned Douche. 'Who's sick?'

'You are! You ran into the door.'

'Door ...?'

'Don't talk – you may damage something.'

'Mm ...?' Now, spotting the silver-lamé uniforms of the crew, he squinted across the foyer in perplexity. '*Ambulance* men, Mavis? Are we doing a piece on ambulance men ...?'

'No, no, Valentine ... they're the crew of Glamour Airlines, don't you remember? They're on "In Town Today" – telecine ... Studio Two ... three thirty! Oh, *please* say you remember ...!'

'Ah!' he said.

'He remembers!' she squealed. 'It's coming back!'

93

'Mm?'

'Oh, it's gone again.'

Valentine gasped, sat up. 'Glamour Airlines! Telecine...!'

'Oh, you *do* remember!'

He shook his head. 'No.'

'Oh, Valentine, *please*...! Take them in! It's terribly late!'

'Certainly.'

He got to his feet, weaved towards the crew, then changed his mind and peeled away drunkenly. 'This way, if you please ... and quiet as you go. I must remind you that live transmissions are in progress and absolute silence must be observed when the red light is showing.'

Noisily the crew and celebrities straggled after him, down one corridor, along another, deep into the heart of the Lime Grove maze.

'That Valentine guy is crook,' observed Bush McKenzie in antipodean idiom, baffling the tipsy Delicious O'Hara who was not acquainted with the Australian expression.

'So – the Mob's got the shake on this joint, too, huh? Hell, is nothing sacred?'

'The Mob?' frowned McKenzie.

'Tell yuh what, though – he don't look so good,' she said, nodding at Douche who was weaving from one side of the corridor to the other, then suddenly stopped and wrestled ineffectually with a massive studio door. 'Go give him a hand, why doncha?'

Bush went to him, dislodging the door with ease. 'Hey, you all right, mate?'

Valentine regarded him blearily. 'Course I'm all right ... go on, in you go ... captain lead the way, please ... take up your positions in front of the cameras, I'll be there in a minute to sort you out.'

Rossiter, flanked by Ramjet and James, shuffled in, closely followed by McKenzie and Boobs Buchanan, the others tagging on behind in a straggly, chattering tail.

In common with most TV studios, a vast floor-to-ceiling canvas curtain, a permanent backdrop, ringed the room, broken only by gaps here and there to admit equipment and

94

personnel onto the studio floor. From the studio door, there-fore, all sight and sound of studio activity is hidden by the curtain.

And so it was with some surprise that Rossiter, arriving at one of these gaps, became aware of the existence of an audi-ence, some two hundred people banked in tiered seats to his left, gazing attentively at some activity or other down on the set.

Peering through a profusion of cameras, props, boom-mikes, and trolleys and a throng of personnel, he was also surprised to find the set already occupied by a group of people seated around an interviewer addressing them from his desk, and at first sight they caused him a certain bewilderment, a certain preposterous inkling that he'd entered the wrong studio.

But then the realization came to him – these people were stand-ins! They were being used for rehearsal ... to establish camera positions – and now that the stars of the show had arrived, they'd get up and go.

Strange, though, that such an unlikely bunch of people had been chosen as stand-ins. For instance, what the hell were four vicars doing there on a Sunday afternoon? They ought to have been in church.

Still, his was not to fathom the vagaries of the TV mind. Maybe they needed the money.

Thus re-assured he sauntered on, drew level with the cam-eras positioned on the edge of the set. At his approach one of the camera operators spun round, gaped at Rossiter .. then at everyone down the line.

Rossiter smiled, realizing the impact their uniforms made seen close-up for the first time, and nodded a friendly greeting. 'Hi, how are yuh? Rehearsal goin' OK? Al Rossiter – Glam-our Airlines ... reckon you can dismiss these guys now, we're all here...'

At the appalling intrusion of Rossiter's voice into his earnest questioning, the interviewer, Gilbert Radish, heavily-and redly-maned, owlishly spectacled, gave a throttled start, shot a hor-rified glance at Camera Two, gaped with saucer-sized orbs at the advancing tribe of hideously-garbed intruders, and shot to his feet, right arm extended like Canute attempting to stay the tide.

'Well, howdy!' grinned Rossiter, mistaking the gesture for a proffered handshake, quickening his stride and taking the hand. 'Al Rossiter – Glamour captain – nice to meetcha. This here's my co-pilot Paul Rogers ... my nav, Crighton-Padgett ...

'Aaaaccchhhuuuggggghhhhh!' replied Radish, rooted with horror.

Rossiter nodded to the assembled clergy. 'Thanks a lot for sittin' in for us. Sorry we're late. Kinda got bogged down over a boozy lunch...'

Suddenly the set was a-surge with frantic people, all flying around in earphones, trailing wires, shouting, 'Cut!! ... Cut!! ... Christ, we've been invaded! ... Well, who the fuck *are* they! ... Sorry, bishop! ...'

Then Gilbert Radish let out a howl of fury and came hurtling round the desk, bellowing, 'Get out of here! Get out! Security! Call the guards! Get off my *set*, you blithering lunatic! Oh, *God*! Get us off the air, you stupid cunt! Cut! Cut!'

Driven backwards by this savage onslaught, Rossiter back-pedalled four or five steps in dismay before finally shaking himself from shock and stopping Radish dead in his tracks with a thump in the chest.

'Now just hold on a minute ...! What the hell's goin' *on* here?'

'On! On!' screeched Radish, widely-known for his manic temper in times of stress. 'You've just *annihilated* a live religious programme, you ridiculous little man...!'

Rossiter's jaw dropped. 'L.. live ... rel ... oh, fuck, no ...'

'Oh, fuck, *yes*!' raged Radish and flung himself from the set.

The audience, the clergy, the celebrities, and crew were in uproar, some screaming indignation, most doubled up with laughter. Rossiter turned, stunned, to Ramjet ... to Crighton-Padgett, realized they were too far gone for any communication, sighed wearily, 'Oh ... shit!' and sank down on Radish's desk to await his fate.

It arrived immediately – in the form of ten uniformed security men.

'Now, look fellas, it wasn't my fault ... hey, leggo, I tell yuh it was *not* my fault ...! Put me ... down! It was not my *fault ...*' he protested volubly.

And was still offering the same excuse when they bundled him on the coach.

8

At least the visit to the ITV studios at Teddington *began* with greater distinction.

Welcomed into the foyer by a bright young thing named Jeremy Love, a white-haired youth in a violet paisley shirt and blood-red trousers, assistant to the producer of the current affairs programme 'NOW!', they were escorted with comforting efficiency along the inevitable network of corridors to Studio One, accompanied by a non-stop commentary of information, explanation, and advice from Love as to where, what, how, and when it would all happen.

'Bobby is an absolute pet, you'll adore him,' he assured Rossiter as they approached the studio door.

'Bobby?'

Jeremy gave a chiding tut. 'Bobby *Shafto* – your interviewer! Dearie me, you really haven't been told anything, have you. Bobby has one of the most ... perhaps *the* most famous chat-shows on tellie over here. I'm surprised you haven't heard of him in America. He has twelve million viewers every Monday night! You do realize, of course, that what is about to happen will be tele-cined and transmitted tomorrow ...?'

'No,' replied Rossiter, still stunned by the ignominy of his departure from the Beeb.

'Well, it will,' said Love, heaving the door open. 'And by nine o'clock tomorrow night the *whole* of Great Britain will know all about you, isn't that lovely?'

'Peachy,' nodded Rossiter.

'Right ... *in* we go.'

Rossiter set a foot over the threshold then stopped so suddenly Bush McKenzie ran into him. 'Hey, kid ... you're positive this is the right studio?'

Love frowned. 'Pardon?'

'I mean, we ain't about to bust into a Baptist singalong or anythin'?'

'Good heavens, no,' laughed Love. 'Would *I* take you into the wrong studio?'

Rossiter nodded. 'It's bin known.'

Even with this assurance Rossiter ventured no further than the nearest camera, leaving it to Love to lead them out onto the floor of a set not dissimilar to the one they had just so hurriedly left.

Again there was the interviewer's desk accompanied by two chairs, flanked, on their right, by a two-tiered, semi-circular, leather couch or banquette, sufficient accommodation for a score or more guests.

To the left of the desk and some ten feet away was a small, slightly raised stage, complete with microphones, amplifiers and speakers, and an extremely long concert grand piano.

Facing the set, to Rossiter's left, rose several tiers of empty seats, designed to accommodate perhaps two hundred people, a use to which he profoundly hoped they would not be put.

'No audience, huh?' he observed to Love as they picked their way through a plethora of cameras, boom-mikes, and snaking cables.

'Oh, but of *course* there'll be an audience,' retorted Love, glancing at his watch. 'Bobby would never work without an audience. But he prefers a quiet chat with his guests before he lets the hordes in. They're being warmed up in another studio right now – about a hundred and fifty of them – then when he's ready he brings them in here. He finds the last-minute switch of studio has an exhilarating effect on them. It's all part of his *exciting* technique – complete spontaneity. Nobody knows *what* will happen on this show.'

'Zat so?' muttered Rossiter, his heart turning cold as the

stirring premonition of another impending disaster clutched his bowels.

A sudden flurry of activity on the far side of the studio brought Jeremy snapping to nervy attention. 'Ah – the great man himself. I just *know* you'll like him!'

Rossiter, detecting the prayer behind the vociferous assurance glanced at Love. Dammit, the kid was secretly terrified. And at that moment he just *knew* he was going to hate Shafto's guts.

The advancing group emerged from the twilight of the studio onto the edge of the set. In its van – a short, fat, heavily-jowled figure in a well-cut grey suit and floral shirt, a personage of immediate impact, struttingly pompous, instantly detestable.

Striding onto the set with a wake of six scurrying sycophants one of whom appeared to be pleading on the trot, Shafto stopped abruptly and rounded on the youth, snarled a rebuke, and punctuated it forcefully with a prodding finger in the chest. 'And I don't give a damn how impossible it is – *do* it! And if it's not done by six tomorrow night – start looking for another job . . . OK?'

'Y . . yes, Bobby.'

Shafto swung round and came on, peering at Rossiter and the group with narrowed, discerning eyes, the flush of anger brought on by the encounter fading to an amused smirk as he recognized his victims.

'Well, now . . . this can only be the famous Cock-up Rossiter and his merry Glamour men . . .'

Rossiter's eyes snapped. 'Where the hell did you get that name?'

Shafto's smirk deepened, indicating that Rossiter's reaction was precisely what he'd hoped for, as indeed it was. For Shafto's technique was founded on insult, sarcasm, and cruelty, the reaction of anger guaranteeing exciting television.

In earlier days he had begun his chat show along bland, conventional lines, employing a geniality so foreign to his nature that it emerged into the nation's living rooms as sickening pretence – and his rating slithered. Then one Monday evening, knowing he was in for an imminent chop, he cast aside all false benignity and in desperation reverted to type, employed heavy-handed cynicism, shocked his guests and riled his audience to such an extent that the show terminated in near-riot.

Within three days the station had received fifty thousand letters and half a million telephone calls, some threatening his very life, many more protesting mere disgust, but the vast majority begging for more.

Shafo had arrived.

Cautioned by the network against *extreme* provocation, he had returned the following week with his current formula of sizzling spontaneity, a technique that kept the entire nation on the edge of its seat every Monday evening, detesting him yet fascinated by him, wondering if it was *this* week that Shafto got what was coming to him.

And had they been present to observe the instant, electrified hatred that crackled between Shafto and Rossiter at that moment, they might well have conjectured that this indeed was the week they'd all been waiting for.

Shafto responded to Rossiter's angry glare with a calm, contemptuous smirk. 'More to the point, captain, where did you get that name? I hear it had something to do with you landing at the wrong Miami airport one night and slicing the tail off a parked DC8 .. a trifle amateurish, old boy, wouldn't you say?'

Rossiter gasped, began to splutter, but Shafto cut him short and addressed the group.

'Attention everybody! My name is Bobby Shafto. I host the most successful chat-show in Britain called "Now!" – and with a viewing audience of twelve million you are all extremely fortunate to be on it. The format is simple – you simply sit over there and do as you're told. I may interview you individually – in which case you will move to the 'special guest' chair at my desk – or I may interview you seated on the banquette. Then again, I may ignore you completely, as the mood takes me. For those of you who can perform, and whom I require to perform, there is the stage over there. There is nothing else you need know. I am intimately familiar with your names, professions, abilities, and social standing, so if

101

there's anyone getting all huffed at this moment and muttering, "Does the bumptious little squirt know who I *am*?" the answer is yes, I do, and it doesn't impress me one little bit. Yes, Miss Fullbrush, you wish to say something ...?'

Gloriana, quivering with outrage, slammed Sam Chortle and Lush Martino aside and stepped forward, drew herself to her full, imperious height and snarlingly proclaimed, 'Yes! I most certainly *do* have something to say, you ...'

'One moment!' Shafto's ringing imperative shocked her, silenced her. 'Before you do say it, Miss Fullbrush, a reminder – that you are currently starring in the film "The Hounds Of Kilimanjaro" due for release on national circuit in this country next week and that your appearance on my show tomorrow night will undoubtedly increase attendance – and therefore your percentage profit and personal popularity – three-fold, four-fold, maybe more. Think about it!'

Silence – Shafto's ringing authority echoing distantly around the upper reaches of the studio. All eyes glued to Fullbrush.

'I ...' bosom heaving labouredly, eyes darting with uncertainty, she computed a lightning calculation of profit potential at ten percent of the gross against a moment of outraged pride and came down heavily in favour of the money. As Shafto knew she would.

His lip curling in a cruel, humourless smile, he nodded slowly at her and waved her back into line with an impertinent flick of his fingers. 'A very wise decision, my dear ... well, now ... does anyone *else* have anything to say?'

No one had, being all tarred with the same dilemma. The crew had no choice in the matter; they were under orders. As for the others, they had everything to gain by suffering a mere hour of this arrogant little despot's insults, and a great deal to lose if they didn't. There was really no choice.

He beamed an insufferably victorious smile. 'Well, then – please be seated and we will commence. Jeremy ...' he whirled on his quaking assistant, 'take over. Audience in ... lights up ... cameras on. I'm going to make-up.'

Slapping his podgy hands together, he paused momentarily to watch his guests dispersing like trained seals to their appointed places, nodded to himself with satisfaction, then strode from the set, murmuring exultantly, 'Shafto ... I do believe you have the makings of a *dilly* of a show.'

Fifteen minutes later – the noise in Studio One now profound, the atmosphere electric.

Moments before, the door had opened to admit an in-pouring of one hundred and fifty souls, galvanized by their pre-programme warm-up into a state of excitation bordering on frenzy, brought to fever pitch not only by the customary prospect of Shafto's outrageous behaviour but also by the opportunity of meeting, in the flesh, the much-publicized Glamour crew and their celebrity guests.

Indeed, so precisely comparable was their demeanour to that of the perfect Shafto audience, that even he, emerging finally and with due fanfare onto the set, could scarcely believe his good fortune. *Now*, he reflected, parading slowly and contemptuously before them, noting with experienced eye the flamboyant, the beautiful, the photogenic, and the patently ridiculous among them, now I *know* I've got a show.

Already sizzling with anticipation, his pompous entrance and disdainful appraisal of them brought them to fresh peaks of excitement, inducing from them nervous laughter, cat-calls, boos, and shouted insults to which he responded with cool contempt, relishing their reaction as does a pantomime demon, knowing his success to be directly proportional to the volume and venom of their abuse.

Pausing a moment longer, insolently impervious to this barrage of spleen, he finally acknowledged it with a mocking bow and held up his hand for silence. The noise died, the insults stopped, silence reigned – but for one final, drawn-out hiss emanating from the back row of the audience, the one lonesome gesture of defiance sounding so pathetically ineffectual it brought the audience to fresh laughter.

Shafto fixed its source with a comical glower, and as the laughter died, commented wryly, 'Put his plug back in and blow him up again, somebody – he'll miss the show.'

Amid fresh laughter, he braced himself and strolled more quickly now along the audience, nodding to himself as he looked them over. 'Well, well ... a right common-looking lot to be sure ...'

A male response from the back. 'What else d'you expect for this show!' And more laughter.

Shafto came back. 'Anymore of that and I'll have your plug removed permanently! It is obvious you are suffering from an excess of hot air!'

The audience loved it.

'Never ...' continued Shafto, reverting to his theme, 'have I seen an assembly of such blood-thirsty-looking ghouls. Look at you ... all sitting there slavering ... waiting for the kill. You know what you are? You're an *anachronism*! D'you know what an anachronism is, madam? ... no, of course, you don't – well, I'll tell you. It is anything out of keeping with chronology ... oh, God, there goes another biggy ... chronology ... time ... it is anything out of keeping with time. Get it? No, she doesn't. She's sitting here with her mouth open. Well, put in terms of child-like simplicity, madam, you lot do not belong to this civilized age – you belong in the time of Nero and the Roman Games! With your blood-lust you ought to be sitting in the Circus Maximus, waiting for the show to begin. Special events tonight ... four hundred pairs of gladiators will fight to the death ... two thousand condemned criminals will be eaten by lions .... and the *star* spot of the show ... fifty beautiful maidens will be raped by donkeys! Now, how does that suit you?'

'Lovely! Get on with it!'

'OK, OK,' laughed Shafto, holding up his hands for silence, then he turned to his floor manager, hovering close. 'Ready yet, Frank?'

Frank, receiving instructions through earphones from the control room, stuck up his thumb. 'Ready when you are, Mister Shafto.'

'OK, here we go, then ... roll intro.'

Frank murmured, 'Roll intro' into his cheek mike and instantly the studio speakers blared out the introductory music of the 'NOW!' show, a big, brassy orchestration intended to shock the nation into the realization that once again the one, the only Bobby Shafto was about to take the air.

104

As the titles rolled, a frenetic announcer proclaimed, 'Ladies and gentlemen ... it's the *NOW!* Show ... and here is your host ... the man you just *love* to *hate* ... Bobby ... Shafto!'

As the floor manager leapt up and down like a caged gorilla, whipping the audience into frenzied applause, the red light on Camera Three winked on, and Shafto's face, cruel with sham-sadism, jumped onto the studio monitors in extreme close-up.

Now, holding a large instruction board to the audience, Frank induced from them a storm of hissing, booing invective which continued until Camera Three had zoomed out and held Shafto in mid-shot, at which point he went into his act and gradually silenced the incensed audience with, supposedly, the sheer power of glowering personality.

'Back you dogs ...!' he snarled, cracking an imaginary whip. 'Back, I say! That's better ... by heaven, we've got a right nasty, vicious lot in here tonight.' Transferring his glower to the lens of Camera Three, he skewered the public with a jaundiced eye and sneered, 'Welcome ... and I mean that most insincerely. Before you joined us I was telling this lot they're an anachronism, more at home in ancient Rome's infamous arena, the Circus Maximus, watching Christians being devoured by starving lions, than sitting in this studio. And that obviously goes for you, or you wouldn't have switched on. Y-e-s, I can just see you all now ... settled in the self-indulgent comfort of your hire-purchased armchairs ... stuffing yourselves with chocolates and crisps and beer and nuts, impatient for the orgy of destruction to begin. *WHO,* you are asking yourselves at this moment, is he going to throw to the lions tonight? WHO ... will limp from his show a mere shadow of his ... or *her* ... former self? *Or* ...' a ghoulish smirk, 'will it be *Shafto*'s turn for destruction. Well, my friends ... all you have to do in order to find out is ... stay tuned to the *NOW! Show!* A-n-d- ... take it away ...!'

As he turned away from camera, the brassy intro blasted out once more, accompanied by an unsolicited storm of applause. Shafto strode purposefully to his desk, seated himself in his luxurious swivel chair, and commenced to shuffle papers as though sorting out his notes, a pretentious piece of business designed to prolong the applause and further unsettle his guests.

'All right...' he said finally, holding up his hand, then, as the applause died, he looked up and levelled a steady gaze at Camera Two. 'Tonight ... a show of *manifold* surprises and *limitless* entertainment...'

A jeer from the audience.

'Shut up, you lot – and get back to your bones!'

'Woof woof!' someone barked, bringing laughter.

'Quiet...! A show ... that will prove, among many other things, the fatuousness of American advertising and the extent to which people will make *clowns* of themselves chasing the Almighty Dollar!'

A ripple of discomfort among the audience and a sporadic muttering.

Ignoring it, Shafto continued, 'For the past week our British newspapers have extensively reported a story whose breadth of ingenuity, height of imagination, and depth of courage is exceeded only by the limitless profundity of its inanity. I refer, of course, to the launching, via the gimmicky vehicle of a world-wide mystery tour, of a new American airline named Glamour. Tonight, we are several times *honoured*...' a snide pause, '... to have as our guests not only the *crew* of the 707 *Glamour Puss*, the pink-and-sequined nightmare in which this round-the-world promotion tour is being conducted, but also several celebrities who are travelling as guests of Glamour for the purpose of attracting publicity for the airline ... and of course as much as they can manipulate for themselves.'

A loud jeer of protest from the audience.

'I'll *kill* him!' seethed Gloriana, ripping her hanky down the middle.

'Not before *I* do honey!' snarled Delicious O'Hara. 'That baby's mine!'

Senator Sam Chortle sat, incredibly, speechless, consumed with rage.

Lush Martino was chuckling away to himself, in full agreement with everything that was being said.

Frankie was fast asleep.

Sydney was picking his nose and flicking it into the ashtray.

Stanley was scraping chewing gum off his boot and flicking it at Sydney.

And Shag McGee was feeding spring onions to the parrot.

'That guy's gotta die!' gasped Cock-up. 'I'm gonna punch his head!'

'The fingers are mine,' muttered Ramjet. 'I'm gonna snap 'em off and shove them, one after the other, up his ass.'

'No room old boy,' drawled James. 'That mike will already be up there.'

'Well...!' gasped Sugar Sweetman.

Both Babs and Wilma were oblivious to the furore. Wilma had her hands full hiding her knickers from a lecherous old ogler in the front row, and Babs was busy showing hers to a dashing young fellow with a Clark Gable moustache in the fifth.

'So...' continued Shafto, delightedly aware of both the anger of his guests and the build-up of resentment throughout the audience, '... publicity being their wish and whim, let us, without more ado, pander to it. Ladies and gentlemen ... render whatever applause you feel fitting to greet our first guest on the NOW! Show tonight. I give you...' swivelling in his chair, he surveyed his guests with taunting languor, noting, with a grim smile, the preening of Gloriana Fullbrush to a state of readiness, the pompous straightening of Sam Chortle's posture, the fixing of Delicious O'Hara's come-hither smoulder, and the alcoholic indifference of Lush Martino's slouch.

Cock-up Rossiter and his crew, he saw, were too angrily prepared to fall victim to any surprise, and so, with a demonic chuckle, he selected ...

'Mister ... Shag McGee ... and the Skull and Crossbones!'

Camera Three jumped in with a close-up of the foursome, earnestly ensconced in their various preoccupations – Frankie, slumped on his spine, mouth open, snoring gently; Sydney still picking his nose and flicking it in the ashtray; Stanley, head back, gulping a stream of extruded chewing gum; and Shag contemplatively scratching his balls.

In the first moment came hearty applause ... then, as the audience became aware of the comical ignominy of the tab-

107

leau, a smattering of laughter, building to hilarity, erupting into knee-thumping guffaws, and finally exploding into a helpless, rollicking roar.

On it went, the cameras cutting to close-ups of the audience in peals of laughter ... to Shafto's lugubrious observance of the group ... to the stiff-lipped resentment of his other guests ... and back to McGee and the others, each in turn receiving his own solo close-up, adding fillip to the hilarity and ensuring the biggest laugh the programme had enjoyed in weeks.

Finally, sensing a diminishing of the hysteria, Shafto roused himself as from hypnosis and waved the audience to silence, his expression rebukeful, as though disapproving the cruelty of their laughter, a tactic he frequently employed in order to allay censure from the network. A dastardly technique, this setting up of ridicule then transferring the onus of fault to the audience, but it worked. For who could blame him, in this instance, for perpetrating anything more nefarious than simply introducing his guests?

'All right ... calm down, now, calm down,' he chided them, allowing a half-smile to temper the rebuke and thus ensuring his audience's continuing support. 'Mister McGee ... perhaps I ought to remind you and the boys that you are now on camera and are therefore, at this very moment, entering the homes of some twelve million viewers ...'

'Oh,' said Shag.

Shafto gave a helpless shrug. 'I mention it – just in passing you understand – in case you wished to nudge your bass guitarist into an awareness of the fact. I'd hate him to miss this golden opportunity to say hello to *twelve ... million ...* potential fans.'

'Oh,' said Shag. 'Yeah.' He glanced along the banquette to Frankie who was slowly slithering off it onto the floor. 'Hey, Stanley ...'

Stanley jawed the last six inches of gum into his mouth and turned his head. 'Mm?'

'Give Frankie a shake, man.'

'Oh ... yeah.' Withdrawing his drumstick from his boot, he leaned across and whopped him on the head.

Frankie woke with a choking start. 'Whhaassamarra ... we

108

on?' He blinked owlishly at the audience who were rocking with laughter, realized he'd missed something funny and joined them with a grin. 'What was it – a joke?'

'Yeah,' frowned Stanley. 'But I think I missed it.'

'Welcome to the show, Frankie.' Shafto smiled cuttingly. 'Ladies and gentlemen, you see before you a pop group of rare uniqueness – progeny of the same genius who devised the concept of Glamour Airlines – Colonel Godfrey Berskin, who, among untold other interests, owns lock, stock, and pelvis, such notable pop-scene Goliaths as Jimmy Silver ... Marc Dart ... and Wensley Picket ...'

'Pocket,' corrected Sydney.

'... someone spoke,' said Shafto, swivelling to the group. 'I beg your pardon?'

'Pocket,' repeated Sydney, finger up his nose. 'Not Picket.'

'You, of all people, are advising *that*?'

Shafto turned back to the roaring audience. 'I stand corrected ... it is, of course, Wensley Pocket – well known to you all as the Scratching Hatrack ...'

'Hey, man ...' Sydney protested. 'He's our friend.'

'I withdraw the remark,' Shafto told the audience. 'Wensley Pocket ... who is *not* well known to you all as the Scratching Hatrack. However, to return to the point ... Shag McGee and the Skull and Crossbones are destined, I know, to make as big an impact on the world of pop as the other three moronic ... sorry, slip of the tongue ... as the three *harmonic* giants just mentioned – and to prove the vastness of their genius they are now going to perform for you one of their own incomparable compositions ... aren't you, Shag McGee?'

Shag's jaw slackened. 'Hm?'

Shafto swivelled to him. 'I said ... in order to prove the ...'

'I heard, I heard,' nodded Shag. 'But we ain't brought our instruments ...'

Shafto smiled paternalistically. 'On the NOW! Show – no problem.' He swung towards the wings, snapped his fingers, and on came five prop men, carrying to the stage a kit of drums and two electric guitars. In a moment everything was ready, the slickness of the operation drawing spontaneous applause from the audience which Shafto deflected towards the group, using it as encouragement to get them to the stage.

'There you are boys ... your audience of *twelve million* viewers awaits. Kill 'em and you're made for life ...'

'Fail and you're dead forever,' muttered Rossiter. 'The bastard! Frankie's still half asleep.'

'No, he always looks like that,' answered Ramjet. 'Still – a foul trick all the same. Skip, I think I'll walk over and smash him in the mouth.'

'I want his scrotum,' growled Rossiter.

'I'm goin' to gouge his eyes out,' put in Bush McKenzie, flexing his great fingers.

Raggedly, Shag and the group approached the stage, discussing with uncharacteristic urgency what they were going to play.

'How about "Bright Blue Bananas and Water On The Knee"?' yawned Frankie, referring to a little masterpiece they'd composed in a public lavatory while waiting for four cubicles to empty.

'Too rustic,' commented Shag, wincing as Marlon's talons dug into his skull. 'Hey, steady boy ...'

'Who – me?' asked Frankie. 'What did I do?'

'No – Marlon. He don't like it in here ... he don't like that fat fella.'

'I can see. He's starin' at him.'

'How 'bout "Sonia's In The Family Way, Her Belly's Like A Ball"?' suggested Stanley, somewhat selfishly as the number incorporated a twelve-minute drum solo.

'Nerts,' replied Shag, wise to his motive.

'I'm dyin' for a pee,' commented Sydney.

Shag frowned. 'Is that one of ours? I don't seem to recall ...'

'No, yuh daft bugger – I *am* dyin' for a pee!'

'You'll be all right when yuh start movin',' said Shag. 'OK, fellas, I got it – we'll do "Slack Maggy's Gotta Hair-lip, She Shaves It Every Night".'

'What key?' asked Frankie.

'H' said Shag, taking the stage.

While the others sorted out their instruments, Shag following strict orders from Colonel Berskin, turned his back to the

110

audience, extracted four linen handkerchiefs from his pocket, and stuffed them down the front of his trousers.

It was at their audition in the basement of Berskin Building that the Colonel had commented, 'I like what I see, kid – the sound's godawful but I reckon the bottom half of ya is promotable. But we've gotta build up your image, you're a bit on the puny side down there. Gotta give the women something to drool over.' And there and then he had sent out for four hankies which Shag had carried ever since.

Hastily arranging the padding into a semblance of naturalness, Shag ran his fingers through his waist-length orange-henna-ed hair, checked that Marlon was securely in position up aloft, ran an eye over the state of readiness of the group, and enquired, 'Ready?'

'Sure.'

'OK – on four.'

With his back to the audience, he suddenly shot his arms and skinny legs akimbo, almost dislodging Marlon who let out a terrified screech, counted aloud, 'A-one ... two ... three ... four!' punctuating the count with violent thumps on the flimsy wooden stage with his tooled-leather pirate boot and on four drove the three-inch heel straight through a knot-hole.

'Oh, *fuck* it ...! Keep goin' ... keep goin'!'

They went.

Amplified some eight thousand times above norm, they filled the studio with a stupefying jangle of diabolical noise, Frankie plucking the guts out of the bass guitar, Sydney ripping wild arpeggios out of the lead guitar, and Stanley, as always, head down to the skins, lost in a flying miasma of hair, his arms going so fast you couldn't see them.

Shag, poor lad, was well and truly stuck.

He pulled and tugged and twisted and shook, flung himself about in epileptic contortions, but still the offending right heel remained steadfastly jammed in the knot-hole.

As the introductory four hundred opening bars came to an end and the time for the lyrics drew near, he twisted so far round he almost sprang his knee-caps, grabbed the mike from its stand, and continued in that corkscrew stance, playing

111

with his back to the audience and alternately twisting to left
and right to relieve the excruciating cramp in his side.

'Slack Maggie's gotta fella who is nearly six-foot-two ...
His arms are kinda stringy and they reach down to his shoe
... He's gotta wooden leg an' his hair's like rottin' hay ...
But compared to old Slack Maggie he is Mister USA ...!
Ohhhhhhh ... yeh ... yeh ... yeh ...!'

The audience loved it, went wild, had never seen such
uniqueness of presentation, such stagemanship – but then,
what else could one expect from an American group?

Gritting his teeth in agony, Shag launched into the second
chorus, relieved to discover his heel had loosened a little –
enough to enable him to make a half-turn and play to the
audience in profile, little realizing that his wiggling and jiggling had caused the four hankies to slip a ludicrous distance
down his trousers and now formed a monstrous phallic bulge
half-way to his knee.

'Good God!' gasped Esme Clatterbrick in the third row,
nudging her blonde friend Ruby Glew. 'It must be a foot
long!'

'Yanks are built like that,' replied Ruby authoritatively,
blowing a mammoth gum bubble. 'I think he's peachy. *Love*
the parrot.'

'Parrot ...? Oh, yes, the parrot.'

'Slack Maggie's only four-foot ten but weighs three hun-
erd pounds,'

screeched McGee, enjoying fresh waves of agony from his captured foot.

'An' fellas she ain't crushed ta death, she sure as hell has
drowned ... She's had a hundred lovers but there's plenty
more to come ... 'Cause when yuh love Slack Maggie yuh
get more meat to the ton ... Ohhhhhh ... yeh yeh yeh ...'

This time the audience joined in the chorus, heartily supporting the group – more out of spite for Shafto than from any appreciation of the fearful racket they were making.

Cheered to the echo, Shag McGee belted out the final crescendo of 'Yeh ... yeh ... yeh-s' and flung his arms up triumphantly. Frankie and Sydney, guessing it was more or less the end of the piece, came to a slithering halt, leaving only Stanley, lost in his own world of flying hair and self-hypnosis, bashing skin and crashing cymbals like there was a month to go before his spring ran down.

'OK, kill it ...!' yelled McGee.

'Stan ... ley!' bellowed Frankie.

'Oi ...!' bawled Sydney.

Finally McGee extricated himself from his captured boot, wrestled it from the knot-hole, and hurled it at Stanley's head.

'OW! Now, whatcha do that for?'

'We finished.'

'Oh.'

Bootless, Shag limped from the stage, acknowledging the applause, whistling, and cheering that accompanied the lads back to their seats.

Shafto, slowly shaking his head, waited until the applause had died, then groaned, 'Oh, my, that was just ... unbe*liev*able! Mister McGee, I congratulate you ... I did not think it possible that anyone on today's pop-scene could achieve a new low-low in imbecilic inanity, but you've just proved me *very* wrong.'

'Gee, thanks,' grinned McGee, thinking maybe Shafto wasn't such a bad guy after all.

Cries of 'Shame!' from the audience bounced off Shafto's impervious hide like peas off armour-plate.

'Yes, sir ...' he continued brutally, 'from that fatuous demonstration I perceive for you a great future over here, bringing ecstasy to the millions of weeny-bopping cretins whose capacity for enjoying such psychopathic trivia will undoubtedly equal your own capacity for producing it. Good luck, my son, you thoroughly deserve each other.'

'Gee, *thanks*,' smiled Shag, now *knowing* Shafto wasn't such a bad guy after all.

'Yuh bum!' someone shouted from the audience.

113

'Pick on somebody your own size!'

Shafto accepted the challenge with a nod, 'All rightee...' then traversed the line of guests with devilish deliberation, finally swivelling to face the audience with an infernal leer.

'Well, now, I confess to finding myself in a bit of a dilemma. I cannot recall ever before being faced with such gathering of wit, charm, interest, and beauty that I could not choose between them. Who indeed shall be my next vict ... er, guest? That liquidinous star of stage, screen, microphone, and hangover ... Vincent Martino ...?'

Amid laughter and jeers and at the distant mention of a vaguely familiar name, Lush jerked from a light doze and blinked at Camera Two which was holding him in demeaning close-up. 'Yeh ... someone call?'

'The bastard!' seethed Ramjet. 'Why doesn't somebody *stop* him?'

'Because they're all enjoying it,' growled Rossiter.

'*Or* ...' continued Shafto, projecting over the din, '... that star, nay, *constellation* of a thousand and one smasheroo box-office successes ... the titles of which appear, distressingly to escape my mind for the moment ... Miss Gloriana Full-brush ...?'

Caught in a close-up of blazing fury, Gloriana at that moment looked anything but the cool and radiant movie queen, and a lot like one of the Macbeth witches who's just spilled boiling bat soup on her foot.

'You ... fat crud!' she spat and the audience rocked with glee.

'*OR* ...' grinned Shafto, delighting in her response, '... that lady of trans-Atlantic renown whose contribution to art and culture appears to lie solely in the performance of an act that every one of us accomplishes every night before going to bed – the removal of our clothes ... Miss Delicious O'Hara ...?'

Whoops and cat-calls and wolf-whistles greeted the zoom-in on Delicious, who accepted the insult with patient disdain, waited for the storm to abate, then hit Shafto with, 'The difference being, Fat Gut, that *I* dare ta do it with the lights on!'

Cheers championed the riposte but quickly diminished out

of eagerness to catch Shafto's retort, but then, into the ensuing quiet burst a blown raspberry of rich, resounding ripeness which sent the audience into fresh paroxysms of laughter and drowned all hope of further wit for a full half-minute.

Shafto did not disappoint them. As the laughter again died, he nodded, calm and confident, and said, 'My opinion, precisely, sir,' evoking even more laughter.

That did it for Rossiter. He shot to his feet, rammed a cheroot into the corner of his mouth, and speared Shafto with a quivering finger.

'That's enough, Shafto! *I* volunteer...!'

Shafto swivelled his chair, a smirk of insolent amusement distorting his face. Then, with a slow affirming nod, 'Well, well ... the gallant captain ... a *worthy* opponent. Ladies and gentlemen ... the commander of the good ship *Glamour Puss* ... Captain ... Alfred ... Rossiter ...!'

Rousing, sympathetic applause greeted Rossiter as he strode pugnaciously to the desk and took the guest-of-honour chair. Settling himself, he snapped a light to the cigar, hooked his right ankle over his left knee, set his jaw aggressively at Shafto, and waited, ready for battle.

Shafto, in pretentious contrast, relaxed, smiled amiably at the audience as though approving their protracted applause, and, as it died, murmured, 'My my ... you appear to have made quite a hit, captain.'

'Yeah,' growled Rossiter, 'but not the one I have in mind.'

Delighted laughter and a shout of, 'Sock it to him, captain!'

Undeterred, Shafto pressed on. 'Captain ... and before we go any further I suppose we ought to establish that you *are*, in fact, a fully qualified airline captain...' A snigger. 'I mean, forgive me, but dressed in that *incredible* Gilbert and Sullivan motley, I *do* have certain difficulty believing in the authenticity of the operation...'

Ramjet was half out of his seat when Bush McKenzie's powerful hand clamped on his arm and pulled him back. 'Take it easy, cock, the Skip can handle him. In any case – *I* bagged first go.'

'I'm gonna tear his head off!'

'Can't be done – not twice.'

With a nonchalant puff of his cigar, Rossiter removed it from his clenched teeth and regarded its glowing tip. 'No, sir, I am not a qualified airline captain. I am an out-of-work house-painter and part-time yo-yo referee. Miss Buchanan and Miss Fluck over there really *fly* the plane – though to be honest they are not really girls at all. Beneath that flimsy disguise Miss Buchanan is an Apache deep-sea diver and Miss Fluck a negro Mafia button-man. There – it's out ... any more stupid questions?'

To delighted laughter from the audience, a rousing cheer rose from the banquette.

'Stick it to him, baby!' whooped Delicious O'Hara, brandishing her pearl-encrusted handbag. 'Give the bum one for me!'

Shafto, still firmly in possession of his cool, though somewhat surprised by Rossiter's, continued as though the interruption had not occurred. 'Yes, one or two ... captain, the object of this ... comic-opera charade is, I take it, to promote worldwide interest in the establishment of a new international airline – an airline which will of necessity have to fly in the face of enormous opposition from existing giants such as PanAm, TWA, British Airways and so on. That being so, what precisely is Glamour Airlines offering to the public that is not already being offered by those other airlines? With what special service ... quality ... tempting tit-bits are you hoping to lure passengers from the already firmly-established companies?'

'In essence – glamour,' gruffed Rossiter.

'Glamour!' exclaimed Shafto, turning to the audience, his manner switching to effusive mockery. 'So Colonel Godfrey Berskin and his merry men have taken it upon themselves to sell *you* – the public – *glamour*. But, my friends, what precisely *is* glamour? Who can define it? Surely to each of us it means a very different thing? All right ... tell you what we'll do – before we go any further we'll have a quick spot-check among the audience for individual definitions of glamour. You, sir, in the front row – the senior citizen with the carnation and the extra-wide parting ... what does *glamour* mean to you?'

Deaf as a door-stop, old Bill Muggeridge sat bewildered,

116

wondering why the fat man was pointing at him, just as he'd been wondering about everything that had happened since he'd arrived at the studios two hours earlier. Afraid to reveal to his daughter, Chrysanthemum, sitting alongside, that he had inadvertently slipped into his deaf-aid an old dud battery, he had so far covered the misdemeanour by reacting as everyone else reacted, laughing when they laughed and applauding likewise, but now, alas, was properly up it.

'Eh?' he winced.

Chrysanthemum, thrilled by the close-up of her father on the TV monitors, crashed an elbow into his ribs and whispered, 'Well, go on, dad, *tell* 'im!'

'Dirty pool, Shafto,' growled Rossiter. 'Hardly typical passenger material.'

Shafto grinned filthily. 'All's fair on a Shafto chat-show, captain. And you did volunteer, remember.'

'What d'he say?' hissed Muggeridge, casting a terrified glance at the boom-mike that now hung two feet above his head like an avenging Sword of Damocles.

'Tell 'im what you think!' Chrysanthemum whispered irritably.

'Tell 'im what I think about *what*?'

'About *glamour*! Didn't you hear 'im?'

'Yers, of course I 'eard him!' retorted Bill, thinking she'd said "salmon".

'May we please have your opinion, sir?' urged Shafto.

'Go on, dad, *tell* 'im!'

'Meself ... I don't go for it!' shouted Bill, forgetting the mike above his head and almost toppling the operator off his trolley.

'Fuckin' roll on,' gasped the operator, banging his ears.

'Oh?' enquired Shafto, delighted by his choice and the fervour of the old man's rejection. 'And why *don't* you go for it, sir?'

"Cause it stinks!' shouted William. 'There's somethin' too damn fishy abart it! And it's all phoney – not the real stuff any more!'

'Ah, the abominations of a plastic world,' Shafto observed sagely. 'But tell me, sir – are you convinced that such would be the case aboard an aeroplane of Glamour Airlines?'

'Eh?'

Chrysanthemum quickly translated.

'Shertainly!' expostulated Bill. 'I find it all too fishy for my tastes! Phoney – the lot of it!'

'Well...' smirked Shafto, 'thank you very much, sir, for your outspoken opinion. So much for a senior citizen, captain. Your promise of *glamour* has obviously not fooled him .... all right, next – the rather lovely young lady in the third row – yes, you dear, in the puce Dior creation and matching nose. What does glamour mean to you?'

Miss Agnes Limp, forty-year-old spinster and part-time chip-shop assistant, sniffed disgustingly into the mike and dabbed at her plum-coloured nose with a soggy hanky. 'Flibbertygibbet,' she intoned adenoidally.

'Interesting,' commented Shafto, inwardly preening at his ability to select precisely the right guest for the required opinion. 'Would you care to enlarge on that?'

'Yes – codswallop! Glamour is ... is ... aaa ... ttcchhooo!'

'Nothing to sneeze at?' suggested Shafto.

Her reply was lost in a welter of snuffling behind the offensive little hanky, and Shafto, sensing audience repulsion, moved on.

'All right ... the handsome young gentleman in the back row ... with the red hair and the black eye. Your interpretation of glamour, sir?'

'Well, it's de birds, in'it?' replied Liverpool rocker Angelo McKnocky, currently out on bail pending enquiries into his alleged breaking-and-entry of Bootle bus clippie Phyllis Rhyll. 'I meanyuhknow, it's de 'old bit – de 'air, de teef, de gams, de tits, de 'ole bleedin' issue, in'it?'

'Er, yes,' nodded Shafto, moving quickly on. 'Well, all right, I think you've underlined the point that glamour is a very difficult thing to define and *is* a different thing to different people. But I will now tell you what glamour is according to the dictionary definition.' He swung round to Rossiter, his manner again aggressive. '*Glamour,* captain is "the *supposed* ... influence of a charm upon the eyes, making them see things as fairer than they are"! And I put it to you, Rossiter, that

118

such is the bill of goods that you and Berskin are currently trying to sell the British public ...!'

Rossiter bristled, shot forward in his seat. 'Are you implying we're purposefully misrepresenting ourselves, Shafto?'

'I'm putting it to you, captain, that you have nothing whatsoever to sell the public that is not already being offered by the other airlines!'

'And *I'm* putting it to *you*, Shafto, that since you haven't fully investigated our service, you don't know what the f ...' cough, '... what you're talking about!'

'Oh, please don't restrain yourself, captain – we can always bleep out bad language. We are on tape remember.'

'I'm not accustomed to using bad language,' rapped Rossiter, sensing the trap and swerving neatly round it.

Smart bastard, seethed Shafto. Nothing like a couple of bleeps to undermine the character of a nauseating goodie-goodie.

'But, by God, *I* am!' shouted Delicious O'Hara, coming to her feet in a heat, tits quivering like dollops of pink blancmange. 'And I'm tellin' ya now, yuh fat crud, lay offa the captain and lay offa Glamour Airlines or I'll flatten yuh where yuh stand!'

A roar of support swelled from the audience.

'You tell him, lady!'

'Give him hell, Delicious ...!'

'My dear lady ...' Shafto protested smarmily.

'I'm no lady, Shafto – an' by Christ, you're no gentleman. I've sat here long enough lissenin' to your insults an' I reckon it's about time somebody shut your big, fat mouth! Yuh call this a chat-show – takin' advantage of a bunch of kids an' a professional flyin' man who's gotta obey orders an' keep his lip buttoned? Well, baby, you're damn lucky these guys *are* under orders or they'da booted your fat ass to London an' back by now. Well, maybe they're under orders but O'Hara ain't! *Stuff* your lousy publicity ... *stuff* your lousy show ... and *stuff* you, too brother!'

And on that she strode across the set, bore down upon him, teeth bared and arm raised, and set about his head with her handbag.

119

The studio exploded in uproar ... shouts, cries, cheers, and yelled instructions blasting the noise-needles clean off their dials. Up in the control box the producers ran amok, some jumping for joy, others bawling instructions to the cameras to hold on the vanquished Shafto who had now slithered from his chair and was cowering in the lea of the desk, on his knees, hands plaited protectively over his head as Delicious rained blow and blow with her pearl-encrusted shillelah.

Finding no protection from the desk, Shafto now began to crawl towards the wings, attempted to get to his feet, but a vicious over-arm chop dropped him on his face, and as he lay there, rolled into a protective huddle, a streak of vivid blue-and-yellow streaked across the set and crashed down on his head.

'Ooooowwwwwww!' yelled Shafto, as Marlon's talons bit. Then 'Yyyooooowwwwww!' as the parrot lined up Shafto's bald spot and with unhurried deliberation biffed it with his beak. 'Get him off ... get him off!'

'Get the parrot in close-up!' screamed the producer up in the box. 'Beautiful! ... beautiful! Thank God we're in colour! Jeezus, Shafto's going to be delirious about this!'

Arnold Bottum now launched himself onto the set in a state of near-apoplexy and dashed around like a hat in a high wind urging his wards to exercise restraint, behave with a modicum of propriety, cease cheering, leering, bellowing, and Shafto-bashing, and generally get the hell back on the bus.

'Outta mah way, boy!' roared Sam Chortle, handing him aside. 'Dang me if that O'Hara woman ain't a sight fo' sore eyes! Lucky for him she got to him fust 'cos Ah wus jurst about ta take the young snapper's hide offa mahself.'

'Push off, Bottum!' rapped Fullbrush, her dark eyes glowing like ebony fires as Delicious caught Shafto another beaut with her handbag.

'Wha's goin' on round here?' enquired Lush Martino, who had just woken up. 'Say ... anybody got just a *teensy* haira that same ole' dawg?'

'Oh, my gosh, she'll *murder* him!' squeaked Boobs Buchanan.

'And a good thing, too,' nodded Sugar Sweetman. 'Talking

120

to the skip like that, damn cheek.'

'Hey, Shag...'

'Yeh, Stanley?'

'Don't you think you oughta get Marlon back, he's peckin' holes in that guy's head.'

'He won't go all the way through, he's fussy what he eats.'

'I'm dyin' for a pee,' groaned Sydney.

'Please ... *please*!' pleaded Arnold, 'everybody out ... *please* get on the coach!'

'OK, I reckon that's enough, Delicious,' smirked Rossiter, catching her arm and saving Shafto a devasting coup. 'Thanks a lot, honey, you were just great. McGee – come an' prise this parrot outta Shafto's head! OK, gang, let's get outta here, I reckon we've done enough damage. So long, Shafto, an' don't think it hasn't bin fun.'

'Damn you!' croaked Shafto. 'Get out! ... get out!'

With a wave to the cheering audience, Rossiter led his troupe back across the set towards the exit, and as they reached the door the audience took up a repeat chorus of a jingle spontaneously adapted from the old Bobby Shafto nursery rhyme by an enterprising wit in their midst.

> 'Ohhh ... Bobby Shafto's shot to hell ...
> Glamour Airlines tolled his knell ...
> O'Hara's handbag made him yell ...
> (Raspberry) ... to Bobby Shaf-to!'

'I'll drink ta that,' grinned Lush Martino. 'Come t'think of it, I'll drink to almost anythin'.'

9

The dinner at the Cinnamon Rooms, Knightsbridge, was, by comparison, a dreary affair – nothing more untoward happening throughout its four-hour duration than a waiter dropping a spoonful of salmon mousse down Boobs Buchanan's cleavage and Lush Martino, true to form, falling backwards out of his chair into a trolley-load of strawberries and cream.

Senator Sam Chortle made a fine, rousing speech which considerably compensated for his having been totally ignored by Bobby Shafto, the resulting applause fixing him in a mood that transcended even the best of humours and deposited him in the realm of irrefutable divinity.

Spoils to the victor, he mused, re-seating himself at Wilma Fluck's side and leaning to her, his hand sliding onto her leg.

'You enjoy that, mah dear?'

'Oh, *yes*, Senator!' she cooed. 'I thought you were just *magnificent*!'

'Splendid ... splendid,' he chuckled, patting her thigh and making a little judicious height. 'Ah do declare this tour is turnin' out quite splendidly after all.'

Make hay while it shines, you fat fumbler, she thought. Daddy, are *you* in for a surprise.

Not alone did Sam Chortle have his thoughts riveted on wee small hours activity. Captain Cock-up was also ensconced in some pretty hairy ruminations regarding the outrageous Lady Penelope Sedgwick-Best. While a little way down the table, Lord Jim, catching the raised brow and lecherous leer of his comrade-in-cupidity seated opposite, paused in the demolition of a strawberry and slid Ramjet a wink of culpable connivance.

'Patience,' James murmured. 'The witching hour is almost upon us.'

'It ain't the witching hour I've got in mind,' grinned Ramjet, throwing half a glass of Mâcon Superieur down his epiglottis. 'It's the three or four after.'

After the speeches there followed a spasm of light entertainment provided by a busty lady singer who rendered 'Fly Me To The Moon' as though in imminent danger of take-off – or blow out, and encored it with an endless version of 'Up, Up and Away', attracting numerous volunteers to quickly help her get there.

Following her, Danny Lang, an up-and-coming self-styled comedian quick-fired a veritable magazine of hilariously unfunny flying jokes, finished with a prat-fall and a ukulele solo, and everyone was delighted he was up-and-going.

Following that the assembly disassembled to the bar for 'a final drink', a euphemism designed by Arnold Bottum as a useful, milling publicity tête-à-tète, but which emerged as a frantic free-for-all for a final drink.

'You fellas thinking of going on somewhere?' asked Bush McKenzie, stifling an honest yawn.

James and Ramjet shook their heads. 'No,' answered Jim. 'Too bushed. And we've got a sickeningly early start tomorrow. How about you?'

'No, I'm beat. As a matter of fact, I think I'll squeeze out now and take a cab back to the hotel. This lot'll be another hour yet.'

'Just what we were thinking,' said Ramjet, stifling a patently dishonest yawn. 'Bin a long day.'

'Share a cab?' invited Bush.

Ramjet caught James's infinitesimal nod of affirmation. 'Sure, why not.'

Ten minutes later they were cabbing along Knightsbridge.

'Well, mates, what d'you think?' asked Bush, stifling yet another yawn, his tenth in three minutes.

123

'About what?' said Ramjet, annoyed that he was catching the habit. 'McKenzie, will yuh stop yawning!'

'About the tour – so far, I mean.'

'Oh, a ball,' replied James, with contrived glumness.

'Wild,' agreed Ramjet.

'Well, I don't know...' grinned McKenzie, bubbling smugly. 'I personally am having a pre-tty good time.'

'Mm?' James looked at Ramjet. 'Is he getting something we're not getting?'

'Must be.'

'Well now, as a matter of fact...' drawled McKenzie, ostentatiously polishing his cuticles on his lapel, 'you hit the nail right on the old proverbial, fellas.'

'Eh?' went Jim.

Ramjet nudged him. 'James ... I do believe the bastard's hit the jackpot somewhere.'

James frowned, disbelievingly. 'You mean – since we got here? It isn't possible.'

'Damn it, look at his face! That is an "I-got-laid-before-you-got-laid" expression if ever I saw one!'

James gasped. 'McKenzie ... you haven't ... you didn't ... you couldn't have!'

'I bloody could,' chuckled Bush. 'And I bloody did!'

'Aw, come on,' scoffed James. 'Where ... when ... how?'

'In the hotel ... within ten minutes of arriving ... and mind your own damn business.'

'Well, by ... no, I didn't mean "how" precisely – I meant "who".'

'I don't think you saw her, you were too busy leching your receptionist. She was standing behind me in the foyer – gorgeous blonde with a belting figure. I bumped into her as I turned round.'

'And fixed it there and then, I suppose?' drawled Ramjet. 'Aw, come on, McKenzie, I know you're fast, but...'

'No, I didn't fix anythin', mate – she did – good an' proper. Came up to the room a few minutes later and told me she was the hotel masseuse. Asked me if I'd like a rub-down.'

James gaped. 'Holy ... and was she a masseuse?'

'Was she heck,' laughed Bush. 'She was a hooker! Neatest

bit of gaffing I've ever seen. She heard the receptionist give me my room number and up she toddled.'

'And ...?' Ramjet enquired eagerly.

'And what?'

'So what happened?'

Bush exploded a laugh. 'Well, what d'you *think* happened!'

'You got screwed.'

'Screwed, blue-ed and tattoo-ed, cock. Wonderful.'

'Well, I'll be ...' Ramjet glanced at James. 'The sod's beaten us to it.'

'Fat chance we've had,' moaned James, dying to grin. 'And a fat chance we're likely to have with this schedule. No wonder you're tired, McKenzie.'

'Tired? I'm mortally fatigued, mate. Fell asleep at lunch and dozed off over dinner.'

'Well, up yours,' pouted James. 'McKenzie, you have no right. *We're* supposed to be the hatchet men of Glamour. You go around doing things like that and you'll ruin our image!'

McKenzie grinned indecently. 'It's every man for himself on this tour – find it when and where you can. Well ... here we are – and in way of celebration, *I* shall pay for the cab.'

They entered the foyer, McKenzie doing a little victory jig, the others feigning misery.

'614, my good man,' Bush effused to the night receptionist. 'Thank you – and a splendid good night to you.'

'He's just come into money,' explained James. '736, please ... and 748.'

In possession of their keys, they entered an elevator and rode up, McKenzie still lording it. 'Yers, nothing like a nice friendly massage for getting the blood flowing, fellas. You really should try it sometime.'

'Shut up, McKenzie,' griped Ramjet, 'or your blood really will be flowing – all over the floor.'

'Jealousy does not become you, Rogers. You must learn to take defeat like a man.' The elevator sighed to a halt at the sixth floor. 'Well, *pleasant* dreams, chaps. I personally don't plan on dreaming at all ...' he effected a gigantic yawn, '... *far* too bushed. Toodle-oo, men, see you at breakfast. And I'd recommend kippers ... hear they're excellent for sexual frustration.' With a guffaw he stepped from the lift and waved a taunting goodnight. 'Ta ta, chumps!'

Ramjet and James held their expressions of scowling miff until the doors closed, then, as the car rose to the seventh floor, fell about with hoots of laughter.

'Oh, poor old McKenzie,' chuckled James, 'if only he knew. As a matter of fact I do believe I'll ruin his day as early as possible and tell him at breakfast.'

The doors opened at the seventh.

'What ... are we doing up here?' enquired Ramjet.

'Quite,' replied James, punching the Lower Ground button.

And six minutes later they were heading for Soho ... and the Phoenix Hotel.

'Phoenix?' repeated Alfred Tulip, London taxi driver. 'Got an address, mate?'

Ramjet shook his head. 'No – just Soho.'

'Mm ...' mused Alfie, tickled to death by Rogers' American accent, his mental meter racking up the prospect of an expensive and unnecessary run-around with a big fat tip at the end. 'Big place Soho ... might take some finding.'

Jim nudged Ramjet, grinned, and leaned towards the sliding glass panel. 'Then you're thinking of the wrong Soho, old boy. The one we want is a tiny place – just off Piccadilly Circus. I'm sure you know it.'

Alfie's rude reply was lost behind the slamming glass panel.

'Still can't believe our luck,' sighed James, settling back in his seat. 'I mean, *two* absolute crackers. I'd be darned hard put to it to choose between them. I, er, presume that you are reasonably satisfied with yours?'

Ramjet grinned. 'Annabel? You're damn right I'm satisfied.' He glanced at his chronometer. 'A quarter to one ... right on time. Say, listen, have you given any thought to ... afterwards? Do we make our way back solo?'

'Safest bet,' nodded James. 'One never knows how long these, er, *interviews* take, does one?'

Ramjet chuckled. 'One certainly doesn't. OK, buddy, we'll play it by ear.'

'Kinky.'

The taxi shot the lights at Piccadilly Circus, circled half of it, and entered Shaftesbury Avenue, turned immediately sharp left into Windmill Street, past the once-famous theatre, crossed Brewer Street into the narrow, alley-like Lexington Street, then twisted and turned through the maze of dark, tiny streets that constitute Soho until even James, intimately familiar with central London, was lost.

The taxi finally came to a halt and the glass panel slid down. 'Phoenix,' muttered Tulip.

James lowered his head to the side window and looked out ... and up. 'Jesuschrist...'

'What's the matter?' asked Ramjet.

'Well, hardly the Savoy, old bean.'

Ramjet joined him at the window. 'Mm ... well, they did say "quiet and inconspicuous", James. If they have erred, it's on the side of caution for our sakes.'

'True. Ah, well...'

They got out. James handed Tulip a pound note and waited determinedly for the change.

'Bin to a fancy dress, then?' enquired Tulip, taking his time finding the coins. 'Whatcha go as – Captain Marvel an' Flash Gordon?'

'No – the crew of Glamour Airways.'

'Oh, them fuckin' idiots. Seen them in the papers. Hear they're headin' this way.'

'Next week,' said James, slipping him a coin.

Tulip did a double-take at it. 'Bloody 'ell, whatcha call *this*?'

'Sixpence – now piss off.'

Bellowing abuse, Tulip departed, filling the narrow, silent street with the roar of angry revs. James and Ramjet stood still until the tail-lights disappeared around a corner, then turned and took another look at the decrepit hostelry before them.

'As you said, James – it is *certainly* not the Savoy ... but understandably so. Shall we investigate the rear?'

'Why not? It can scarcely be less inviting than the front.'

A short way along the block they came upon a narrow alley, entered it, and moments later emerged into a back street, if anything, less salubrious than the one they'd just left, a dark

127

and dismal place of overflowing garbage cans and dense, threatening shadows.

'Wonderful,' gulped James. 'For a moment back there I was beginning to have doubts.'

'James, I don't like it ... something is *wrong*. I have the distinct feeling we have fallen victim to some cruel hoax ... a practical joke.'

'And I concur, Ram old jet. It's highly unlikely...' He paused. 'Hang on ...'

'Mm...?'

'Over there – is that or is that not a fire escape ... and would that not be the rear of the palatial Phoenix Hotel?'

Ramjet peered into the eerie gloom. 'James, you are correct on both counts. Well, now ... shall we stroll cautiously in that direction and see what befalls us?'

They did ... and what befell them was a sudden upsurge of hope, joy, and blood pressure, for there, waving down to them from two adjoining open windows on the first floor were the girls!

'It's them!' gasped Ramjet, grabbing Jim's arm. 'All is not lost! A pox on us for doubting their veracity.'

'Coo ... ee!' waved James.

A warning 'Ssssshhh!' floated down to them from the lovely Delphinia in the right-hand window. Then: 'Quickly – come on up!'

James in the lead, they mounted the double flight of iron approach stairs and tiptoed along the latticed cat-walk.

'Hi!' he whispered to Annabel's head and shoulders showing through drab red-cotton curtains.

'Hi!' she grinned. 'Glad you found us!'

'We would have torn London apart!' answered James, turning to give the thumbs-up to Ramjet. 'See you later, son!'

'Much,' nodded Ramjet. 'Hi, babe ...'

'Hi, yourself. Come on in.'

Ramjet cocked a leg over the sill and was quickly gone from view. James moved on.

'Delphinia ...'

'You're right on time, you *clever* men.'

Taking her hand, he climbed into the room, experiencing a

128

delicious surge of excitement as his eyes took in the double bed over by the wall.

The room, he was relieved to find, did not altogether perpetuate the promise of imminent collapse exuded by the building itself. Hardly Hilton, granted, but sufficiently wholesome to enable him to dismiss it from his mind and concentrate on the adorable creature before him.

Poised at the now closed window, she regarded him with a warm and welcoming smile, her almost Oriental beauty quite demolishing his cool and starting a thunder in his bosom that was destined to continue for several hours to come.

'Delphinia ...' he croaked, 'you look fabulous ... quite fabulous.' His eyes drifted over her slender, sensuous body draped in a tight-fitting embroidered silk Oriental gown, split to the thigh and clinging like a second skin, and just knew his journey had not been in vain.

'Thank you ... and so do you.' She moved towards him with a graceful, silent glide. 'You realize, of course, what a devastating effect that uniform has on us poor helpless females?'

'No,' he lied. 'Tell me.'

She indicated an armchair, set close to the bed. 'Sit down, I'll get you a drink.'

Flinging his cap on the bed, he sat down, his eyes following her hungrily as she crossed to a rickety chest-of-drawers.

'Scotch all right?'

'Perfect,' he replied, his mind very much elsewhere. He doubted if he'd ever seen a nicer bottom.

She laughed. 'Good – it's all I've got.'

'Oh, I wouldn't say that.'

She turned her head, smiled at him through a curtain of dark, gleaming hair. 'James, you're staring ... it's naughty.'

'It's beautiful. All of you is beautiful.'

'Now, now, Officer Crighton-Padgett – remember this is strictly business.'

'Of course,' he chuckled.

She padded to him, lithe as a lynx, handed him his drink then sat, almost demurely, on the edge of the bed in front of him. 'Well ... to the success of Glamour Airlines.'

'Thank you ... and to the success of this ... interview.'

She sipped her drink. 'Oh, this will be successful all right. It has to be.'

'Oh? Why so imperative?'

She shrugged. 'It's my job. My magazine is banking on it.'

He sighed mockingly. 'Ah, the sacrifices one has to endure for profession. It means so much to them, hm?'

'Of course. For what other reason d'you suppose I'd have gone to such underhand lengths to get you alone?'

He grinned. 'Why else indeed?'

'You and Ramjet Rogers are the undoubted "stars" of the tour – so far as women are concerned. You are the essence of glamour.'

'Well, that's very nice of you, but ...'

'But what?'

A pause ... then a self-conscious grin. 'Nothing.'

They both laughed. 'False modesty doesn't become you, James. Be honest, you know you're a knockout.' She leaned towards the pillow and from under it drew out a pad and pencil, then sat with her back against the wall, knees drawn up, knowing, as his eyes flashed to her naked thigh now exposed through the split, that James DeCourcey Crighton-Padgett was already a very dead duck.

'Ready?' she enquired.

'For anything.'

'Then let us begin.'

And in the adjoining room, at a distance no greater than the thickness of the wall against which Delphinia sat, Annabel Bear, exotically attired in a deep-green gown of thinnest jersey wool, her golden hair tumbling sumptuously around her shoulders and spilling carelessly over the jutting plateau of her breasts, raised *her* glass of Scotch to the handsome hunk sprawled indolently in the armchair before her and also proposed a toast to the success of Glamour Airlines.

'Thank you,' grinned Ramjet, quite delighted by the way things were going. What a set up! The little pigeon exuded sexuality like a humming generator. The dress she was wear-

130

ing! ... so thin and clingy he could see every curve and mound, nook and cranny as clearly as if she'd been naked.

The outcome, he knew, was a foregone conclusion. No girl would sit there as she was sitting, her back to the wall, knees drawn up high to tighten the dress round her fabulous ass unless she was ready to offer everything he could plainly see!

Well, the sooner this laughable interview was over the better, then – down to the real business of the evening, the prospect of which was making him feel quite dizzy.

'And here's to your interview,' he replied, nodding towards the pad and pencil at her side in the hope it would get her started. 'I hope it, too will be successful.'

She smiled, smokily, over the rim of her glass. 'It will be.'

'You sound very certain.'

'My job depends on it.'

He frowned. 'An interview with *me* is so critical?'

A wry laugh. 'Oh, come now – false modesty is hardly your style, Paul Rogers. You know darned well there are only two men aboard *Glamour Puss* that interest women – you and James Crighton-Padgett.'

He responded with a self-effacing, 'Well, that's very nice of you, but ...', the pretence laying great strain on his integrity.

'But what?' she sighed, mockingly.

He shrugged. 'Nothing.' And they both burst out laughing.

'That's better,' she said, laying aside her drink and picking up the pad and pencil.

'It's still unbelievable...' he said, lighting a cigarette and looking one-eyed at her through the smoke.

'What is?'

'You ... me ... us ... this.'

'Why so? Look, this is a hellishly competitive world Delphinia and I operate in. This Glamour tour is a once-in-a-blue-moon godsend to women's mags. It embraces so many things women are interested in – travel, men, fashions, men, romance, men, adventure, men...'

'How about men?'

'Them, too,' she laughed, then shook her head. 'You fellows are crazy, you know ... any self-respecting journal would have offered you a nice fat fee for an exclusive...'

'*Now* she tells me!'

She smiled at him, her eyes suddenly aglow with promise. 'Oh, you won't come out of this unrewarded, Ramjet Rogers.'

His heart skipped a beat. 'I won't?'

'No ... but the fee is something to bear in mind for the remainder of the tour.'

'It's pretty much out of our hands, I'm afraid. We don't even know where we're going next. And there'll be an agent like Arnold Bottum waiting everywhere we land who'll have organized everything.'

'Too bad. Still ... maybe you'll have the good fortune to bump into someone like me at each stop-over.'

He shook his head, hypnotized by the amber fire of her eyes. 'Impossible ... a fella doesn't get this lucky twice.'

'Thank you. How's your drink? Help yourself to another.'

'How about you?'

She shrugged, 'Why not?' and drained her glass. 'After all ... we have almost six and a half hours.'

'Y ... es, ma'am.'

'And one can get an *awful* lot down in six and a half hours.'

'Yes, *ma'm*!' he chuckled, then crossed the room for the drinks without once touching the floor.

IO

Hilton Hotel – Room 623 ...

'One fifteen!' muttered Cock-up Rossiter, glancing at his captain's chronometer as he paced across the room to the door, then turned and paced back again to the dew-encrusted ice-bucket in which reposed a bottle of ostentatiously expensive bubbly. 'Dammit, if that dame don't turn up, I'll ...'

He abandoned the threat, common sense telling him that if she didn't turn up there was nothing he *could* do, and continued his furious pacing.

Dames, he thought bitterly. The first bit of promising crumpet he'd come across in a coon's age and it looked like an eleventh-hour wipe-out. Granted, it had all seemed a bit unbelievable when it had happened. Stupendous-looking canaries were not in the habit of falling over themselves to climb into his bed – especially stupendous-looking *titled* canaries – yet there had been that argument about her being a chairman-screwer to comfort him. Dammit, why *else* had she made that play at the lunch table? – a five-star, grade A come-on if ever he'd seen one, pulsing with pullulating promise. The bird was a raver, no two ways about it ... and now this!

'Oh ... fuck it!' he cursed aloud and changed course for the bathroom, deciding to call it a night.

But the furtive tap-tap-tap on the bedroom door caught him before he could set a foot over the threshold, both arms slamming into the wall to stop his forward plunge.

133

'Oh, my God...' he gasped, his stomach looping-the-loop as it did whenever he hit an unexpected air-pocket and dropped five hundred feet like a stone. Exultantly, he tore across the room, wrenched open the door. It was she! – clothed completely in black, her face hidden by the voluminous black-fur collar of her coat.

'You came!' he cried.

With a quick last glance up and down the corridor, she entered, sighing with relief as she pulled away the mask of fur and threw the coat back loosely upon her shoulders. 'God, I was suffocating in there. You have simply no idea what a time I've had getting here unseen.'

'Oh, I have, I have!' Cock-up breathlessly assured her. 'Here, let me take your coat... I have champagne on ice, I'm sure you need it.'

'I need it,' she nodded, shucking off the coat to reveal a honey of a dress in multi-hued floral silk that sent him cuckoo with desire.

'Oh, Penelope, you are altogether too much,' he chuckled, throwing the coat into a chair and hastening to the champagne. 'I was beginning to despair that you'd never get here,' he said, wrestling with the cork.

A chiding smile. 'Alfred, I'm not *that* late.'

'Oh, no... no, I wasn't implying... I mean, I was only... well, put it down to my impatience to see you again. Each minute after one o'clock seemed an eternity.'

'How very sweet. Er, Alfred... are we destined to drink that tonight?'

'I'm... all thumbs,' he laughed nervously. 'Can't seem to...'

'Here, let me.'

She relieved him of the bottle and with a deft, experienced flick of her thumb sent the cork exploding across the room and the champagne gushing all down his silver-lamé trousers.

'Yipe!'

'Oh, Alfred, I'm *so* sorry,' she pleaded, redirecting the stream into a glass.

'Now, don't worry... don't worry...'

'But your uniform!'

134

'It's spill-proof. I'll get a towel . . .'

He shot into the bathroom and returned with a hand towel, rubbing at his flies as he came.

'No . . .' she smiled, setting down the bottle and reaching for the towel. 'I'll do that.'

'Mm . . .?'

'After all, I am responsible . . .'

Stunned by the offer, he dumbly handed over the towel and stared wide-eyed as she dropped to her knees in front of him, wrapped her free arm round his legs, and commenced to stroke the damp patch directly over his knob with slow, deliberate strokes.

'There . . .' she whispered, her demeanour suddenly and strangely intensely preoccupied, almost hypnotized, as though that tiny area of his being held an all-important fascination for her to the exclusion of the rest of him. '*There* . . .' she went again, a warm and tender sound, the mew of an adoring mother comforting her child. 'Oh, Alfred, you naughty boy . . . you're getting an erection.'

'I . . .' croaked Rossiter, almost sick with excitement.

'*Shame* on you . . . fancy doing a naughty thing like that to a lady you hardly know. What would you do to a lady you *did* know, for heaven's sake . . .?'

'I . . .'

'Oh, my, look how *big* he's getting, Alfred! I think if I'd known this was going to happen, I'd certainly have had to think twice about coming here. But since I *am* here . . . I think we'd better have a look at him.'

Riiippp went his zipper and in went her hand.

Cock-up buckled at the knees, emitted some strange, unintelligible sounds as though he was being garrotted.

Plink! From the confines of his Y-fronts out shot his pride and joy, cradled in her warm and trembling hands.

'Ohhhhh . . .' a plaintive, adulating sigh. 'Isn't he just the most adorable . . .'

Cock-up shut his eyes, grabbed the ice-bucket for support, then damn-near fainted as her hot breath scorched his scrotum and her sizzling tongue tickled him from root to tip.

135

'Penelope...!'

'What is it, Alfred?'

'I want you ... I *want* you!'

'Then you shall certainly have me – but all in good time. Come ... let us drink some champagne ... and leisurely contemplate what we shall do to each other.'

And while this situation was developing nicely ... Room 806.

Merde, but I am tired, thought Monsieur Jacques Camembert, in French, naturally.

Bad food always exhausted him and the food they'd served at dinner had been so bad it had drained him of all verve and rendered him positively comatose.

Shuddering with horror as he recalled the *côtelettes de veau*, he wound his wrist-watch, noting abstractedly that it indicated one twenty, yawned wearily, and decided a deep, hot bath was what he needed to cleanse his memory of the vile *légumes assortis* and wash away the tragedy of their diabolical *poires étuvées au vin rouge*.

So deciding, he entered the bathroom, filled the capacious tub to the overflow hole, flung away his clothes, and immersed his sensitive soul to the neck. And in less time than it takes to knock up a *soufflé glace aux framboises* was fast asleep.

While simultaneously ... in Room 669.

Senator Sam Chortle, all of a dither with excited anticipation, looked at his watch for the umpteenth time in ten minutes, cursed its crawling progress, and nervously inspected his appearance in the wardrobe mirror, also for the umpteenth time in ten minutes.

Fahn figure of a man, he modestly allowed, adjusting the flap of his grey double-breasted suit over his bulging belly and straightening the loops in his leather-thong cowboy tie. Yessirree, a fahn figure of a man ... an' by golly Miss Wilma Fluck would know the full weight of the argument before anuther hour had passed or his name was not Samuel Washington Chortle.

With a self-congratulatory chuckle he abandoned his preening and crossed to the side table on which stood two ice-buckets, each mothering a bottle of pricey bubbly with which he intended to execute the Fluck seduction.

Given to frequent bouts of sexual fantasy, and with five minutes to kill, he seated himself and encouraged his mind to wander yet again over the sequence of events about to take place, savouring with voracious appetite each thrilling nuance of the progress towards the final ecstatic consummation.

Moments from now he would gather up the bubbly, open the door, and cautiously proceed along the corridor to the rear stairs, then ascend two flights to the eighth floor and cautiously proceed along that corridor to room 806.

A discreet knock.

The door would open ... and she would be standing there, attired for seduction ... a flimsy night-gown of some teasingly sheer material of baby doll design, scarcely concealing the womanly ripeness of her naked body.

'Mah dear...'

'Senator! Come – quickly!'

'Have no fear, no one saw me ... and make it Sam, if only for tonight.'

'Thank you.'

Her room – an enchanted oasis, heady with the lingering perfume of her bath, romantically illuminated by soft bedside lights. Her bed – a beckoning host to wanton sport ... and she upon it, languorous with love, eager for delight.

'How lovely you look in chiffon, mah dear...'

A breathless whisper. 'Do I please you, Sam? I did it all for you.'

'Please me? ... you excite me clean outta mah boots, child.'

'Take them off, Sam ... take everything off, then ... un-dress me ... *please*!'

'How impatient is youth. First – a drink, the night is very young.'

'Will it be nice and long, Sam?'

An obscene chuckle. 'On that, honeh, you can bet your daddy's plantation...'

Chortle roused himself from reverie, checked his watch a

137

final time, slapped his great hands together, and came to his feet in readiness.

Zero hour ... was in exactly thirty seconds.

'Oh, Alfred...!' With a cry, Lady Penelope released herself from his embrace, her hands flying to the buttons of her dress.

'I know ... I know...!'

With haste bordering on desperation they clawed the clothes from their bodies and carelessly flung them aside, then, starkers, they paused the merest moment, breast and bosom heaving, absorbing the other's attributes and thrilling to the sight.

'F .. fabulous!' gasped Cock-up.

'Lover!' she cried, extending her arms towards him and back-pedalling for the bed.

Throwing herself upon it, she flung her thighs asunder and beckoned him to take refuge in their hirsute midst, a quite unnecessary invitation since the good captain was already in the air.

'Penelope...!'

'Oh ... *Al*fred ...! Take me ... take me ...!'

And as he took aim for the plunge, the telephone rang.

'Oh ... *no*!' he cried.

'Ignore it ... ignore it!' she implored.

'Yuh're danged *right* I'm gonna ignore it! You don't think a mere phone call could stop me now?'

'My hero ...'

'Unless, that is ... it happened to be a telephone call from a certain Colonel Berskin in New York!'

Despair. 'Oh ... Alfred!'

He backed off, knelt between her legs. 'Dearest, the man is mad – completely fruitcake! If I don't answer it he'll send someone up to bang on the door, thinking I'm asleep. Honey ... it won't take long.'

'Oh ... *Al*fred ...'

'I know, I know ... but see how persistent he is. How can we concentrate on love with that thing blasting us? I'll get rid of him fast ... I promise!'

'Go, then!' she commanded huffily. 'I will smoke a cigarette and pretend it hasn't happened.'

'Such devotion.'

He clambered off the bed and with quickly wilting erection answered the offensive instrument.

'Yeah!'

'I have a call from New York, Captain Rossiter ... hold the line, please.'

He clapped a hand over the mouthpiece and turned to Penelope, already half-hidden in a cloud of billowing Disque Bleu smoke. 'It's him!'

'Fuck him.'

'Now, don't you worry, angel, I'll have him off this phone so fast you won't notice I've bin gone. After what I've been through today I'm in no mood for any protracted crap from Berskin, I can tell you ... hello ... yes, this is Rossiter ... who's that ... oh, Miss Destry, how are yuh? Yeh, I'm just beautiful. Say, I thought Berskin was supposed ta call me at seven thirty London time. I waited here half an hour for ... oh, he did, huh? Well, ain't that too damn bad. OK – put him on ...'

Again he covered the mouthpiece and turned to Penelope who was looking more furious by the minute. 'How'd yuh like that guy – had me waiting here at seven thirty for his call and *he* decided to take a nap after lunch ... hello ...?'

'I'm putting you through now, captain ...'

'I can't wait.'

The phone clicked and cracked in Rossiter's ear, then Berskin was on, demanding, 'That you, Rossiter?'

'Sure it's me. It's bin me since seven thirty tonight ...'

'Never mind that – just tell me what the hell's goin' on over there! I've had Gloriana Fullbrush on my back bitchin' she's not gettin' the star treatment ... Sam Chortle was on bitchin' because he didn't get a look-in on either of the TV interviews ... that ass-hole Bottum was on complainin' he's gettin' the minimum co-operation and the maximum grief from everyone ... I've had "In Town Today" on complainin' you fucked up a live religious programme ... and some nut named Shafto is threatenin' to sue me for personal injury inflicted by Delicious O'Hara's handbag and Shag McGee's parrot! Now, what in

Christ's name is goin' *on* over there?'

Rossiter exhaled a sigh of stupefied weariness and sank disconsolately in a chair. 'Berskin ... do you have any conception of what *time* it is here in London? It is half past fucking one in the morning ... !'

'I *know* what time it is, Rossiter, and since when did you work nine-to-five? I want a full report on what's bin going on and I want it *now* – so kick that dame outta your room and commence reportin' – or, by God, I'll have your replacement at the Hilton by breakfast time! And if *that* threat don't shift your ass into high gear, may I remind you of a certain *tape recording* that I have in my possession ...'

Rossiter gasped. 'F'Godsake, Berskin, not over the phone ... !'

'OK!' barked Berskin. 'So fire away – from the top!'

Rossiter cast a glance of pitiable apology at Penelope, now fuming behind a veritable smoke-screen of Disque Bleu obfuscation, and offered her a helpless shrug, detecting in her responding scowl how little it compensated for the erection whose return she so yearningly awaited.

'Honey ...' he pleaded.

'Oh ... *knickers*!' she rapped, and threw them at him.

Phoenix Hotel:

'A *fascinating* story,' smiled Delphinia, laying aside her pad and pencil. 'James ... another drink.'

'Let me get them.'

'No, stay right where you are, you look so comfortable.'

They had, in fact, changed places – at Delphinia's recent insistence – she taking the armchair while he, jacketless, bootless, and tieless, stretched indolently upon the bed in the attitude of a patient reclining upon his psychiatrist's couch.

Relaxed by the whisky and the warmth of their rapport, he lay cocooned in rosy well-being, careless of time and place, mindful only of the delectable girl now about to sit at his side.

'Here you are, sir – one Scotch and Scotch.'

'I must say the service in this hotel is absolutely marvellous.'

'We aim to please.'

'And by jove you do ...' His hand dropped lightly to her naked thigh, exposed beneath the flying panel of her gown.

She smiled softly. 'And so do you. You really are an outrageously attractive man.'

'Would you ... do something for me?'

'Of course.'

He offered her his glass. 'Please put that on the floor.'

She took it from him, placed her own alongside it, out of the way. 'Anything else, sir?'

'Yes ... come here.'

She went. She fell upon him, their mouths blending, gently at first but quickly passionate. She broke away, gasping, Wow!'

'Delphinia...'

'Yes, James...?'

'I want you.'

'And I you, James.'

'You do?'

'This instant.'

'How perfectly super.'

He sat up, abandoning his shirt. She came to her feet, performed a lightning contortion, and the gown whispered to the floor. James swung his legs from the bed, quickly shed his trousers.

'One moment...' she insisted, taking them from him, then quickly gathering up his Glamour jacket, cap, shirt. 'They'll be horribly crumpled for tomorrow if we don't hang them up.'

'How terribly thoughtful.'

'I'll hang them in the bathroom, it's damp in there. The humidity will bring the creases out.'

'I have never known such kindness.'

She shrugged. 'It's only good sense. You have a big photographic session tomorrow. Can't have you looking like a bag of washing.' She gave a nod, indicating the T-shirt and shorts he was still wearing, and her eyes crinkled sexily. 'Take those off – I'll be right back.'

Taking a wooden hanger from the wardrobe, she arranged the uniform on it and disappeared into the bathroom. Moments later she was kneeling on the bed, at his side, a vision of erotic womanhood desirous to please.

'Are you ... familiar with the Sumatran ways of making love, James?' she whispered, her voice as gentle as the fingers that trickled across his chest, caressed the flinching ripple of his stomach, then captured the iron hardness of his throbbing manhood.

'N .. no,' he croaked.

Smiling, she slowly lowered her face towards him. 'Well, to be honest, they're no different from the English, French, American, and Spanish ways of making love ... it's the girl that makes the difference. I will make it different for you, James ...'

'How .. D .. Delphinia ...?'

A low, erotic chuckle. 'Well, to start with ... like this.'

And then she swallowed him.

'Ramjet ...' she sighed, laying aside her pad and pencil. 'I believe that concludes the interview. It was marvellous.'

'You've got all you want?'

She smiled smokily. 'For the article – yes. Let's have another drink.'

She got off the bed and went to the chest-of-drawers. Ramjet roused himself from the armchair and moved close behind her, placed his hands on her shoulders. 'And ... in other matters?'

Abandoning the drinks, she turned into him, slid her hands to his waist, and murmured, 'I think you know me as an honest woman?'

'Honest ... beautiful ... and ravishingly sexy,' he grinned. 'I don't know how I've kept my hands off you for the last half hour.'

'They're on me now ... do you hear me objecting?'

'You are disarmingly honest, Annabel ... quite takes my breath away.'

'I'll take your breath away,' she growled, squeezing him.

'That sounds decidedly like a threat.'

She shook her head. 'No ... it's most decidedly a promise.'

She eased away from him, doe-eyed and heavy-lidded,

reached for the buckle of his jacket, and slipped it loose. 'I ... think we'd better take care of this ... it's going to get awfully creased. Take it off, Ramjet ... all of it ... I'll hang it in the bathroom.'

He frowned. 'Bathroom?', fingers fumbling.

'It's humid in there, it'll bring out the creases.'

'How very thoughtful.'

She gave a shrug. 'You have a heavy photographic session tomorrow ... we can't have you looking as though you've slept in the park.'

'No ...'

Quickly divested, she hangered the uniform and went into the bathroom, pausing at the door to raise a critical brow at the shorts and T-shirt he was still wearing. 'Ramjet ... you're *still* over-dressed.'

'Oh ... sure.'

Bubbling with excitement, he discarded the garments, then, hearing a sound behind him he turned, finding her also very naked.

'Annabel ... my God, you're lovely.'

She came to him, fell into his arms, reaching hungrily for his mouth and groaning at his burgeoning hardness against her belly. She broke away, gazing down at him in wonderment, then urgently took his hand and led him to the bed.

'Lie down,' she gasped, her voice a hushed command. 'And lie quite still ... there are things I wish to do to you.'

'What ... sort of things?'

She knelt beside him, gazing in awe at his throbbing rod, then slowly reached out and took it tenderly in both hands.

'Well, for a start, my Ramjet ... this.'

And then she consumed him.

II

Meanwhile, back at the Hilton ... Room 669.

With both arms full of clattering ice-bucket, Sam Chortle eased the door of his room open and peered out into the corridor. Fahn! It was deserted – an omen, perhaps, that everything else was gonna be jurst fahn.

Soundlessly whistling 'The Days of Wine and Roses', he tiptoed down the corridor to the emergency stairway, pushed through the swing doors and ascended two floors, growing more confident as each flight of stairs was safely negotiated that the Fates were on his side.

Emerging with extreme caution into the corridor of the eighth floor, he paused, impatiently, for a quick recce, decided the silence was to be trusted, and proceeded down its endless length on the sides of his boots, looking far more like a bow-legged cowboy searching for his horse than a lover hastening to a romantic tryst.

820 ... 818 ... 816 ... by golly, his luck was holdin' out. Not a soul or a sound – not so much as a wayward snore.

812 ... 810 ... 808 ... and finally ... 806! Nerves all a-jangle he reached her doorway and paused to corral his rampaging wits. Wonder of wonders, he'd made it. He was here! A quick glance back along the corridor and then he turned his attention to the door.

Slipping one of the ice-buckets between his knees, he rendered the door the most diplomatic of taps, anticipating, as in his fantasy, its immediate opening. Transferring the bucket again to his arm, he braced himself, fixed a smile of disarming smarm upon his face, and prepared his lips for the opening line, 'Mah dear . . .'

Long moments passed. The smile slid from his face and his teeth snapped together irritably. Again he transferred the freezing bucket to his knees and fetched the door a harder rap.

Still no response.

Eleventh-hour failure loomed at his shoulder like a horrifying spectre, rousing his indignation – and the old Chortle fighting spirit. Hell's bells, she couldn't be out! . . . couldn't have stood him up! Not Sam Chortle!

Maybe she'd fallen asleep!

Yeah, that was it – the poor darlin' had had a mighty hard day. She wus so plumb tuckered out she'd fallen asleep waitin'.

His hand fell to the doorknob . . . turned it . . . pushed. Jumpin' mint-juleps, it opened!

With clamouring heart he peered in, all fear of failure rapidly receding as he espied the low, romantic lighting and the sliver of bright light beneath the bathroom door.

So . . .! His fantasy had not been wrong after all – merely ten minutes fast. The angel was still at her toilette.

With a devilish titter he closed the door and tiptoed to the bed, silently put down the ice-buckets on the side table, then, cat-like, headed for the bathroom door.

A quick listen.

Tap . . . tap . . . tap. 'It is I, honeh chile . . . ole Sam has arrived . . . bearin' gifts!'

Monsieur Jacques Camembert awoke with a start, dropping his arm into the water with a splash, amazed at the vividness of his dream. *Mon Dieu*, but the water was cold, he would be catching his death. Quickly he scrambled out, hazy with sleep, and wrapped a big, warm, fluffy towel around his shivering body. Then he removed the bath plug.

And while the water was sucking noisily down the hole, Senator Sam Chortle, quite giddy with excitement, feverishly

145

removed his clothes and slipped between the cool white sheets, naked as a skinned Longhorn.

Count down to seduction ... had begun.

While down in Room 623 ...

'Alfred, for God*sake* ...!' raged Penelope, smashing her fag into an ashtray and leaping off the bed in high dudgeon.

Rossiter's head snapped round, his eyes huge with horror. 'Penelope ...!'

'What?' barked Berskin.

'Er ... just one moment, Colonel, the, er, chambermaid's here ...'

'At one-forty in the mornin'!'

'I mean ... it's the waiter ...!'

'Named *Penelope*?'

Rossiter laughed ridiculously. 'Pen*e*lope! Did you think I said "Penelope", Colonel? No sir, I said "Napoli" – he's an Italian guy ... five-two, black hair, and a limp ... would you excuse me one moment, colonel, I've gotta pay him for some cigars ...'

Rossiter slammed the phone onto the desk and rushed across the room to Penelope who already had one foot in her knickers.

'Penelope ... darling!' he cried, attempting to take her in his arms. 'You're not leaving!'

'Certainly, I'm leaving!' she seethed, hopping away from him, trying to get the other foot in. 'Damn it, Rossiter, what d'you think I am? I take a terrible chance creeping up to your room ... with the express intention of giving you the f ... the evening of your life ... and you spend it rabbiting over the phone to that idiot B ...'

'Sssshhh! Oh, beloved don't go ... take them off again, I beg you! I'll get rid of him *fast*, I promise!'

'No, you won't.'

'I will!'

'You can't.'

'I can! Dammit, I *will*, you watch me.'

'Well ...' she pouted, uncertainly.

'Good girl ... here, let me help you ...'

'Rossiter!' shrieked the phone.

'Oh...'

'Go on – get rid of him!' Penelope whispered.

Rossiter set his teeth and strode purposefully back to the phone, snatched it up. 'Now, look here, Colonel, I must...'

'Where the fuck have *you* been? Dammit, d'you know how much this call is costing me, Rossiter ...?'

'Colonel, I must...'

'OK – get back to your story.'

'Colonel, I must...'

'So yuh keep sayin'! OK – *what* must you, Rossiter?'

'I ... that is ... if it's all the same to you, Colonel ...'

'Rossiter, are you pissed?'

'Colonel, how dare you...'

'Well, somethin' funny's goin' on over there. You've got a dame in that room, Rossiter!'

'I have not!'

'Oh, yes you have!'

'*Oh*, no, I haven't.'

'Well, somethin' screwey's goin' on.'

'What is going *on*, Colonel, is that I've had one hell of a damn day and I'm out on my feet! I am *tired*, Colonel ... bushed, tuckered, exhausted and fucked and I desire most urgently to climb back into my bed and...'

'OK, OK...'

'... because I've got *another* hell of a day comin' up tomorrow...'

'OK, Rossiter, OK...'

'And after all the treking around London with those photographers, I've still got to fly the goddam plane...'

'I said *OK* Rossiter!' bellowed Berskin. 'Yuh made your point – nine times over! Well, keep that bunch of idiots under better control in future ... an' don't forget I'm payin' Gloriana Fullbrush a *fortune* to fly this trip. Make use of her! And get Chortle more coverage or there could be political repercussions! And...'

'Al-*fred*!'

Rossiter slapped his hand over the mouthpiece. 'Coming this instant, beloved ...!'

'Who was that!' demanded Berskin.

'Who was what?' enquired Rossiter.

'That! I distinctly heard a female voice shouting "Alfred".'

'Crossed line. Heard it myself. These English phones are real weird.'

'In a pig's eye. OK, Rossiter, just don't let me hear of any more trouble, I want a clean operation from now on.'

'Clean, yes, *sir* ... well, g'bye, colonel ...'

'And don't think you can hide anything from me just because you're on the other side of the ...'

'World, no, sir, certainly not, colonel ... well, so long, colonel, I ...'

'I've got spies everywhere, Rossiter. You can't drop a fart without me knowin' about it, yuh hear?'

'Yes, sir, I hear – loud and clear! So g'bye, colonel, I've gotta get some *sleep*!'

'OK, g'bye ... oh, yeah, one more thing, Rossiter ...'

Rossiter crashed the receiver into its cradle and rushed to Penelope who had one leg off the bed again, threatening departure.

'Beloved ...!'

'One more second, Alfred, and no amount of persuasion ...'

He fell heavily onto the bed, gathering her in his arms. 'Thank you, thank you for staying ... you won't regret it, I promise.'

The warmth slowly returned to her smile and finally she kissed him teasingly on the nose. 'No more phone calls?'

'Not on your life.'

'No more interruptions?'

'How can there be?'

'Of *any* kind?'

'No way ... oh, that is *nice*, Penelope.'

'Well, it hasn't *all* been wasted time, Alfred.'

'No?'

'No ... I've been sort of lying here thinking of things to do to you when ... or rather *if* ... you finally got off the phone.'

'Oh? And ... what did you come up with?'

A throaty, threatening chuckle. 'All *sorts* of lovely things.'

'Such as?'

She slid sensuously and slowly down the bed, pecking his torso with fleeting, affectionate kisses, until at last she arrived once more at his pulsing pylon.

'Well, for starters ... how about *this*?'

'Right on ... centre line,' gasped Cock-up ... and abandoned himself to heaven.

Phoenix Hotel ... Room 14.

'Oh, James ...' Delphinia sighed plaintively, gazing with unseeing eyes at the decrepit ceiling, 'you do that *so* beautifully.'

James raised his head and smilingly shrugged. 'One good turn deserves another, I always say.'

'Do you always say that? I always say that, too. I knew we had a great deal in common the moment we met. Oh, I'm so glad we had the courage to go through with our little scheme. You really are the most accomplished lover.'

'As you are, my sweet. What would you like me to do now?'

'Enter me, James. Just lie upon me and I will do the rest.'

'Consider it done, angel.'

Rising between her widespread thighs, he supported himself on his hands, smiled down at her, teasingly witholding his favours.

'Hi, down there.'

'You ...' She reached for him, gasping as she clutched the rock-hard realization of her desire. 'Oh, James, *please* ...'

'What if I decided you can't have him?'

She bared her teeth. 'You would not get out of this room alive.'

He chuckled. 'That sounds pretty desperate.'

'I *am* desperate. James, *please* ...'

'If there's one thing I can't refuse it's the plea of a desperate woman. OK, angel, but ... sl-o-w-l-y ...'

At the first tentative touch she released a low, plaintive groan, arched her hips to meet him, but with a cruel laugh he backed away, probed again, withdrew, advanced, retreated, teasing her unmercifully, until, with a cry, she grabbed his buttocks and pulled him sharply inside her, bullseye, first time.

'Oh, God . . . !' she cried. 'James, that . . . is wonderful !'

'That is the word, love.'

'No – don't move! Just . . . lie there . . . oh, James, you're so *big* !'

'Good, hm?'

'So *hard* . . . ohh . . .'

'What?'

'I don't think I'm going to last very long.'

'There's no penalty for speed, Delphinia. Take it as it comes . . . no pun intended.'

'Can you . . . hold?'

'For as long as you wish.'

'You're wonderful . . . ohhh . . . James! . . . it's coming! . . . it's here! . . . OOHHHH !'

'Wey hey . . . ! Ouch . . . !'

'I can't help it! Ohh, you have no idea how good that feels . . .'

'I'm . . . beginning to get the idea !'

'It's just fantastic . . . I think I'm going to faint with pleasure! . . . I'm going to cry! . . . James . . . James . . . go *faster* . . . !'

'Faster . . . yes, love.'

'And *harder* . . . !'

'Certainly, dear . . . ohh, my God . . .'

'What . . . you, too?'

'Me, too . . .'

'How soon?'

'Soon !'

'Super !'

'Like . . . right now !'

'Wonderful !'

'OhhhhhHHHHHH ! !'

'Oh, James . . . James . . .'

'Yoooowwwww !'

'Fan . . . *tastic* !'

'Un . . . be*lievable* . . .'

With an exhausted grunt he collapsed upon her, then snuggled to her side. 'Aw, baby . . . I think my back's broken.'

'You really socked it to me, James . . .'

He snuggled closer still, caressed her shoulder, hugged her tight. 'Aaawww ... I could sleep for a week ...'

'Good, then sleep.'

He shook his head. 'No ... I'd never wake up in time.'

'I'll wake you.'

He laughed. 'And who's going to wake *you*?'

'Oh, I won't sleep. I'll just rest awhile then freshen myself with a shower.'

'You ... are not going to move. I like you right where you are.'

'Oh, I shan't go just yet. I'll wait until you're asleep. There ... close your eyes and sl-e-e-p. You've had a long, hard day ...'

'We'll see,' he murmured drowsily. God, he felt bushed ... maybe just ten minutes would do it ... just ten minutes ... can't be late for the photographic session ...

The horror of being asleep while Rossiter combed London for Ramjet and himself temporarily roused him – but it was very temporary. Lulled by Delphinia's warmth and her softly caressing hand his alarm quickly abated, and, as sleep began to overcome him, his thoughts drifted languorously to his buddy next door, discovering with some astonishment that he hadn't given Rogers a moment's thought since he'd climbed through the window.

A smile touched his lips as he pictured the great attempted seduction in progress just beyond the wall ... Rogers Victor Maturing himself into a frenzy ... even playing scenes from the Old Master's films to break down her resistance.

Ah, well, he chuckled ... slipping deeper into oblivion ... if Ramjet didn't have what it took to get it without five hours of histrionics, that was his problem ... his own was well and truly solved. Well ... and ... truly.

And on that thought he fell asleep.

But in that regard James could not have been more wrong, for at that very moment Ramjet Rogers was doing quite all right for himself. In all his travels he had not encountered a more lively, adventurous and totally uninhibited chickadee than the lovely Annabel who was currently mounted across his

151

thighs, impaled to the limit of his prodigious offering, a grin of ecstatic glee lighting her amber eyes and the joy of pending orgasm reflected in her laboured breathing.

'Ohh, Ramjet . . .'

'Anything I can do to help, honey?'

She shook her tangled head. 'No, no . . . ohh, it's just too incredible . . .' she clutched her heart. 'I feel you right up here!'

He laughed, not overly offended. 'Angel, that would make me two feet long . . .'

'So?'

'Ha!'

'Oh, Ramjet . . .'

'What is it, lover?'

'I'm coming . . .'

'Well, good for you.'

'Ohhhh . . . aaahhhh . . . OHHHH!'

'Go, baby, go . . . !'

She went.

With a cry, she kicked . . . shot ahead of the field, coming out of the saddle to lighten her stallion's load, then slapping down hard again to drive him on. Up . . . down . . . up . . . down, teeth a-grit and golden hair flying, post coming up fast. Tally-ho!

'Aaaaaaahhhhhh!'

With an exultant cry she thrashed her head, seized by a shuddering climax, racked by shattering spasms, then with a final, 'Oooohhhhhh!' collapsed upon him. Smack! She hit his heaving chest, kissed the salt from his skin, murmuring over and over, 'Fabulous . . . fabulous . . . fabulous . . .'

He gave a chuckle. 'It's the only way to fly, baby – the Glamour way.'

'That . . . is no lie. It's what I'm going to tell all my readers . . .'

'Eh?'

She groaned. 'Oh, if only I could . . . you really deserve the publicity.'

Smiling at him, she raised herself up and regarded him tenderly. 'Ramjet . . . it's so much better than I imagined . . .

and I imagined it was going to be quite miraculous.'

'Aw, shucks ...'

'I mean it.'

'You're too much, Annabel ... hey, where're you going now?'

'Up here.' She sat erect, wincing. 'Wow ... and you say *I'm* too much. Oh, Ramjet ...'

'What, love?'

'I do believe I want you again.'

'You do? How ...?'

'Well, being just a plain, old-fashioned girl at heart ...'

'Ha!'

'... I'd like you the plain, old-fashioned way.'

'You mean ... missionary?'

She dipped her head. 'And this time ... all the way?'

'It's yours.'

Hastily they rearranged themselves.

'Oh, Ramjet ...'

'Yes, love?'

'Please ...'

'What?'

'Hard!'

'Yes.'

'Fast!'

'Certainly.'

'Now!'

'This instant!'

'Aaaaaahhhhh!'

'Yooooowwwwww!'

'Eeeeehhhhhh!'

'Wooooowwwwww!'

Panting, he collapsed upon her, eased his weight to her side and there they lay, breathless, welded together, engulfed by their body heat.

'Un ... believable ...'

'Out of ... this world,' she agreed. 'Ram ... jet ... how aptly named.'

A low chuckle. 'Right now ... it ought to be limp lettuce leaf.'

153

'Sleep.'

He shook his head. 'Can't ... early start ...'

'I'll wake you.'

He laughed. 'And who's going to wake *you*?'

'Oh, I won't sleep. In a few minutes I'll get up and take a shower ... you sleep.'

'Terrible temptation ... had a mighty hard day ...'

She laughed and snuggled closer. 'To say nothing of the night. Go on, close your eyes, you deserve it. You've got several hours yet.'

'Well ... if you're sure ...'

'Of course, I'm sure.'

'Is there any limit ... to your sweet perfection?'

Her response was a light and loving caress upon his face that soothed away all lingering resistance and slowly eased him down into deep untroubled sleep.

12

Simultaneously ...

'Sacre *bleu*,' muttered Monsieur Jacques Camembert, gazing blearily at his haggard reflection in the bathroom mirror. 'Camembert, you look like 'ell. Your complexion 'as ze consistency of a dish of *groseille à maquereau avec crème fouettée* and your eyes bear a distinct *resemblance* to a brace of redcurrants. Get some sleep!'

Naked as day, he pulled open the door and strode with portly purpose into the bedroom, the hairs on his nape rising in violent protest at the sight of an equally fat and flabbily naked Sam Chortle propped up in his bed puffing a cigar.

Camembert came to a speechless, pop-eyed halt.

Chortle shot erect, dropping two inches of scalding ash into his navel. 'Yooooowwwwww!'

'What ... who ...' stammered Camembert, in French, naturally. 'Sacre bleu – un pouff!'

'Oh, mah Gard!' cried Chortle, flinging back the sheet to reveal a huge erection still nine-tenths viable.

'Aaagggghhh!' bellowed Camembert, his Gallicly heterosexual soul outraged that this smarmy pig could have possibly misread him for a fag. 'Stay vere you are! Don't moof! Come no closer or I vill ...'

'But mah dear Camembert ...!' protested Chortle, swinging a tree-like thigh off the bed.

That did it.

With a howl of horror at Chortle's advancing erection, Camembert fled for the bathroom and snatched up his open, cut-throat razor.

That also did it.

With a similar howl at Camembert's obvious intention, Chortle wrenched the blue cotton counterpane from the bed, whirled it around his shoulders, and dived for the door, gained the hallway with barely an inch to spare and set off down it at one hell of a clip and in entirely the wrong direction.

'Bah! I teach ze big fat pouffter a *leçon* 'e nev-er forget!' cried Camembert, dashing back into the bathroom for the towel, draped it hurriedly around his middle, then ran for the door, emerging into the corridor just in time to spot the tail-end of Chortle's counterpane disappearing round the distant corner.

'Come back 'ere, you ... you *sédiment odorant*!' he cried, then took off after him.

'Oh, mah *God*...!' whimpered Chortle. 'Gotta hide ... gotta *hide*!'

In desperate panic he plunged for the knob of Room 849, gave it a twist, praying hard. His prayer was answered. The door opened! In he went, barely closing the door behind him before Camembert flashed round the corner, crying, 'Eet iss no good to 'ide, my cock-a-doodle-doo – I shall 'ave it off wiz one stroke!'

Chortle stood trembling in the dark, utterly bemused by what had happened. How *could* he have made a mistake in the room number! Why, on the other hand, was that crazy Frenchman in her room!

Now, from behind him in the absolute blackness – fresh terror. A grunt, a stirring of bedclothes, and a sleep-drugged demand.

'Uh ... who ... who's there? Wh ... who's in this room?'

Chortle swallowed, the gulp sounding ludicrously loud in the black silence. 'Ah ... ohh!'

The room filled suddenly with startling light.

In the distant bed – a distinguished, grey-haired old fogey of military bearing, iron-jawed, grimacing angrily, his manner threatening in the extreme. 'And who the hell are *you*, sir?'

'Sir, Ah...'

'A burglar!'

'Sir, Ah...'

'By gad, a bloody thief ... in *my* room!'

'*Sir*, Ah...'

'Well, by Jove, we know how to deal with *you* johnnies ...!'

Ripping away the bedclothes, General Sir Mortimer Nevercombe-Hardleigh, attired in peacock-blue Kowloon-silk pyjamas, leapt from the bed and strode stiff-backed to the wardrobe, extracted a silver-knobbed ebony walking cane, gave the knob a deft twist, and withdrew from its scabbard a hellish three-foot rapier blade with which he had once despatched two rampaging Khyber thugs intent on converting him to one-inch beef cubes.

'Now, sir...'

Chortle was gone.

But Nevercombe-Hardleigh was swiftly after him, out of the door and into the corridor, almost colliding with a flushed, razor-waving Camembert who, espying the rapier, put two and two together and cried, 'Aha! 'E try it on you, too!'

'Aha!' halloo-ed Sir Mortimer. 'A man after my own heart!'

'No – after 'is! Quickly – zis way!'

'Tally-ho!' cried Sir Mortimer. 'Thief! Thief! Stop that man!'

''oo are you shouting to?' asked Camembert, and fell into a gallop alongside Mort.

'Mah God, this is *madness*!' gasped Chortle, rattling door-knobs as he fled along the corridor. He had to find the stairs ... get back to his own room ... but he'd left his key in his clothing in 806!

'There he is!'

Sir Mortimer's triumphant shout behind him sent Chortle scuttling round yet another corner and through the first door that opened to his hand. Barely had he closed it when the hunting party whooped round the bend and thundered past, Sir Mortimer slightly in the lead, his rapier poised for the stick in best pig-pinking tradition.

'Who's that ... who's there?' The matronly demand spun

Chortle round to face this new invisible nightmare. 'Dolittle ... there's someone in the room! Come up from there this instant and investigate!'

Chortle gasped as the blinding light went on.

Mrs. Henry J. Betworthy of New York, New York, an owlish lady of unprecedented ugliness and untold wealth, ogled the newcomer with myopic uncertainty while awaiting her butler/handyman to emerge from wherever he'd been.

An ascending hump surfaced between her widespread legs and a balding head appeared above the sheets, blinked perplexedly at the cowering, counterpaned hulk of Sam Chortle and remonstrated sniffily, 'It is possible, sir, you have the wrong room. Be so kind as to remove yourself this instant!'

'Aaaaggghhh!'

Chortle removed himself.

They finally cornered him by the Emergency Stairs, a flood of irate phone calls to the management regarding premeditated door-knob rattling swiftly bringing an army of security men converging on the eighth floor.

'There he is ...!'

'Stay right where you are!'

'Got him! Jack, circle round behind.'

'What on *earth* is going on?'

'Sex maniac on the loose. He actually rattled *my* knob!'

'Looks a vicious swine. Just look at those eyes.'

'My God, he must be *naked* under that thing!'

'D'you reckon he's a real live rapist?'

'Get the glint outta your eye, Marjorie, an' come back to bed.'

'Yeah, *I* should be so lucky.'

'And whose little tum-tum is this?'

Lady Penelope gave a girly giggle. 'Alfred, don't be silly.'

'A-n-d whose little belly-button is this ...?'

'Alfred, stop, you're tickling!'

'A-n-d whose little hairy-furry forest of fun-feathers is this ...?'

'Alfred ...!'

'As my dentist says ... open wider. *There's* a girl ...'

'Oh ... Alfred ...' (Wonderment).

'Up ... and ... down ... and round ... and round ...'

'*Al* ... fred!' (Delight).

'Now, let us apply a t-e-e-n-s-y touch of massage ... here.'

'Oh, *Alfred* ...' (Gathering ecstasy).

'Then just a t-e-e-n-s-y bit higher ...'

'Oh! Alfred ...!' (Approaching delirium).

'Hittin' the button, hm?' he chuckled.

Her hips writhed in rhythm with his tender stroke and her breathing broke in stifled gasps. 'Oh ... ohhh ... ohhhh!'

A terse whisper. 'Somethin' happening, honey?'

'Uh huh ... ohhh ... ohhhh!'

'Really taking off down Runway Joy?'

'Uh huh ... hm hm ... ohhh ... ohhh.'

Lift off gettin' close?'

'Yes ... *yes* ... ohhh ... ahhhh!'

'Are you there ... are you there?'

'Yes ... *yes* ...!'

And at that intempestive moment ... the telephone rang.

Penelope gaped as though she'd been shot.

Cock-up froze as though he'd been pole-axed. 'Oh, no ...'

'Oh, bloody yyyeeeessss!' she cried, biffing him on top of the head with her fist.

'Oh, *honey* ...!'

'Oh, *honey* ...!' she mimicked cruelly. 'Why the fuck didn't you *tell* me you were running the Park Lane Answering Service!'

'Angel ... beloved ... my heart bleeds ...!'

'And it *ought* to, you crumb – all over the bed! Well, *answer* the sodding thing!'

'Aw, baby, baby ... I'll get rid of him – fast! Don't go ... I mean, keep going ... don't go off the boil, I'll be right back!'

'You *must* be joking!'

Rossiter flung himself from the bed and snatched up the receiver. 'Yeh, what is it?'

'Captain Rossiter ...?'

'Of course it's Captain Rossiter – who'd yuh expect – Billy the Kid?'

'Captain, sir, I'm *very* sorry to disturb you ... this is the management. I'm afraid one of your guests has been making rather a nuisance of himself ... cavorting around the hotel, rattling door knobs and entering rooms, wearing nothing but a bed counterpane ...'

Rossiter's eyes bulged 'A *what*? Oh, my sainted aunt ... who is it? – Shag McGee ... Vincent Martino ...?'

'Er, no, sir ... I'm very much afraid it's ... Senator Chortle.'

'Chortle! F'fuc ... for Godsake, are you sure?'

'Absolutely positive, sir. And I felt, in the circumstances, that I'd better notify you before I call the police ...'

'Police! Hey, now hold on ... look, there must be some rational explanation ... I mean, the guy must have locked himself out of ...'

'His room? No, sir, Senator Chortle's room is on the sixth floor. His astonishing cavortings took place on the eighth.'

'Well ... is he *drunk*?'

'Sober as a judge, sir – though at the moment a little incoherent, possibly from shock. It appears he was chased for some time by two armed guests who thought he was a burglar.'

'Oh, my *God* ... all right, don't do anything till I get down there. Where are you holding him?'

'In the manager's office, sir.'

'Be right down.'

With a groan Rossiter slammed down the phone and turned to Penelope who was curled up into a distraught ball, furiously puffing her way through another Disque Bleu.

'Dearest ...'

'Just ... don't say anything, Rossiter ...!'

'I must ... I must! My God, how awful for you – right on the brink. But, baby, I got problems. Senator Chortle has gone berserk ... he's been dashing around half-naked rattling door knobs and ... angel, I gotta go and sort this mess out. Promise you'll stay until I get back?'

'Ha! So you can disappoint me again?'

'I won't ... I won't, I *promise*! Dammit, how can anything else happen after this! Tell you what – I'll take the phone off the hook so they *can't* disturb us. Oh, please say you'll stay!'

'I don't know ... I'll have to think about it.'

He went to her, knelt on the bed, and stroked her face. 'Please, baby ... can *I* help it if I'm flyin' around a plane-load of nuts?'

'You'd better go,' she replied coolly.

'Promise you won't leave while I'm gone.'

She gave a shrug, her manner off-hand but scheming. 'It ... depends ...'

'On what, angel? Ask it – it's yours.'

A glimmer of a smile. 'On what you plan doing for me when you get back.'

An obscene chuckle. 'Penelope, have I got something lined up for *you*!'

'What?'

'Oh, no ... I want it to be a big surprise ... baby, look, I've got to go ...'

'All right ... but don't be long.'

'Greased lightnin'!'

He got off the bed, hurriedly threw on his uniform, and made for the door, came back, kissed her on the left nipple, and made again for the door.

As it closed behind him, Penelope killed her DB in the ashtray and slid down the bed, mad as a snake that she'd passed up the entire French tennis team for this inept twit. Well, he was going to pay for all the anguish he was causing her. By heaven, she'd screw the little runt into a stupor yet or her name was not Penelope Sedgwick-Best.

The decision to stay having been made, she lit another fag and turned her thoughts to a visiting Spanish hockey team due over in September, chuckling to herself as she began to formulate a plan for their total doodlefication.

It was going to be a *very* sporty autumn.

13

Time: 2.30 a.m.

Place: Room 12 ... Phoenix Hotel.

Ramjet Rogers, dreaming he was fighting a horde of jealous husbands on a South Sea island, turned boisterously in his sleep, and struck the wall a hefty crack with his arm, the blow not only jerking him from slumber but also waking James Crighton-Padgett in the adjoining room.

Grinning at the thought of what was going on next door, James responded with a loud hand-smack on the wall to let his chum know he could *hear* what was going on next door.

This in turn produced the familiar da-di-di-da-da tattoo from Ramjet, to which James added the end da ... da, and thus their line of communication was established.

Both now turned onto their backs, hands behind heads, and listened with smiling contentment to the sound of shower water coming from their bathrooms, the memory of such recent pleasures massaging their egos and evoking natural comparisons between their own performance and that of their less accomplished buddy next door.

Amateur, reflected Ramjet with a pitying shake of the head. A certain top-drawer charm, to be sure – fine on the build-up, but when it came to the plunge ... nah, he simply couldn't imagine James exciting a woman to nail-clawing acstasy the way he (here a wince and a gentle probing of his lascerated shoulders) had turned on Annabel. In fact it was difficult to imagine James doing it at all without his hat and boots on.

Poor Delphinia, he continued ... if she only *knew* what she'd missed by choosing James. There was Annabel, showering happily away, as sublimely satiated as a woman could ever hope to be, while Delphinia ... sad ... really sad.

Positively criminal, reflected James, gazing thoughtfully at the peeling ceiling. Poor old Annabel ... she really got the sticky end of the wicket. Ramjet might be fine on the prelims – all that eyebrow arching and lip curling – but when it came to the gritty, well, he simply couldn't imagine Rogers bursting a bird at the seams as he (here a pause to massage his aching pelvic bone) had just disintegrated Delphinia.

Listen to her, bless her, happily showering away, as patently plentified as a pigeon could ever hope to be. A fine night's work, James ... absolutely spot on.

Glowing with satisfaction and grinning with devilry, he turned to the wall and tapped out, in Morse, the message: 'How goes it?'

Back came the reply. 'Currently – solo.'

'Where is Annabel?'

'In the shower.'

'Mine, too. How went it?'

'I haven't the strength to reply.'

James laughed and lay back against his pillow, and, overcome by exhaustion, drifted once again into slumber.

He awoke with a start, conscious of passing time and the continuing hiss of shower water. He rolled over, took up his wrist-watch. Good God ... two forty five! The girl would dissolve herself. She'd been in there for half an hour.

He swung his legs from the bed and padded across the threadbare carpet.

'Del ... phinia ...'

No response. Obviously she couldn't hear him above the noise of the shower. He rapped on the door. 'Del ... phinia!'

Still no response. His brows knit.

Thump! Thump!

'Delphinia!'

And again nothing.

163

Sudden concern swamped him. She'd fallen ... fainted! Was she lying in there face-up, her mouth filling with water? He reached for the knob, turned it, flooding with relief as the door opened. Good God, the room was freezing! Its window was wide open! What a crazy way to take a shower.

'Hey ...!' he laughed. 'You'll catch your death ... of ...'

The uninhabitedness of the room hit him. There was no movement, no sound from behind the curtain. He lunged for it ... yanked it aside.

The shower was empty.

James gaped, gasped, glanced at the open window, ridiculously supposing for the briefest moment that she might have left via the fire-escape, but in the next instant dismissed the preposterous idea and went to close it. Yet, nevertheless, motivated by the crazy hunch, he popped his head out and checked the fire escape, seeing, of course, nothing.

Shutting the window, he went back into the bedroom, bewildered as to where she could be. Could she ... no, hardly likely she'd have nipped next door to confer with Annabel. And yet ... he *had* fallen asleep. It was possible she could have slipped out. Hell, what other alternative was there!

Well, there was only one way to find out.

He crossed again to the bed and brought his knuckles to bear on the wall.

'Oi, you awake?'

He could almost hear Ramjet give a start.

'I am now,' came the reply.

'Is Delphinia with you?'

Ramjet's bellowed laugh came faintly through the wall. 'Are you kidding?'

'No – serious. She's disappeared. Is Annabel there?'

'Of course. Mine don't run away.'

'Where is she?'

A pause, perhaps contemplative. 'In the shower.'

James frowned. 'Still?'

'So – she's a clean dame!'

James's heart beat faster. 'Check.'

'Repeat.'

'Check the shower.'

'What for?'

'Check the bloody shower!'

Now fiercely attacked by the premonition that something was wrong, James got off the bed and paced across the room, his bewildered mind fighting for the solution but managing only to produce lurid and ludicrous images of her fate.

The fire-escape ... the open window ... a desperate sex maniac sees her from the road below ... creeps up ... climbs in ... knocks her cold and ... bloody ridiculous. There *had* to be a simple explanation ...

Ramjet's summoning slap brought him up sharp and sent him scurrying back to the wall. 'Well?'

'Mine's gone too!'

Jim's jaw sagged. Something was *very* wrong! His mind raced, utterly confused, half a dozen possible solutions tumbling over one another ... and then, into this confusion popped one lucid impression, something he had not consciously seen but which he had subconsciously registered, and with an appalled gasp he turned and ran to the open bathroom door, freezing at its threshold as the reality of his dread socked him under the heart.

'Oh ... bloody hell ...'

The room was empty.

Completely empty.

His uniform was gone.

The knuckle-smash on the bedroom door shocked him from his stupor. 'Jim ... open up!'

He ran to it, pulled it open, and in shot a wide-eyed Rogers, attired in vermilion shorts and a white T-shirt.

'The bitch has gone!' he gasped.

James shut the door. 'Mine, too – and my bloody ...'

'Uniform. So has mine. Jim, what the *hell* is going on?'

'God knows.' Still in shock, James made for the bed and sat down hard. 'Ramjet ... we've been had.'

'Taken.'

'Conned.'

'Dry-gulched. Oh, I thought it was too good to be true ... two fabulous birds like them ...'

'I know, I know ... but *why* ...?'

Ramjet shrugged and slumped dejectedly. 'Obviously for our uniforms...'

'Oh, *brother*...'

'We should've known, Jim ... a crummy dump like this...'

'Cock-up will go stark, raving spare. We'll have to miss the photo session...'

'But who *were* they, Jim? Certainly not journalists, that's for sure.'

Jim shook his head. 'Students, maybe...? D'you reckon this could be a Rag Week caper? They get up to some pretty stupid tricks. Or a bet ... or a practical joke...?'

Ramjet sighed and nodded. 'Could be anythin' ... what a goddam mess. Our only uniforms ... Jim, what are we gonna *do*? What are *you* gonna do? Hasn't she left you any clothes at all?'

James gave a start, realizing for the first time that he was stark naked. 'Oh, blimey ...' In panic he searched the rumpled bedclothes, dropped to his knees, and looked under the bed, exclaimed, 'Aha!' and hauled out his candy-striped shorts and pale-pink vest. 'Thank God for small mercies,' he sighed, putting them on.

'Anything else?' asked Ramjet. 'How about your boots?'

James shook his head. 'Nope, she's pinched the lot.'

'Me, too,' said Ramjet glumly.

'And I reckon we can kiss them goodbye forever, mate. Whatever the adorable bags were up to, they succeeded admirably. You know, I mightn't feel *so* badly if I knew what it was all about! I mean ... there *were* compensations...'

A quick grin lit Ramjet's dejected countenance. 'Yeah ...' but dejection quickly returned in the face of their dilemma.

'OK' sighed Ramjet, 'let's ... just ... calm down and give some thought to this mess. Problem number one has to be – how do we get outta this dump and back to the Hilton?'

'Taxi?' offered James, but dismissed the suggestion instantly with a shake of his head.

'No way,' agreed Ramjet. 'Firstly – we cannot approach the management of this rat hole, even supposing there *is* a management, which is doubtful. The joint looks as though it's condemned, awaiting demolition. We cannot approach them be-

166

cause we're not supposed to *be* in here ... and in any case, at first sight of us dressed like this they'd phone the cops and we'd be even further up it.'

'Agreed,' nodded James. 'All right – taxi – out.'

'Mm,' Ramjet pulled his lip. 'You got any money?'

'Not a bean. It was all in my uniform.'

'Me, neither. And no dough means no telephone call.'

James frowned. 'To whom?'

'I was thinking of Rossiter.'

James winced. 'Wow ... can you imagine the reception we'd get waking him at three in the morning to tell him a couple of hookers have pinched our uniforms?'

'I prefer not to. But heck, Jim, he's going to find out soon enough – like at breakfast time.'

James groaned. 'Ohhh, what a day this is going to be! Ramjet, the full horror of the situation is only just beginning to get through to me. We, old chum, are in a *frightful* stew! How are we going to get back into the Hilton? ... what's going to happen with the photo session? ... how are we going to get out to the plane? ... and into it! Are we destined to fly round the world in our bleeding underpants! We, old son, have well and truly copped it!'

'Mm,' agreed Ramjet, 'though the distant future doesn't worry me *so* much. We can get a couple of uniforms made at our next port of call. It's the immediate future that concerns me – like you said, how do we get back into the Hilton. The photo session ...' he shrugged, 'well, we'll have to miss it, say we're ill or something. The trip out to the airport ... we'll have to buy some civilian clothes and fly in them. Rossiter, of course, will be hairless, but screw him. It's happened and it can't be unhappened. OK – that's our real problem, then – how to get back to our rooms.'

'Mmm,' said James, and went into a big think.

Silence reigned unbroken for a full minute ... then suddenly James came to life.

'Got it!'

Ramjet looked up expectantly. 'What?'

'Saw a film once,' Jim said excitedly, coming to his feet. 'A bunch of officer-cadets were taken out into the country on one of those initiative training things ... they were supposed to be escaping prisoners of war held in enemy territory. With no money, no maps, and dressed in British army uniform, they had to make their way back to camp without being caught – and they all made it.'

'Yeah? How?'

James gave a gleeful grin. 'By stripping down to their shorts and vests, cock ... daubing numbers on their backs ... and pretending they were long-distance runners! They ran straight through the enemy villages, right past the police station – and the police actually cheered them on!'

'Brilliant!' exclaimed Ramjet. 'By God, you've got it!'

'A cinch!' laughed James. 'It's not all that far back to the Hilton. We cut up to Oxford Street, trot along to Marble Arch, and down Park Lane – I reckon three miles at the most. We'd be there in half an hour.'

Ramjet shuddered. 'Make that an hour. I haven't *run* any-where in twenty years.'

'But you like it?'

Ramjet nodded. 'I love it. OK – what do we use for numbers?'

They scanned the room, James's eye alighting on the ash-tray. 'That!'

'Mm?'

'Ash! – mixed with a little water.'

Ramjet grinned with unabashed admiration. 'James, I take my hat off to you – and don't I wish I could. *And* my trousers, jacket, boots ...'

'Well,' sighed James, 'we'll face *that* dilemma around break-fast time. Come on, I'll mix up a malodorous paste and paint a number on your back – then you can do mine. Then it's hot-foot down the fire-escape and Hilton-ho. When we get there we'll tell the desk-clerk we've been for a jog round Hyde Park – part of the Glamour training programme.'

Ramjet shook his head. 'James ... the infinite capacity of your brilliant deviousness leaves me constantly astounded.'

'Gee, thanks,' laughed James, and took the ashtray into the bathroom.

'Beloved ...!' whispered Rossiter, kneeling at her side.

'Hm!' Penelope woke with a start. 'God, I fell asleep.'

'And divine you looked in the arms of Morpheus, so innocent ...'

'Are you drunk? What time is it?'

'A mere three fifteen – the night is but a pup.'

'Rossiter ... you've been gone hours!'

'A small exaggeration, sweet lady – a half hour only.' He got off the bed and began peeling off his uniform. 'Honey, you've no idea what I've bin through. There was a crazy old cunt down there who wanted to run Chortle through with a sword-stick! And that French chef of ours was tryin' to screw Chortle on a brown-hatter charge!'

'Well, why *was* he running around in a counterpane, rattling door-knobs?'

Rossiter sighed wearily. 'It would seem the Senator developed hot-pants for our over-developed airstew, Wilma Fluck, and arranged a secret assignation with her during lunch. In an attempt to cool his ardour the silly cow gave him the wrong room number and when Monsieur Camembert emerged from his bathroom he discovered Chortle disporting himself in his bed with two bottles of bubbly and an erection as big as the Post Office Tower. Naturally mistaking Chortle's intention, Camembert grabbed up his cut-throat razor with the idea of whittling the Chortle morsel down to size and in the ensuing chase ... and why I am wasting precious time babbling on about this when I could be whispering sweet nothings into whatever takes my fancy and generally compensating for all the heart-ache I've caused you tonight ...?'

'Oh, Alfred ...' she sighed, covering his advancing nakedness with smouldering approbation. 'If Chortle's is compared to the Post Office Tower ... what on earth would you call *that*!'

'The Empire State?' he grinned, launching himself onto the bed. 'Oh, Penelope ...'

'Oh, Alfred ... promise me there won't be *any* more interruptions?'

'See – I've taken the phone off the hook.'

'Oh, thank you ... oh, that is lovely ...'

'Worth waiting for?'

'Every wretched minute ... oh, masterful! ... Alfred – fly me to the moon.'

'The moon ... the stars ... and beyond, my darling – way off into outer space ... into the black void of infinity ... into the endless reaches of unimaginable eternity ... into ...'

'Alfred, f'Godsake shut up and get it in.'

14

'There...' said Ramjet, putting the final touches to James's number.

'Good man.' James looked at his watch. 'Three fifteen ... good, we'll be home before the hotel wakes up. A quick shower and ...'

Ramjet winced. 'Please! Don't ever mention the word shower to me again.'

'Sorry. Well ... ready?'

Ramjet nodded and put down the ashtray. 'As I'll ever be for a three-mile run.'

'OK – quietly does it.'

Jim lifted the sash window and peered out, whispered, 'All clear,' and swung a leg over the sill. 'Oooh!'

'What's the matter?'

'This iron's freezing! I wish she'd left my socks.'

'Do long distance runners run in socks?'

'Oh, no ...'

Ramjet climbed out after him and silently they crept along the fire-escape and descended to the street.

'D'you know where we are?' whispered Ramjet.

James shook his head. 'No.'

'Then how'd you know which way Oxford Street is?'

James tapped the side of his nose. 'Instinct, old boy. You don't live all your life in a city without developing an instinctive sense of direction. This way...'

Off they started down the dark and silent street, picking their way along the filthy sidewalk with all the confidence of two cross-country runners negotiating a field of thistles.

'Yerk!' Ramjet broke into a hobble.

'What is it?' hissed James.

'I hate to imagine. I *hope* it was only a decaying banana peel.'

He paused to scrape his sole against the edge of the pavement and off they went again, turning left into a narrow offensive alley, right into another, left into yet a third, finally breaking out into a vaguely familiar street – at the rear of the Phoenix Hotel.

'Ha!' panted Ramjet. 'So much ... for your instinctive sense of direction! Eight miles and we're back where we started!'

'It's these back streets!' protested James, wheezing like a rusted pump. 'Once I find Wardour Street we're home and dry.'

'Some bloody navigator,' scoffed Ramjet. 'At this rate we should be nicely in the outskirts of Birmingham by dawn.'

'Oh, very droll. Come on – I think I know where we went wrong.'

'So do I – landing in bleeding London!'

Off they set again, this time turning right instead of left, and within a hundred yards emerged into a street of vaguely more prepossessing appearance.

'Ah!' exclaimed James.

'Know where we are now?'

'No.'

'Great. Birmingham – here we come.'

'This way.'

'Y'know ... for a guy who's totally lost you have the damndest arrogance, Crighton-Padgett.'

'OK – that way, see if I care.'

'No, no, I'll leave it to you, James. After all it *is* your city.'

'Thank you.'

'On the understanding that when this happens to us in New York, *I* do the navigating.'

'Just have a little faith, Rogers. If we don't hit Oxford Street *right* on the nose, my name is not James D. Crighton-Padgett.'

It was some fifteen minutes later that they finally broke from the labyrinthine maze of dark, threatening streets into the startling brightness of a major thoroughfare.

'Aha!' cried Ramjet, with profound relief.

'Oh,' gulped James.

'What's up?'

'Erm...'

Ramjet narrow-eyed him. 'Crighton-Padgett ... you've *boobed* again!'

'Well .. just a little.'

'Where the hell *are* we?'

'Shaftesbury Avenue.'

'Shaf...'

'It's of minor importance, however ... all we have to do is trot down to Piccadilly Circus, then along Piccadilly itself – and we're there.'

Ramjet regarded him askance. 'You wouldn't fool a guy, would you?'

'Scout's honour, we're almost there.'

'Just how almost?'

James shrugged. 'Two miles...'

Ramjet groaned. 'Well, let's get to it, my feet are blue.'

'Right. Troop ... yo-o!'

The police car overtook them at Green Park Underground station.

Suddenly confronted by two uniformed giants, our heroes slowed, continued falteringly for another few steps, and finally came to a halt in the towering lee of Sergeant George Munster, heavyweight wrestling champion and professional cynic.

'Well, well, well...' sneered Munster, most unpleasantly, 'and what do we have here – a couple of floor-walkers from Simpson's lingerie department? 'Ave you ever seen anything like this in all your born days, Constable Pike?'

Constable Pike, a six-foot-four amateur champion caber-tosser with a chin like a trouser press and a beard reminiscent of a burst sofa, sauntered with casual disdain to the rear of the

173

shivering duo, shaking his head.

'Funny you should ask that, serg, because I was just this moment thinkin' to myself – Pike, in all your born days have you ever seen anything like this.'

'N .. now, sergeant,' stammered James, 'there *is* a rational explanation.'

'Aha! Did you hear that Pike? – there *is* a rational explanation as to why these two gentlemen should be trotting along Piccadilly at harf past three in the mornin' dressed in their underwear.'

'I am profoundly relieved to hear it, sergeant. For a moment there I was somewhat tempted to believe it wus just a *teensy* bit abnormal.'

'Obviously not, Pike, obviously not. All right, sir ... before we escort you back to the station for a chat with our resident psychiatrist, why don't we take a moment to hear your ... rational explanation?'

'W .. well, w .. we ... that is Mister Rogers and I ... we .. we're in training! We're in training for the, erm, ah! – the London to Brighton run ... you know, the ... London to ... *terribly* hard on the old feet, you know, so we're sort of toughening up our soles ...'

'Arseholes,' nodded Munster.

'... so to speak ... er, aren't we, Paul?'

'Indubitably,' croaked Ramjet.

'Uh, uh,' grunted Munster. 'And you ... belong to some kind of club, I take it.'

'Oh, yes!' grinned James, pointing a thumb over his shoulder. 'See – the number. Yes, we're all at it.'

'And the name of the club?' Munster asked pleasantly.

James coughed. 'It's the ... well, it's not so much an actual *club*, you understand, as a ... well, what exactly *would* you call it, Paul? It's more of a ...'

'Yes, certainly ... more of a ...'

'Sort of a ...'

'I see,' Munster nodded amiably. 'I'm beginning to get the picture. More of a ...'

'Precisely!' laughed James. 'Well, sergeant, if there's nothing more we can do for you ... got to get the old soles toughened up, you know . . .'

'Fully understand, sir. And *far* be it for me to stand in your way. There's just one *tiny* point I'd like to clear up before you proceed, sir . . .'

'Anything, sergeant, anything at all.'

'This . . . London to Brighton thing . . . race . . . it *is* competitive, of course?'

'Oh, fiercely! My word, yes, keen as mustard.'

'Ra*ther*,' added Ramjet, breaking into an on-the-spot trot. 'Fight to the finish all the way.'

'Which is why, presumably,' Munster continued blandly, 'you all have different numbers on your backs.'

'But of course,' smiled James. 'How else could they tell who'd won?'

'How else indeed?' agreed Munster. 'And you always wear the same number?'

'Always,' replied James. 'Mister Rogers here is always number seven, and I . . .' James frowned, faltered.

Ramjet cut in quickly. 'And Mister Crighton-Padgett is always . . . number . . . oh, my sainted . . .'

James shot round, gaped at him. 'You . . . Ramjet, you didn't!'

Ramjet nodded, mortified. 'I did.'

'*Seven?*'

'Seven.'

Munster chuckled triumphantly. 'Well now . . . it would seem that these two clowns are all at sevens and sevens, hey, Pike? Right you are, gentlemen . . . if you'd be so *very* kind as to step into the car, we'd be delighted to save some wear and tear on your poor old feet – *and* on your imaginations. What a load of old codswallop.'

'Oh, *Al*fred . . .'

'That feel good, honey?'

'Delectable! . . . a*dor*able!'

'Does it make up for all the interruptions?'

'More . . . much more. Thank heaven there won't be any more of those, I simply couldn't stand it.'

Rossiter shook his head, a difficult manoeuvre in the circumstances. 'Not a chance.'

'Alfred ...'

'Yes, angel?'

'Would you ... do something for me?'

'Anything – just name it.'

'I ... don't know how to ask you – in case you think I'm ... kinky.'

Alfred came up for breath. 'You – kinky? Never. Call it ... an adventurous spirit. What is it you want?'

'Would you ... do it for me in your uniform? Oh, not the trousers, naturally ...'

He laughed, 'Naturally.'

'Just your jacket and your lovely cap.'

Rossiter shrugged. 'Sure.'

'Oh, you are kind ... so understanding.'

'What is life all about if we can't do these little things for one another? Don't go away, I'll be right back.'

He slid from the bed, picked up his jacket with its four brave stripes and slipped it on, then perched the cap at a sexy angle and presented himself to her. 'There – how's that?'

'Fabulous! Oh, you *do* look outrageous.'

I feel a right cunt, he thought, glancing at himself in the mirror.

'Just ... one more thing?' she implored. 'Would you put your boots on, too?'

He nodded. 'Boots coming up. There ...'

'Oh, Alfred, you look *quite* divine. Now, would you ... play a little game with me? Would you pretend that I'm a lady passenger who's sneaked on board without paying my fare ...'

Aye aye, thought Rossiter.

'... and I *refuse* to pay it, so you, as the captain, have to get tough – I mean really *mean* with me ... and you insist on having your way with me as payment for the fare and ... I struggle ... but you are *far* too strong for me and finally overpower me and really do the most *awful* things to me and ... Oh, Alfred, darling, *would* you ...?'

Rossiter laughed, bashfully. 'Well, I ...'

'Oh, *please* say you will, it would mean so much to me ... and it *would* make up for all those horrid interruptions.'

176

'Well, I guess I owe you for that. OK . . .'

'Oh, *scrummy*! Right . . . I'm sitting here reading a magazine, very aloof and forbidding. The stewardess has just reported to you that I haven't paid my fare . . . now in you come – and don't forget you're a *really* mean man.'

'Mean,' nodded Cock-up. 'Right . . .' He gave a cough, braced himself and advanced on her with a mean swagger, his lip curled meanly and with a mean look in his eye. 'So! – you're the dame who hasn't paid her fare, huh?'

Penelope lowered her imaginary magazine. 'I *beg* your pardon! Are you addressing me, by any chance?'

'By every chance, lady. What the hell d'you mean by sneakin' aboard *my* plane without payin' your fare?'

'Push off, you silly man. Leave me alone.'

'Now, that simply won't do, lady – *every*body pays aboard my ship – one way or the other.'

She looked up. 'What *do* you mean?'

'Very simple – cash or kind, don't make no difference to me. But *pay* you will.'

'K . . kind? What do you mean by that?'

'Can you possibly be that dumb? I mean *you*, lady! You screwed me for the fare – so I screw you for the fare.'

A gasp. 'You . . . unmitigated swine! How *dare* you suggest such a thing!'

'Easy – to a good-lookin' doll like you. I fancy yuh. Put that magazine down.'

'I will do no such thing!'

'Yes, you will.'

'D . . don't come near me! Don't touch me! Stay away from me!'

'Funny – I get strangely deaf when I'm aroused,' he growled, climbing onto the bed. 'OK – here goes . . . one first class return to paradise!'

He plunged.

She fought, kicked, scratched, and screamed (silently), all the while cleverly allowing him home between her thighs.

'Ohhh! Ohhh. You rapist!'

'Sure, I am – it's more fun than bowling.'

'Get that . . . *vile* thing out of me!'

'All in good time, baby ... the ship's on auto, we've got an hour yet.'

'Ohhhh ...! How will I live down the shame?'

'Try enjoyin' it.'

'Oh, Alfred ... that is fantastic! Oh, my God ...'

He stopped. 'What's the matter?'

'Alfred, I'm coming ...'

'Great.'

'Alfred ... I'm *coming*!'

'Terrific.'

'Over the moon ...!'

'Way out.'

'Beyond the stars ...!'

'Right on.'

'Ohhhh ... *Alfred* ...!'

She didn't make it.

At that unbelievably unfortunate moment a furious battering on the door shocked them to an instant halt. 'Captain Rossiter ... CAPTAIN ROSSITER ...!'

Penelope gaped at the startled face above her, her own crumbling into horrified disbelief. Her mouth dropped open twisted, then a low spiralling cry, terrible in its torment, heart-rending in its bitter anguish, broke from her, threatening to bring the roof down.

Rossiter, sensing the imminent storm, snapped from his coma and quickly placed his hand over the erupting orifice.

'Yes!' he bellowed.

'Captain ...' cried a distraught, subdued voice. '... it's the management! I tried to telephone you ... couldn't get through! Please open the door!'

'Wh .. what *for*? What the hell d'you want this time of the morning!'

'Captain ... it's the police! Two of your crew have been arrested!'

Rossiter gasped, choked. 'Two of my ...'

'Crew, sir! ... Rogers and Crighton-Padgett ... they ...'

'Aaaaaagggggghhhhhuuuuggghhhh!' roared Rossiter ... and collapsed on his face beside the suffocating Penelope.

178

15

Time: 4 a.m.

Place: A London taxi – proceeding along Piccadilly.

'Now ... I have travelled around this big, wide world more than just a piece,' recited Rossiter, his voice quavery with passion yet ominously calm, reminiscent of a hissing fuse insidiously progressing towards a vast stockpile of TNT. 'I have been to Aachen in Germany, and Zyyi in Cyprus, and a million odd-ball places in between ... and on my journeyings I have met some p-r-e-t-t-y stupid people, believe me, yes, sir, some real grade A, five-star, thorough-goin' ding-a-lings ... but never ... *NEVER* ... in all my days have I met a pair of jumped-up, full-blooded *morons* like *you* two!'

'Now, Cock-up...' protested James.

'Shut up!' raged Rossiter, his fury finally engulfing his self-control. 'Look at you! – a disgrace to the airline! Two supposedly mature, intelligent officers ... poncin' around the streets of London in your sweat shorts! ... taken, conned, hustled outta your uniforms like a couple hick rookies! What in *hell* were you thinkin' about? – no, don't answer that, I *know* what you were thinkin' about! The day you guys think of anything above the navel – pigs will fly 707's!'

Some do now, thought Ramjet, skulking beside James in the rear seat.

'And *what* ...' continued Rossiter from the jump-seat, gnashing his cigar to shreds ... '... about the photographic

179

session? You two got any ideas how we're gonna explain your appearance outside Buckingham Palace in sweat-shirts and T-shorts ... sweat shorts an' T-shirts? Hm? Hm? What's the matter, Crighton-Padgett, suddenly lost your tongue?'

'I ... feel sick,' groaned James, grimacing at Rossiter's foul smelling cigar.

'*You* feel sick!' ranted Rossiter. 'Well, then, just imagine how *I* feel! I'm in *charge* of this maniac tour! And so far, to our credit, we have two aborted TV interviews ... one disgraced United States senator ... a run-in with the London police ... and a washed-up photographic session! If this keeps up we're gonna blaze a trail of destruction around the globe that has not been equalled since the rampaging of Ghengis Khan! Well, God help us when we get back to New York. If I know Berskin he'll have our severance pay waitin' at Kennedy – plus extradition papers to Siberia – and frankly *I'm* thinkin' of quitting somewhere around Melbourne.'

The taxi swirled into the forecourt of the Hilton and stopped.

'OK,' rapped Rossiter. 'You guys get your asses up to your rooms *fast* – an' f'crissake stay there until you're collected. I wanna know where at least *two* idiots can be found.'

Ramjet and James alighted and trotted into the foyer, startling the night duty clerk.

'Eh, here, I say ... you can't come in here dressed like that ...!'

'Just been for a spin round the park,' panted Ramjet, trotting on the spot. 'May we have our keys, please?'

Open-mouthed, the clerk handed them over and the lads continued their trot to the elevators.

'*Well* ...' gasped the clerk to Mavis Clutter, cleaning lady. 'Did you ever see anything like that before?'

Yes, thought Mavis with a sigh ... but never inside a pair of vermilion shorts.

With great weariness of mind and body, Cock-up Rossiter approached his bedroom door knowing that, of course, Lady Penelope had done a bunk. And who could blame her? To have had her sexual gratification severed at the brink once was bad enough, twice – a matter of understandable distress, but *three* times ... well, that was totally unforgiveable.

Sure, she'd done a bunk. The moment he'd left the room she'd have been flying for her knickers, unable to get out of there fast enough – away from what to her must have seemed a den of rollicking incompetence inhabited by the fumbler of all time.

Imagine his surprise, therefore, to say nothing of wild delight, as he opened the door and found her just where he'd left her, half-hidden behind a Disque Bleu pea-souper, blandly reading the telephone directory and scratching her leg.

'Darling!' he gasped, quickly closing the door. 'You ... you stayed!'

'Yes, Alfred,' she replied nobly, setting aside the directory. 'To be frank, my first instinct was immediate flight, but then ... well, a cool shower quenched my fury and with calmer mind I saw things as they really were. It was not your fault – none of it. The fault lies in the very things that attracted me to you in the first place – your rank, your position, your burden of responsibility. Penelope, I said to myself, don't be a cow. Leadership is a lonely role – don't add to Alfred's problem by ditching him.'

'How ... *incredibly* thoughtful,' exclaimed Rossiter, unable to decide whether she was for real, drunk, drugged, or merely taking the mickey. Did women still *talk* like this? 'Penelope ...' he said fervently, sitting on the bed and taking her hand, 'you won't regret this, I promise. Time is running very short, I know – it's almost dawn – but what little time we have left together I am devoting to your uninterrupted delight ...'

A wan smile. '*Un* ... interrupted, Alfred?'

'My God, what *else* could happen between now and seven o'clock!'

'I don't know – but it *does* seem we've had this conversation before somewhere ...'

'Cross my heart, I will allow *nothing* to come between us this time – *nothing*! I don't give a damn if the hotel catches fire ... if Chortle rapes every danged female in the building ... if every single member of my maniac crew runs stark naked down the Mall – I shall not desert you.'

181

'Oh, Alfred, you are sweet. I just knew I'd picked a winner. Hurry, get out of your trousers and back to where we left off.'

He kissed her on the nipple. 'All right...'

'No!'

'Hm...?'

'I have an even better idea! Let us pretend this time that I am a sweet, demure young thing applying for a job as an airstewardess. This is your office ... you are a mean, lecherous captain in charge of hiring the girls ... and, oh, I want the job *so* badly. But you...'

Rossiter raised his hand. 'Say no more – I got the picture. OK – where's my desk... the dressing table. Right...'

He crossed to it and sat down, pretended to become immersed in paper work.

Penelope slipped off the bed, her good humour fully restored and her imagination working overtime, determined to salvage *something* out of this disastrous night.

'Knock knock...!' she cooed, sickeningly demure.

'Yeh, who is it?' growled Rossiter.

'It is I – sweet Jenny Wren from Clacton-on-Sea.'

'Whadaya want, I'm busy.'

'I ... I've come to apply for a job as airstewardess, sir ...'

Rossiter turned in his chair, gave a start at the ravishing beauty of the maiden, ogled her lasciviously, and twirled an imaginary moustache. 'Well, now, come in, my dear ... maybe there's something I can do for you.'

'How fan*tastic*! Oh, I do *so* want to be a stewardess.'

'*How* so?'

'With all my heart, sir! I've dreamed of nothing else since I was a little girl.'

'That right? Well, it ain't easy ... there bein' four hundred applicants for every vacancy. It's gonna cost yuh, honey.'

She widened her huge, innocent eyes. 'Cost me, sir? How much?'

'Well, now, I ain't referrin' to coin of the realm.'

'Then ... to what?'

Rossiter rose slowly from his chair and advanced upon her, mean-eyed. She gave a gasp and cringed from the gleam, covered her naked breasts and backed off a step or two.

'There are other ways of payin' your union dues, honey...'

'Like what ... for instance?'

'Like *this*!' he laughed and grabbed her.

'You ... beast ... you *beast*!'

'Ha! ... ain't I, though.'

'Let ... *go* of me!'

'Not until I've had my way with you, sweetheart. Come on – on the bed ... now don't fight it ... just let it happen...'

'You ... filthy ravisher...!'

'That's me, baby.'

'How *dare* you take your trousers off in front of a lady!'

'So – turn round.'

'I ... shall call my father!'

'Call him what? There ... trousers away.'

Penelope's eyes popped. 'Ohhh! Oh, you *dirty* old man!'

'Less of the old. Come on – on the bed with you!'

'Ohhhh ... I'm so helpless against your brutal strength...'

'That's the way I like it. Now ... open up, there's a good girl ...'

'No!'

'Open ... *up*!'

'Never!'

'See ... that wasn't too difficult.'

'Take that filthy thing from my sight!'

'My pleasure ... there.'

'Ohhhh!'

'Yuh just can't please some people.'

'You fiend ... you brute ... ohhh, Alfred, you're doing it again!'

'Hittin' the old spot, angel?'

'Ohh, right on ... right on.'

'And this time, baby, you're going all the way! No Sam Chortles ... no Godfrey Berskins ... no Rogers and Crighton-Padgetts. Like I said, honey ... this time I don't give a damn if the hotel catches fire, I ... now what in Christ's name is *that*!'

At that very moment the room was rocked by the ear-splitting wail of sirens and whoopers and bells – a fierce, mind-blowing cacophony that shattered their genital bliss and had them stumbling to the window in nine kinds of panic and staring down into the street below.

'Fuckin' ... mother ...!' bellowed Rossiter, 'the hotel *is* on fire!'

'You did it!' raged Penelope, beating him over the head with her fists. 'You opened your big fat mouth! You wished this on us, Rossiter ... you and your damned mouth!'

Rossiter opened the orifice to respond for the defence but before a syllable could be uttered there came a great thumping on the door.

'Captain Rossiter! ... CAPTAIN *ROSSITER* ...!'

'What the hell d'you want *NOW*!' roared Cock-up, striding to the door.

'Come *quickly*, sir ... it's Officers Rogers and Crighton-Padgett ...'

'Ohhhh *NO!* What did they do *this* time – set fire to themselves!'

'No, sir, no ...' wailed the clerk. 'Much worse! They're committing suicide on the seventh floor!'

'They ... *WHAT*?'

'Oh, dear me, it's *terrible*! They're hanging by their finger-tips from a window-sill on the seventh floor!'

'B .. but ... they're not *on* the seventh floor, man! They're on this floor!'

'I know, I know ... but they're hanging out there all the same.'

'Well ... how d'you know it's *them*?'

'By their uniforms, sir. They ...'

'Uniforms!' thundered Rossiter. 'Now look! ... I don't know what the hell's goin' on, but it's a dollar to a doughnut it ain't them! Why don't somebody open the door and haul them in?'

'We can't, sir! They've blocked the keyhole! But it *is* them, captain – there's a note on the door! It says they're ashamed of the disgrace they've brought upon Glamour Airlines and they're going to end it all.'

'HA!' guffawed Rossiter. 'Now I *know* it ain't them! Who called the fire brigade?'

'Someone spotted them from the street, sir ... oh, *please* come quickly, captain ...'

'Oh ... Jesus!' With a despairing sigh he turned to Penelope. 'Honey ...'

'Ahhhh ... shut up!' she yelled, and hurled the telephone directory at him.

Minutes later, Rossiter emerged from the hotel to discover a crowd of large proportions gathered behind the fire ladder, every face turned skywards to the seventh floor.

Walking backwards, he manoeuvred this way and that, his view of the window in question blocked by the towering ladder. So he kept on walking backwards until he trod on Sugar Sweetman's foot.

'Ow ...! Here, watch where you're going, you ... captain! Oh, captain, am I glad to see you. My God, isn't it *terrible*! Whatever possessed them to do such a thing? I mean, *suicide ...*!'

Rossiter shook his head. 'I don't believe it is them, Sweetman,' he said, bobbing and weaving to get a glimpse of the window. 'There's something mighty funny goin' on here ...'

'Funny, captain? What ...'

At that moment Babs Buchanan and Wilma Fluck hove to, clad in such fetching shortie nightgowns it momentarily diverted Cock-up's attention from their tears of anguish.

'Oh, *captain* ...' wailed Babs, clutching his arm. 'Isn't it *awful ...*'

'Poor James ... poor Ramjet ...' sobbed Wilma.

'Now, girls, don't give up hope ... look! the firemen have got a coupla nets set up. If they do fall, they won't hurt themselves ... much. I'm gonna take a closer look. You stay here ...'

Forcing his way through the crowd, Rossiter reached the front, only to be stopped by a burly fireman in an over-large helmet.

'Sorry, sir, you can't go any closer ...'

'Listen, those are my boys up there. I'm Rossiter of Glamour Airlines.'

'I don't care if you're Toad of Toad Hall, sir, you can't go any closer. You might impede the rescue.'

'OK – but just let me get a look at them, will yuh?'

The fireman thought about it, finally conceded. 'All right ... move over here. There they are – up on the seventh floor ... damndest suicide I ever saw.'

'Whadya mean?' asked Rossiter, edging around the ladder truck and finally catching sight of the dangling duo. 'My God ... they really *are* hanging by their finger-tips!'

'Precisely,' nodded the fireman, his helmet falling over his eyes. 'It's inhuman,' he said, pushing it back. 'Those chaps have been dangling like that for ten minutes or more ... it's just not possible. Besides, that is *not* the position to adopt prior to suicide ...'

'Oh – there's a regulation position?'

'Invariably,' nodded the fireman, blinding himself again. 'I must get this changed, I think my head's shrinking. Usually they crouch or stand on the ledge and think it over for a while ... give the crowd and the press time to assemble. Hanging by the fingers like that is far too risky. You could easily fall.'

'Yeh,' grunted Rossiter, not even listening. He was staring hard up at the two dim and distant silver-lamé-ed figures suspended motionless from the sill, faces to the wall. 'Listen ... don't they seem awfully still to you? Have you seen them move at all?'

The fireman shook his head and this time the helmet shot sideways at right-angles. 'Not a muscle – not so much as a flinch since we arrived. Y'know, I've got a sneaky feeling my wife boils washing in this. I reckon it's stretched.'

A sudden barrage of startling flashes illuminated the building.

'There you go,' remarked the fireman.

'There I go where?'

'The press, sir. Huh, someone's rallied them in a hurry. Can't say I blame them, though – this'll make the picture of the year.'

Rossiter's eyes narrowed. 'Right ...' he nodded, the seeds of gross suspicion beginning to germinate in his own cunning mind.

'Reckon this should hit all the front pages tomo ... I mean

186

today,' continued the fireman.

'Right again,' said Rossiter. 'How long are you guys gonna take getting them down?'

'Not long, sir, but it can't be rushed. One false move and we could panic those chaps.'

'Yeh,' said Rossiter, with complete lack of conviction.

In silence they watched the huge extension ladder swing slowly towards the face of the building, a lone fireman perched high at the top, all but lost to view in the pre-dawn murk. Inch by cautious inch he approached the two rigid figures, mere silver-lamé smudges against the off-white face of the hotel.

'Why don't you get some spotlights on them?' enquired Rossiter.

'Too risky, sir ... the sudden bright light could bring them down. The press shouldn't be allowed to shoot off their flashes like that, either.'

'Yeh, well I wouldn't worry too much about it if I were you ...' muttered Rossiter. 'I reckon if they ever intended takin' a dive, they'd have done it by now ... hey, your boy's almost on them.'

'Yes, sir, he's just about there.'

The murmur of the crowd intensified as the ladder touched the face of the building only inches from the left-hand figure. Another barrage of flashes lit the scene like day as the fireman reached out a hand towards the first dangling man. He could be seen to gesture, cajole, persuade the figure to make a move towards him, swing a leg onto the ladder, but there appeared to be no response. Then suddenly, in seeming desperation, the fireman lunged, caught the figure by the wrist, wrenched the left hand from the sill. The figure swung out ... dangled sickeningly in the fireman's grip. A great gasp went up from the crowd. Photo-flashes now lit the scene continuously. Cries of anguish sounded from the crowd. 'My God, he's going to fall ...!' ... 'He can't hold him ...!' And then, in realization of their fears, the fireman appeared to overbalance, fell heavily against the rail, all but toppled over it and in desperation released his hold on the figure and grabbed the rail to save himself.

A horrified scream from a hundred spectators heralded the

figure's nightmare plunge. Over and over it turned, cartwheeling rigidly, its arms and legs straight as boards ... down ... down ... down ... down ... twang! into the waiting net, shot six feet in the air, did a couple more cartwheels and smashed into the hotel wall, its right arm severing at the shoulder and its head catapulting horrifically into the arms of a dumbfounded fireman.

Six women fainted on the spot.

Rossiter, taking advantage of the restraining fireman's temporary paralysis, dashed forward, skirted the ladder truck and leapt into the midst of the firemen crowding around the dismembered suicide.

He heard a gasp. 'Well, I'll go to our 'ouse ...!'

Another: 'Would you bleedin' believe it!'

'Let me in! Let me in!' insisted Rossiter. 'That man is one of my crew!'

They looked up at him, as though he was mad, and one chuckled. 'What you flyin', captain – Harrod's window?'

With a laugh they moved away, allowing him in, and as he crouched, open-mouthed, to the mutilated figure, a plaster dummy's head came whistling over his shoulder to land with a thump on the body.

'There,' laughed the fireman who'd caught it, ' 'e'll need that if he's flyin' your plane, skip – no good without the brains.'

Rossiter stared furiously, astounded, at the corpse ... a bloody window dummy! Now, who the ... how the ... what the ...

'Clear the way, now, sir ...' requested a fireman. 'Another member of your crew is about to make a landing ... ha ha ha.'

Rossiter backed away and looked up. The fireman on the ladder was preparing to send the second dummy crashing down into the net. Rossiter continued to watch as he backed further and further away and finally came to a halt when he trod on Ramjet Rogers' foot.

'Ouch! Oh, hi, skip ...'

'Hi, skip!' said James cheerily. 'What on *earth's* all the excitement? We've just arrived.'

'Rogers!' spluttered Rossiter. 'Crighton-Padgett! What the *hell* have you two been up to?'

'Who ... us?' They looked at each other.

'Yes, *you*! How come these dummies are wearing your uniforms!'

James gaped. 'Our ... you mean ... we've ... they're *our* uniforms?'

'As if you didn't *know*!'

'*Honest*, skip ...'

'God's honour, skip ...' added Ramjet.

At that moment they were deluged by well-wishers. Babs Buchanan and Wilma Fluck, streaming tears of relief, flung their arms around the lads and kissed them passionately.

'Oh, James ...!' squealed Babs. 'I'm *so* glad you're alive!'

'Eh?'

'Ramjet ... *baby* ...' sniffed Wilma, 'we really thought it was you.'

'Me ...? What ...?'

Now a loud gasp from the crowd as the second figure came hurtling down, bounced into the net and stayed there, standing on its head.

'Look ... will someone *please* tell us what's going *on*!' demanded Ramjet.

Rossiter speared him with a fierce eye. 'You mean you really don't know?'

'Of *course* we don't know, skip ...'

'Captain Rossiter?' demanded a stern officious voice.

Cock-up turned, came face-to-face with a small, grey, moustachio-ed man in a fawn raincoat and a battered trilby hat.

'Yeh, what is it?'

An identity card appeared in the man's hand as if by magic. 'Detective Sergeant Grimmet of the Metropolitan Police, sir. May I have a word with you ... in private?'

Rossiter groaned. 'OK – where?'

'Over here, sir.'

They moved away from the crowd, faced each other, the detective surreptitiously perusing Rossiter's uniform with a wince of disbelief. 'All right, sir ... like to tell me what you know about all this?'

'Certainly. Nothing. May I go now?'

'No, sir, you may not. How did two of your uniforms get up there, on those dummies, on the seventh floor?'

'I don't know.'

'Who do the uniforms belong to?'

Rossiter nodded. 'To the two officers standing over there in their dressing gowns – Rogers and Crighton-Padgett.'

'Do they know how their uniforms got up there?'

'They said not.'

'How many uniforms do you each have?'

'One.'

'I see ... so somebody took their *only* uniforms without them knowing and ...'

'No.'

'Explain that.'

'They knew somebody had taken their uniforms all right. It happened tonight. They were led astray by two phoney girl journalists who seduced them to a down-town hotel and nipped off with their clothes. Nice-lookin' dolls, I'da been tempted myself.'

Grimmet heaved a sigh. 'Captain Rossiter ... you are currently flying a world-wide promotion tour for Glamour Airlines, right ...?'

'Spot on, Inspector.'

'Detective Sergeant ... the purpose of the tour being to attract as much publicity for the new airline as possible, right ...?'

'On the nose, Grimm, on the nose.'

'Grimmet ... in that event, doesn't it seem just a *trifle* more than coincidence that you have managed to attract tonight what is conceivably the publicity scoop of the decade?' He swung round and pointed. 'You see that group of newspaper men and photographers over there ... must be fifty of them. Can you explain to me how that many pressmen can get to know about – and so quickly assemble at the scene of – a four a.m. mock suicide attempt? Doesn't it seem just a *little* bit premeditated to you?'

'Frankly, I wouldn't know, Grimmet ...'

'Really? Well, I *would*!' snapped Grimmet. 'This business stinks to high heaven of PR skullduggery and I intend to get to the root of it. Who's your promotion consultant in London?'

'A guy named Arnold Bottum.'

'Pardon?'

'Don't blame me, I'm not his father.'

'Arnold Bottum of...?'

'It's his own outfit. He's got a place in New Bond Street. But if you think Bottum had anything to do with this, you're way off.'

'Oh – why?'

'Because it just ain't Arnold's style. He's strictly small-time – frightened of his own shadow. He couldn't go through with a thing as bare-faced as this if yuh pumped him full of H. Hell, he damn-near dieda shock at the airport when one of our guest celebrities demanded a Rolls-Royce!'

'Mm,' said Grimmet grimly. 'Well, we'll see.'

'Look, sergeant...' sighed Rossiter, 'I'm sorry the fire boys have been brought out on a phoney call, but it is only one ladder and it doesn't seem to me a hell of a lotta harm has been done. Now, we take off from Heathrow at 16.00 hours ... so why not forget the whole thing and let everybody get some sleep? Personally, my ass is draggin' so low I need plasters.'

Grimmet regarded him with a cold, disapproving eye. 'There would seem little alternative *to* forgetting the whole thing, captain. As tasteless as the incident *personally* appears, it nevertheless constitutes no more than a practical joke ... and since the Fire Department was summoned by an anonymous caller, we cannot take action in that direction. So – your wish is granted. You are free to retire and apply whatever medicament to your posterior you feel necessary.'

'Thanks a lot,' scowled Rossiter.'

'Just ... *one* small thought before you go, though...'

'Yeh, what's that?'

'If this ... *ignominious* charade *was* designed to attract favourable publicity for Glamour Airlines, I'm very much afraid it is destined to fail.'

'Oh? Why so?'

Grimmet permitted himself a snide smile. 'Ask yourself,

captain ... would *you* rush to buy seats on an airline whose officers – no matter how remotely – are prone to spectacular suicide?'

Rossiter's jaw dropped. 'Hey, come *on*, now ...!'

'Oh, *we* know they're not, Rossiter ... but where there's smoke, as the saying goes. Personally, I believe those headlines and photographs in the mid-day papers are going to nicely put paid to any hope you ever had of selling Glamour to the British. Good morning, captain.'

And on that infuriatingly victorious note, Grimmet about-turned and disappeared into the dispersing and disappointed crowd, leaving Rossiter bludgeoned with despair and very seriously contemplating his own spectacular demise.

16

In profoundly melancholy mood, Rossiter returned to his room and stood gazing through the window at the encroaching dawn, his mind tormented by Grimmet's prophecy. He was right, damn him. Whoever perpetrated this stupid stunt *had* put the mockers on Glamour's chances of captivating Britain.

He knew the press of old and could envisage to the last dotted 'i' and crossed 't' the heyday they'd have with this story. Past-masters at manipulating the truth to suit their circulation figures, they'd make a mountain out of the figures suspended from the window-sill, the attempted rescue, and the hideous plunge into the nets, and such a tiny molehill out of the fact that the figures were dummies, that by the time the public got to that part the damage would already have been done.

Sure, Grimmet was right. No matter *how* it was explained, Glamour would come out of this smeared with suspicion, for even if the public didn't react to the suicide angle, they'd sure think badly of officers who played tasteless games with their uniforms.

Goddam it, Berskin would go bananas. At that very moment news of the stunt was probably flashing across the Atlantic from a dozen vindictive sources. He could see Berskin, hairless, ranting and raging, and simultaneously working on seventeen different ways of de-masculating the leader of the pack – Alfred B. Rossiter. The end, he knew, was nigh. One phone call from Berskin, so imminent that he threw a reflective glance at the instrument expecting it to ring, and it was curtains for him. And knowing Berskin's power and influence, he'd fix it so that Rossiter would never fly again – for anybody!

Ah, well, he mused exhaustedly, there was always rabbit-breeding. He'd go back to Mrs. Wesolowski, his New York landlady, and plead with her to let him set up business on her roof again. But as quickly as he formulated the plan, he abandoned it, remembering the vehemence with which she had promised to annihilate both him *and* his crapping rabbits if they ever set paw over her threshold again.

He glanced at his watch, not really caring, and saw it was five o'clock. Two more hours and the day would begin ... a day promising such an abundance of excitement the thought of it forced his jaws apart in a mammoth yawn and sent him toppling to the bed.

Eight-thirty – Hyde Park Corner, he languidly recalled. Nine o'clock ... Buckingham Palace. Nine-thirty ... The Mall. Ten o'clock ... Houses of Parliament. Ten-thirty ... Fleet Street. Eleven o'clock ... Trafalgar Square. Eleven-thirty ... Piccadilly Circus. Twelve o'clock ... lunch. And then, thank God ... out to the airport.

Never in all his life would he be so glad to board a plane.

Ah, well ... at least nothing could go wrong with a simple photographic session The very most that could assail him during that was boredom ... beautiful ... enervating ... boredom.

And on that comforting thought he drifted into an exhausted doze, little realizing, poor devil, how unprophetic his supposition would prove to be.

'Everybody ...!' trilled Arnold Bottum, resplendent in olive-green flares, burnt-orange jacket, and a stunning bright orange velour fedora and matching shoulder-bag, 'could I *please* have you outside in the landaus!'

'Anywhere, ducks, looking like that,' joked Sugar Sweetman.

Arnold almost blushed. 'Ooh, d'you like it?'

'*Heavenly*, pet. Where *did* you get that hat?'

'Marcus and Cyril – Knightsbridge. Cost a *fortune*, but I just had to have it.'

'Divine!' enthused Sugar. 'Here – what's all this about landaus?'

Arnold winked naughtily. 'Just a little thought of mine ... thought it might catch the eye. I hired four open carriages and had them painted pink and candy-striped. Ought to look *fab* trotting along Fleet Street. If that doesn't pull some press, I don't know what will.'

'Huh! After last night, d'you think we're going to need more press?'

Arnold gaped and clutched his arm. 'Wasn't it *aw*ful! I didn't hear about it until the seven o'clock news. I'm absolutely shattered! I mean, who could have *done* such a thing!'

'Done such a thing as what, Bottum?' asked Cock-up Rossiter, wiping egg from his chin as he approached.

'Well, the whole *thing*, captain! ... stealing the uniforms, renting the room on the seventh floor, smuggling in those dummies, calling the press and the fire brigade. I mean, *really* ... I simply can't imagine who would go to all that *trouble*!'

'Yuh can't, hm? Seems to me, Bottum, a first-class PR man might go to all that trouble – considerin' the publicity potential involved.'

'Well,' sighed Arnold, 'he'd be a very misguided PR man, then. I'm absolutely *distraught* about the effect this might have on our campaign. Good heavens, we couldn't have *wished* for more adverse publicity than a joke suicide! I'm certain Colonel Berskin will go *mad* when I report it to him.'

'Oh, you're, erm, reporting to him, huh? Er, might I enquire when, Bottum?'

'Immediately you depart from Heathrow, captain. I have to give him an up-to-the-last-minute resumé of how it's all gone.'

'Oh, *after* we take off,' said Rossiter, flooding with relief. 'Well, that's fine.' He shook his head. 'Sure as heck beats me who'd do a thing like that, though. Then again the world's so full of goddam nuts it coulda bin anybody.'

He moved away, now completely convinced that Bottum had had nothing to do with the prank and seriously considering

195

the possibility that it might have been PanAm, TWA, or British Airways – and conceivably all three!

'Now, please ... into the landaus everybody!' urged Arnold. 'They're right outside ... oh, *do* please hurry, we're behind schedule by five minutes already. It's a lovely morning for a carriage ride, I'm sure you'll all enjoy it immensely. In the lead carriage I'd like Captain Rossiter and Officers Rogers, McKenzie, and Crighton-Padgett ... second carriage – Steward Sweetman, Stewardesses Buchanan and Fluck, and myself ...'

'*Su*per!' murmured Sugar.

'Third carriage – Miss Gloriana Fullbrush, Miss Delicious O'Hara, Mister Vincent Martino, and Senator Chortle ... and last, but by no means least, in the fourth carriage – Mister Shag McGee and the Skull and Cross Bones – not forgetting, of course, Marlon, the parrot.'

'Knickers!' squawked Marlon.

'So ... could we please have you all outside right away – the photographers are already waiting at Hyde Park Corner.'

Across the foyer to the hotel entrance sauntered the celebrities, to where four outrageous pink and candy-striped landaus, each drawn by four immaculately-groomed black horses and attended by a groom bedecked in silver-lamé livery, awaited them.

'Now, *that* ...' slurred Lush Martino, monumentally hungover from the night's libations, 'is what I call style.'

'Indeed,' sniffed Gloriana Fullbrush, once again outraged at being relegated to the third carriage. '*I* would call it insufferable ostentation.'

Martino nodded. 'So might I – if I knew what it meant.'

Time: 8.45 on a morning of surpassed beauty, the sky a vault of unblemished blue and the sun warming up nicely.

'Ah, *what* a day!' sighed Bush McKenzie, flexing this and stretching that, filling his capacious chest with the cool, clean London air and generally feeling top-hole. 'Trust you slept well, skipper? Personally I slept like a bug in a rug, didn't hear a thing of that rumpus last night. Eight solid hours of deep, dreamless, fully-restorative oblivion ... by God, I feel

196

marvellous ...!'

'Fuck off, McKenzie,' scowled Rossiter, sliding onto his spine and tilting his cap over his eyes. 'Gimme a shout when we hit Hyde Park Corner, you guys.'

Bush frowned at Ramjet. 'What'd I say?'

'We all had lousy nights,' yawned Ramjet, propping his leaden head in his hand.

'Skip ...' droned James, finding it difficult to speak. 'War-risit?'

'Hate to break it to you ... but we're here.'

'Huh? Where?'

'Hyde Park Corner.'

Rossiter sat up. 'Already! Jeezus, we haven't bin goin' more than a minute!'

'Nevertheless, we are here.'

The landaus drew to a halt on Rotten Row, just inside the park gates, where a score of photographers – national press and magazine – eagerly awaited them, and for the next twenty minutes the crew and celebrities were shunted from position to position, posed against familiar backgrounds – the park gates, Wellington Arch, the Hilton Hotel – until the gamut of possibilities had been run, then it was back in the landaus for a fast clop down Constitution Hill to Buckingham Palace, followed by the press in cars.

Here, at the palace, a similar routine was followed – everybody out, pose, click, flash, next one ... individual shots here, a group shot there – in front of the splendidly ornate gates of the palace, against the miraculous Victoria Memorial, and with a back-drop of the endless, sunlit Mall. Then everybody in again.

Now down the broad pink ribbon of The Mall itself, a quick stop for shots against the now-distant palace and Victoria Memorial, then on again to the Admiralty turn-off, cheered all the way by a multitude of summer tourists heading up towards the palace.

'Genius!' exclaimed Sugar Sweetman, patting Arnold on the knee to emphasize the point. 'Sheer genius, Arnold, painting these landaus pink – just *look* at the attention we're attracting!'

197

'Thank you,' Arnold smiled modestly. 'When I heard the long-range weather forecast, I thought what a dreadful shame not to make the most of all this lovely sunshine. No good hiding your light under a closed-in bus, is there?'

Sugar sighed admiringly and shook his head. 'Beats me where you get all these ideas. You've certainly done a wonderful job of promoting us in London – despite the setbacks.'

Arnold's ebullience abated. 'Yes,' he said glumly. 'I'm very much afraid anything I've managed to achieve is going to be seriously diminished when the mid-day papers come out.'

'Poor Arnold,' Wilma sympathized, leaning forward to pat his hand consolingly. 'But nobody can possibly blame you for what happened last night. Colonel Berskin has just got to be pleased with what *you've* done.'

Arnold shrugged helplessly. 'Berskin only accepts success, Wilma – it won't matter to him that I had nothing to do with that dreadful incident. He's only interested in one thing – did Glamour Airlines successfully sell itself in London. And I'm very much afraid the answer is going to be "no".'

Babs Buchanan turned from waving to a troop of wolf-whistling wolf-cubs. 'Now, Arnold, don't burn your bridges before they're hatched. Things may turn out better than you think. There's nothing you can do about it, anyway – so why not just sit back and enjoy the ride. Coo-eeee!'

Moments later they were turning into Parliament Square. Here they executed a bold circuit of the square, cheered by the milling tourists, and finally came to a halt in the forecourt of the Houses of Parliament.

As the chimes of Big Ben struck out the hour of ten, they disembarked and arranged themselves for shots outside Westminster Hall, moved thence to Big Ben itself, then crossed St. Margaret Street to the ancient and glorious edifice of Westminster Abbey, completing the session on the stroke of ten thirty.

Things were going very well indeed.

And things continued to go very well indeed as they trotted flamboyantly along Victoria Embankment, turned north to Ludgate Circus, then proceeded along Fleet Street towards Trafalgar Square.

It was in the famous square itself, alas, that the black thunder clouds of impending disaster rolled in to mar the sweet perfection of the day.

'My Gard, just look at all them pigeons!' exclaimed Frankie, gaping bass guitarist.

'Ouch!' replied Shag McGee, wincing hard as Marlon began a needle-sharp fandango on his head. 'Hey, Marlon, cut that out, will yuh!'

'What's the matter with him?' enquired Stanley.

'I dunno. Maybe he don't like pigeons.'

An incorrect and unjust assumption on Shag's part because Marlon adored pigeons. He also adored ... no, a wild understatement – was absolutely fruit-cake about pigeon's food – the delicious, succulent assorted seed currently being dispensed in open cans to the public by several vendors for the purpose of attracting the ultra-tame birds on to hands, arms, heads, and shoulders while being photographed – to which attraction the birds were responding with greedy alacrity.

The vision of all this heavenly food lying scattered around the square in abundance and of eighty thousand disgustingly fat pigeons gorging themselves to bursting point was almost more than Marlon could bear, and yet he did not abandon his hirsute perch and join the free-for-all. For above all Marlon McGee was a professional – and long months of theatrical discipline were not to be denied. And besides, he knew such an expression of frivolous self-indulgence would be rewarded with a clobbering from Stanley's drumstick and that hurt. And so, although not without protest, he maintained his appointed station.

'Hold still, man!' winced McGee. 'Jeez, I'm gonna have to cut your toe-nails!'

'Gee, don't them fountains look *cool*,' sighed Sydney. 'I sure could use a shower right now.'

'An' break the habit of a life-time?' frowned Stanley. 'Come on, fellas, let's get down an' feed the birds.'

Sydney was right – the fountains did look cool, for there is no cooler-looking, cooler-sounding oasis in all London on a scorching summer's day than Trafalgar Square, the spray from the towering breeze-blown plumes providing exhilarating refreshment to the sweltering crowds and its pools of sparkling turquoise water offering a dire temptation frequently overcoming obligatory restraint.

'Over by that fountain, please!' directed Arnold Bottum. 'They'd like some shots against the National Gallery and St. Martins. Er, Miss Fullbrush ... would you mind doing a few shots feeding the pigeons?'

Gloriana's lip curled. '*How* feeding them? You mean just scattering a bit of corn?'

'Well, no, I, er ...'

'On my head! Get lost, sonny ... Fullbrush does *not* pose in public with pigeons on her head!'

'Well ... how about just on one arm?'

'No!'

'A ... hand?'

'No! I'll toss some on the ground but that's it – take it or leave it.'

Arnold gulped. 'Well ... all right, I'll go and buy some seed.'

His reappearance a moment later with no fewer than *ten* cans brimming with all-together irresistible goodies sent Marlon into prancing paroxysms of frustration that all but drew blood from Shag McGee's scalp.

'Marlon! ... f'chrissake quit that, will yuh! What's the matter with this bird, Stanley?'

Stanley shrugged. 'Maybe he feels outnumbered. Maybe he's gettin' an inferiority complex with all these pigeons.'

'Rollocks!' squawked Marlon.

As Arnold handed a can of seed to Gloriana, several photographers rushed forward. 'Right, Miss Fullbrush ... could we have you right over by the fountain, please ...'

Gloriana moved to the low stone wall encompassing the huge shimmering pool and indifferently began distributing the seed to a horde of strutting, cooing pigeons, her disenchantment with the mangey, flea-ridden creatures patently reflected in her expression.

'A little happier, please, Miss Fullbrush ... could we have a few smiles?'

Gradually she began warming to the project, her awareness

200

of total attention from the photographers subduing her loathing for the birds and the ignominy of her role. And correspondingly, the photographers, sensing her developing co-operation, became more bold in their requests as their inspiration flowed.

'Could you just ... throw some seed into the air, Miss Fullbrush ... maybe get a pigeon hovering close?'

Gloriana obliged.

'Wonderful ...! Great ...! Hey, how about a two-shot of that with Mister Martino?'

'He flies a little, but I don't think he hovers,' she cracked.

'Yes – why not.'

'Thank you very much. Er, Mister Martino ... would you mind if a few birds perched on your arm?'

'So long as it ain't my drinkin' arm,' grinned Lush. 'Hokay, li'l pigeon, come to poppa ... atta boy ...'

'Aw, terrific ... fantastic!'

'Senator Chortle, sir, would you like to join them?'

'It would be mah pleasure,' Chortle responded readily, anxious to expiate the notoriety of the night in a welter of effusive co-operation.

Click! Clack! Flash! The cameras peppered them with shots, the unpredictability of the birds' movements resulting in gratifying spontaneity.

'Captain Rossiter, sir ...! Would you mind joining the group?'

'Mm?' Rossiter was asleep on his feet. 'Oh, sure ...'

'And how about your crew? Would they kindly ...'

In came the crew, collected tins of seed and began feeding the birds which by now surrounded the entire group in a strutting, hovering, swooping, fighting cloud, perching on anything, even each other, that offered a claw-hold and attacking the tins with gluttonous gusto.

And then – a lone voice above the clamour – that of Bert Shifty from 'Shutter Bug Monthly'. 'Say, I've got a great idea ... everybody up on the wall! I'd like a long, angled shot of everyone in semi-profile, fanning forward. Please – would everybody climb on the wall? Cummon, it's not very high ...'

'OK, pal,' said Lush Martino, throwing a handful of seed

201

into his mouth thinking they were bar peanuts. 'Man, these coulda done with another five minutes. C'mon, everybody, up here!'

Martino climbed up and made a big thing of pretending to overbalance into the knee-deep pool, wobbling back and forth until it seemed highly likely he would fall in. Then, as groups will, they were all in on the act ... Ramjet Rogers grabbed Martino's coat-tail ... Delicious O'Hara began doing a mock strip in preparation for the plunge ... Sugar Sweetman dipped his toe in and shivered ... everybody was doing something for the amusement of the huge spectator crowd and to the delight of the photographers who were crashing off shots as fast as they could re-wind.

'Fabulous ... hold that, Miss O'Hara! A touch lower ...'

'This way, Senator ... how about a wave?'

'Could you wobble like that again, Mister Martino ...?'

'One more time with the push, Mister Rogers ...'

And then ... it happened.

Theatrical discipline or no theatrical discipline, Marlon McGee had had a *bellyful* of watching fat slob pigeons stuffing themselves with all that top-grade seed. Hell, speaking bird-wise, wasn't he the *star* of the show? So how come he was the only feathers around there who wasn't reapin' any benefits?

A glance below indicated that Shag and the lads were having too much fun to be overly concerned with his momentary absence. He could be there and back with a beakful before anyone even missed him. And so ... lining up on the nearest available tin – which just happened to be clutched close to the bosom of Miss Gloriana Fullbrush – he counted a mental three and took off like a rocket, straight for the source of supply.

Now, the sight of a huge blue-and-yellow parrot coming straight at them at four hundred miles an hour would cause anyone to take evasive action, but when that someone happens to be Gloriana Fullbrush and the parrot happens to be Marlon who so recently bit her on the left boob, a great deal more than simple evasive action can be anticipated.

Gloriana, in fact, let out a shriek that frightened eighty thousand pigeons into the air, staggered three steps to the rear, discovered a sickening absence of solid ground after the first two, grabbed wildly at Senator Chortle's coat with her right hand and Lush Martino's arm with her left and brought them hurtling off the wall. They, in turn, in reflexive self-preservation, locked onto Cock-up Rossiter and Delicious O'Hara, they onto Ramjet and Bush McKenzie, and so on down the line and before you could shout 'Man overboard!' half of the group were flat on their backs in the briny.

Gentlemen to the core, in plunged Sugar Sweetman to rescue the floundering, spluttering Gloriana Fullbrush ... simultaneously, in went Lord Jim to render assistance to the half-drowned Delicious O'Hara ... then, not to be outdone in the gallantry stakes, in dived Shag McGee headfirst to offer aid to Babs Buchanan, in jumped Stanley to lend a hand to Wilma Fluck, and, seeing no reason why they should be left out of the fun, Sydney and Frankie also took a header into the shallows.

And that was all the encouragement the spectator crowd needed. With a whoop and a holler a tidal wave of sweating humanity was over the wall and into the pool, splashing and kicking and throwing it at one another until the water boiled and the staid and ancient fountain more closely resembled Blackpool Baths on August Bank Holiday.

Then, suddenly ... the turquoise water was turquoise no more. It was bright orange – and so was everybody in it.

Shrieks of dismay from the women and gasps of horror from the men in silver-lamé as their uniforms quickly turned a rather fetching shade of tangerine.

'Wh .. what happened?' spluttered Rossiter, wringing out his apricot cap.

'It's .. it's *him*!' cried Gloriana Fullbrush, levelling a dripping finger at Shag McGee, sitting up to his waist in a spreading circle of ginger ochre. 'It's his bloody henna!'

'Oh, sweet Jesus!' gasped Rossiter. 'Quick – everybody out! ... everybody out!'

As the half-drowned figures clambered from the pool, the photographers leapt into action, ripping off shots at a rate that made their previous output seem torpid.

'Oh, no ... no!' cried a demented Arnold, rushing from one to the other. 'No ... please ... not this! Oh, my *God* ...!

Quickly – everyone back in the landaus! Back to the hotel! Back to the hotel...!'

But worse was yet to come.

It was Bush McKenzie who first noticed a certain 'tightness' under the armpits. As he, Ramjet, and Lord Jim dripped back across the square towards the waiting landaus, he had occasion to inhale an extra large chestful of air, his exertions in the pool evoking the need, and ... ping! ... a button exploded from his jacket.

'Aye aye,' he remarked, easing his great shoulders within the strangely confining garment. 'Something wrong here...' He stretched out his arms ... looked down at his trousers ... and let out a gasp. 'Oh, bloody 'ell ... hey, mates, now we're *really* up it! Now we've *really* gone and done it!'

'That ...' nodded Ramjet, gaping first at Bush, then at Jim, and finally at himself, '... is no lie.'

'Oh, my aching back,' gulped James, watching with incredulity his trouser-cuffs literally creeping up his legs and his sleeves racing up his arms.

At the sound of a snort, they turned and beheld a rapidly approaching Rossiter, and next moment they were doubled up with laughter, for their captain's trousers had shrunk so much they were practically Bermuda shorts.

'OK ... OK!' bellowed Rossiter. 'Jesus H. Christ, let's get the hell out to that airport before Bottum calls Berskin! If he don't have me assassinated for this, I'm Sweetman's half-sister! Driver ... back to the Hilton – at the gallop!'

17

Twenty minutes later, having been landau-ed to the rear entrance of the hotel and smuggled as inconspicuously as possible through to the elevators, the crew and celebrities were safely in their rooms.

For the celebrities, the problem deriving from their henna-ed soaking was relatively simple – they merely changed their clothes. At least, all but the Skull and Cross Bones changed their clothes. The lads were so delighted with the result of the dyeing they decided to adopt the yellow streaking as part of their costume and kept them on.

For the crew, however, the problem looked, at least at first glance, insurmountable. Since each male member now resembled a grossly over-stuffed cushion about to burst at the seams, it was obvious the uniforms had to be discarded.

But what was to be worn as an alternative?

It was simply not on – even supposing they could be purchased in time, which was doubtful – that *Glamour Puss* should be flown by personnel in civilian clothing. And yet there had to *be* an alternative.

The solution came (a stroke of genius) from Arnold Bottum. Leaving a distraught Rossiter showering orange from his person, Bottum descended to the foyer and conferred with management, who went adroitly to the kitchens and conferred with the head chef, who in turn conferred with his staff, who eventually provided the answer. And minutes later Bottum was proudly exhibiting his solution to the dripping captain.

Rossiter choked. 'Kitchen whites! Bottum, it may have escaped your notice, but I happen to be an airline captain – not a fucking short-order cook!'

Bottum gulped, inately hurt. 'I thought it was *such* a good idea. At least from a distance they'll *look* like airline uniforms. Far, *far* better than civilian clothing, you must agree.'

'Yes, well...' muttered Rossiter, reluctantly accepting the practicality of the argument.

'And the public will see so little of you from now on,' persisted Arnold, detecting a chink in Rossiter's opposition. 'I mean, we can load you on the coach at the rear entrance ... you can keep out of sight during the drive to the airport ... and then you're practically home and dry!'

'And don't I wish I *was*!' growled Rossiter. 'OK – so we make the plane – then what? Maybe our next stop is Paris – only an hour away! What happens when we hit Orly!'

Arnold offered a comforting, secretly-knowledgeable smile. 'I ... wouldn't worry about that if I were you, captain. I happen to know your next stop is *not* Paris.'

Rossiter narrow-eyed him. 'Oh, you *do*, do you? Now, how in hell...'

Arnold restrained him with an upheld hand. 'Captain, *somebody* has got to know where your next stop is.'

'Well, certainly they've got to know – but why you, Bottum?'

'Because ...' said Arnold superiorly, '*I* have to communicate with my PR counterpart in that country. I have to advise him on ... well, many different aspects of your British visit. It's far too technical to go into now, but believe me, captain, I *do* know where you're heading.'

'OK,' shrugged Rossiter, 'so you know where we're heading – but that still leaves us landing in cook's whites!'

'Landing – yes,' smirked Arnold. 'But publicly appearing – no. As I told you, I have to report to Colonel Berskin the moment you depart Heathrow. I shall inform him of your mishap and he will have new uniforms flown out to ... to your next stop-over – before you get there.'

'Oh, really? Just like that, hm? And, er, how come you're

so sure of that, Bottum?'

'Simply because there's no alternative, captain. If Colonel Berskin wishes the tour to continue, he'll have to do it.'

'Uh huh,' nodded Rossiter, eyes narrowed cunningly. 'Well, thanks for the tip-off, Bottum ... mighty good of you.'

'Tip-off?' queried Arnold. 'About what?'

'About our next drop down. I've got a pretty good idea now where we're heading.'

'Wh ... why – *I* didn't tell you anything.'

'As good as. If Berskin is going to be able to get new uniforms to our next port of call before *we* get there – then he's got to be geographically nearer to it than we are – right?'

'Well ...'

'Sure, it's right. And as we will undoubtedly continue flying in an easterly direction ... so Berskin will have to fly our uniforms out in a westerly direction ... which makes our meeting point somewhere on the other side of the world ... say in ... Australia?' He grinned brazenly but Bottum shook his head emphatically.

'I am not saying a word, captain! It will not get back to the colonel that I divulged information about the mystery tour!'

'OK, OK, nobody's gonna snitch on you, Bottum. You tried to do a good job for us here – it wasn't your fault everything got fouled up. Boy, I sure don't envy you havin' to report in to Berskin this afternoon. The headlines in the mid-day papers will be bad enough, but when he catches an earful of what happened in Trafalgar Square ...! Well, rather you than me, kiddo.'

Arnold stiffened. 'One's duty is one's duty. It will not be shirked.'

'Well, bully for you. Now – push off and let me get dressed. And as soon as the others are ready we'll get going. The sooner I'm aboard that plane the better I'll like it. I just hope an' pray they don't have any goddam fountains in Wagga Wagga.'

Time: 12.55 p.m.

Place: Rear entrance of the Hilton Hotel.

'All the luggage aboard, Bottum?'

'Everything stowed away, captain.'

207

'Right – let's get everyone aboard and make it fast.'

Bottum disappeared into the hotel and almost immediately the outflux of Glamour guests began. First to arrive were the twenty members of the public, led by fluttery Miss Minnie Wattle, retired librarian from Boston, her arm linked in that of chubby Karl Makepiece, pork butcher from Idaho, both of whom looked and sounded as though they'd been at the sauce bottle again.

'Why, Captain Rossiter . . . !' exclaimed Minnie, agog at his strange garb. 'I thought for a moment you were the gentleman who brought in my morning tea! Whatever happened to your lovely uniform?'

'A slight accident, Miss Wattle . . . I spilled some orange on it.'

'Aha!' she teased, wagging her finger. 'That's what you get for soft-drinking. Now, if that had been straight gin, it wouldn't have shown!'

'I'll remember that next time. Now, climb aboard quickly, please . . .'

'Great little stop-over, captain,' winked Makepiece, grabbing Rossiter's arm. 'Know what I mean . . .?'

'Glad you enjoyed yourself, Mister Makepiece.'

'A *ball* is what I had . . . know what I mean? A reg'lar hoedown. Sure hope all you fly guys had yourselves a fine time last night, you sure deserve it.'

'I . . .' Rossiter sighed. 'I can safely say it was a night in a million, Mister Makepiece . . one never to be forgotten.'

'Attaboy!' chuckled Makepiece. 'Sure like to hear of folks havin' themselves a good time. Come on, now Minnie, up you go, mind them steps, now . . . woops! Now, Minnie, I *told* yuh ta mind those steps . . .'

Rossiter suffered in crack-faced silence as each of the twenty guests trundled past, made a comment, observation, remark, or quip about his cook's uniform and entered the coach.

Then came Monsieur Jacques Camembert, steely-eyed and still vengeful, who gave a start as he espied Rossiter's outfit.

'Sacre bleu, vat iss zis! You intend 'elping out wiz ze cooking? I warn you, keptain, you stay out of my galley or zere will be . . .' he drew his finger ominously across his throat, '. . .

208

much trouble! My patience is at an end! First I 'ave ze poufters to contend wiz – and now a keptain who vants to take over ze cooking...!'

'Relax, Camembert, I ain't takin' over the galley. And watch where you're wavin' that cleaver on board, I want no trouble between you and Chortle on the next leg out.'

'Well, you keep him away from me – or it vill be *his* next leg out – out of ze window!'

Next it was the turn of the American press, bristling with jokes, puns, cracks, and witticisms, all cock-a-hoop with the material the Trafalgar Square debacle had provided.

'Two fried eggs – sunnyside up, captain...!'

'Two rashers streaky – beans on the side, chef...!'

'Who's this – Doctor Kildare's stand-in?'

'Yeh, yeh...' grimaced Rossiter, 'Ver-ry funny. Just keep it movin'.'

And with the last of the press finally aboard, out swirled Gloriana Fullbrush, fit to burst with the humiliation of her Trafalgar Square soaking and the degredation of this back-door departure.

Throwing a glance at Rossiter's get-up, she snorted a laugh and sneered, 'How *very* fitting. By the time I've finished re-porting your handling of this tour, Rossiter, that'll be the only job left open to you – kitchen help!'

'Sure, sure,' nodded Rossiter. 'Can *I* help it if the parrot hates the sight of you? Climb on board, please.'

She climbed – followed closely by her three studs.

Next to emerge was Senator Chortle, an obsequious shadow of his former insufferable self.

'Captain...' he nodded, avoiding Rossiter's eye, but then, as he sidled closer, 'Er, captain ... about last night...'

'Yes, senator?'

Chortle lowered his voice to rumble. 'Captain ... as a man of the world ... a man accustomed to and familiar with the vi-ciss-itudes of life ... a man of experience, understandin', and wisdom ... a man all too acquainted with the vagaries of human relationships ... the frailty of the flesh ... the capri-ciousness of the heart ... a man who...'

Rossiter stopped him with a yawn. 'What can I do for you, Senator?'

Chortle coughed. 'Well, suh ... seein' as how last night's, er, somnambulations have so far miraculously escaped th'attention of the press, I wus wonderin' ... that is ta say, I would regard it as the *greatest* personal favour ... the embodiment of truest inter-human graciousness ... the ...'

Again Rossiter dammed the flow. 'I gather what you're askin', Senator, is will I keep my trap shut?'

Chortle grinned, most contritely. 'In as many words, suh – yes.'

Rossiter nodded. 'Consider it shut.'

Chortle swelled visibly, the colour of restored confidence returning to his puce-dappled cheeks. 'Captain, I regard that, suh, as a most *touchin'* gesture of loyalty ... an' a gesture that will not go unrewarded, believe you me. I ...'

'Think nothin' of it,' muttered Rossiter.

'Oh, but Ah do! An' if the time should ever come that old Sam Chortle can use his *con*-siderable influence to return the favour, why – you can bet yuh sweet life it will be done ...'

'Thank you, Senator ...'

'Yes, siree. Right from the start of this here tour you impressed me as a man of rare vision ... of tender-hearted concern fo' his fellow traveller on life's stoney path ... a man of conscience, judgement, and down-right kindness ... in short – a very *real* human bein'. Yes, suh, the moment I ran inta you in the Glamour hangar ...'

'Yes, well ... thanks a lot, Senator, but could we have you aboard, we're running kinda late.'

'Certainly, certainly, yoh wish is mah command. Yessir, just say the word and ...'

He disappeared into the coach, chunnering to himself, greeting his fellow travellers with the sickening effusion of high relief.

Rossiter heaved a sigh and passed a weary hand across his face.

'Why, captain, honey, you look plumb tuckered out!' Up slunk Delicious O'Hara, looking breath-takingly wanton in a flimsy organdie creation through which all of her liquid assets and most of her hidden liabilities could be seen. 'Heavy night, baby?'

'Huh – *I* shoulda bin so lucky.'

'Right – you shoulda been. Next time – come up an' see Delicious, why doncha? She'll make it right for you.'

Rossiter grinned. 'I'll remember. Enjoying yourself?'

'Lissen, there ain't no place on earth Delicious don't enjoy herself. Drop me off at the North Pole an' in ten minutes I guarantee I'll have those eskimos howlin' like snow wolves.'

'I'll bet,' laughed Rossiter. 'Delicious, you're a shot in the arm. Stay close – I need the laughs.'

'Like skin, baby.'

As she entered the coach (a supper-show in itself), up rolled Lush Martino, so dishevelled he looked as though he'd dressed himself in a broom cupboard.

'Hi, captain, old buddy ... say, one thing's bin kinda puzzlin' me ... not that it matters a helluva lot, y'understand, but just f'the record – where the heck *are* we?'

Rossiter laughed. 'You're in London, Mister Martino.'

Lush's ruby eyes widened. 'No kiddin'! London, hm? Say ... could you tell me where a fella might find a li'l snort around here?'

'Sure – at the airport. You can have one as soon as we hit the Departure Lounge.'

'Oh ... we flyin' somewhere?'

'Yes.'

'Where?'

'I dunno.'

Lush nodded understandingly. 'Tha's good enough for me.'

He entered the coach, crooning, 'I've got plen'y of bourbon ... an' bourbon's plan'y for me-e. Got a glass ... I got some ice ... I'm in good compan-eeee ...'

Up came Shag McGee and the group, not forgetting, of course, Marlon.

'Hi, captain,' said Shag. 'Say – pretty fancy threads you're wearin'.'

'Glad yuh like 'em,' scowled Rossiter. 'Now, lissen, you keep that parrot under control during the flight or I'll have to lock him in a cupboard. He can't go around bitin' birds on the boobs, it ain't healthy.'

'Don't worry, I told him that ... told him he gotta stick to grapes. I reckon he thought that's what it was. I think he's short-sighted.'

'Maybe it'd help if you took that patch off his eye,' suggested Rossiter.

'An' ruin his image? Don't worry, I'll watch out for him.'

'Knickers!' screeched Marlon.

The group climbed aboard.

Now, finally, the crew emerged from the hotel, the girls unchanged, since their see-through plastic skirts had fortuitously been unaffected by the Trafalgar soaking. But the four men resembled the kitchen night staff coming off duty, Bush McKenzie looking particularly preposterous in a set of whites three sizes too small for him.

'And v-e-r-y smart, too,' sneered Rossiter. 'A credit to the airline, every one of you. But a word of warning – watch out for Camembert – he may attack on sight in a fit of jealousy.'

'Aw, come on, skip...' groaned McKenzie. 'I can't wear this clobber. I can't even sit down!'

'Then fly it standing up.'

'I *refuse* to disembark at our next stop, and that's all there is to it,' sniffed James. 'I will not be seen dead in this ... this ...' Words failed him.

'Well, you won't have to,' said Rossiter comfortingly. 'I have Arnold Bottum's word that he'll get Berskin to fly new uniforms to our next drop down. They'll be waitin' there when we arrive.'

James brightened. 'Really!'

'Thank *heaven* for that,' tutted Sugar Sweetman. 'I mean, *how* can I possibly steward an aircraft looking like a Walthamstow fish-fryer?'

Ramjet's brow beetled thoughtfully. 'Now, how in heck is Berskin gonna manage *that*? Even supposing he's got spare uniforms already made – which, knowing him, he could have – and even if he hasn't, he'd damn-well get them made in an hour – but even supposing that, how's he going to get them out to our next drop down before ... we ... get ...'

His voice tailed away as enlightenment dawned.

'Precisely,' nodded Rossiter with a crooked smile. 'It means we're in for a long haul, fellas – possibly . . .' a glance at Bush, '. . . Australia?'

'Aussi!' cried McKenzie, exploding the shoulder seams of his jacket. '*Oho!* Lads . . . !' he smacked his soup-plate hands together, '. . . stand by for a tiny riot . . . !'

'Now, hold on, hold on, McKenzie,' cautioned Rossiter. 'We don't *know* it's Australia, we're only guessing. And even so, you can can that riot idea. We've had enough bloody riot-ing on this stop-over to last us six world tours. From now on the behaviour of the Glamour crew and guests is gonna be sedate, circumspect, and entirely above suspicion – get it!'

'Of course, skip, of *course* . . . anything you say, skip, natur-ally,' grinned McKenzie, winking at Ramjet and James. 'Wee hee . . . Sydney, here we come!'

'McKenzie, will yuh cut that out!'

'Certainly, skip, this very minute – absolutely.'

'OK . . . here comes Bottum for his farewell kiss. Get on board you lot . . .'

As they climbed up into the coach, McKenzie whispering *sotto voce* regalements of the delights of Sydney's night-life to Ramjet and James, Rossiter went to meet the approaching Bottum whose bearing resembled that of a jockey who'd just fallen off a 100-to-1 winner three yards from the finishing post.

'Cheer up, Bottum,' said Rossiter, 'it coulda bin worse . . . though off-hand I can't think how. Maybe we'll have more luck in the next place. We sure as hell couldn't have less.'

'Failure is *not* a joyous event,' Arnold replied glumly. 'Per-haps it's better that you don't see the mid-day papers.'

Rossiter nodded. 'You can say that again. Ignorance bein' bliss, I intend to remain ecstatic. Well, so long, Bottum . . . give my love to Berskin. Handle it as you like, I don't care, but don't forget those uniforms, hm?'

'I won't forget. Goodbye, captain . . .'

Rossiter shook the limp hand then swung aboard the coach. 'OK, Sterling, take it away . . . so long, Bottum – see you in the dole queue. And if you're ever passing through New York . . . do yourself a big favour an' keep going!'

213

With a glimmer of a smile, Arnold waved them off, watched them out of sight, then, with a sigh, turned back into the hotel.

Entering the foyer, he crossed to the news-stand, slowing nervously as he approached the piles of mid-day papers displayed there. His eyes widened ... chin dropped. Staring apoplectically at the assorted headlines, he drew copies from each mound, absently handed over the money, gasped a shocked, 'My ... *God*!' and rushed from the foyer, out to the taxi rank.

Fifteen minutes later, from his New Bond Street office, he was booking a call to New York. And learned with no sense of relief whatever that there would be a one-hour delay.

18

Time: 3 p.m.

Place: The cockpit of *Glamour Puss*.

Occasion: Captain's and Co-pilot's Pre-Start Check.

Those present: Captain Cock-up Rossiter, First Officer Paul Rogers and Second Officer James Crighton-Padgett. Engineer Officer Morton McKenzie being stationed below on the tarmac conducting his own Engineer Officer's Pre-Start Check of the fuselage and landing gear.

'Aaaawwww!' With a heart-felt groan, Rossiter lowered himself into the captain's seat, fell forward onto the control column, and cuddled it lovingly. Aw, baby . . . baby. I tell you, you guys, I never thought I'd ever be so damn glad to see this hunk of metal. It's a sight for sore eyes.' He sat erect again and heaved a settling sigh. 'Well, let's get through the Pre-start and the hell outta here – where*ever* we're goin'.'

Ramjet, in the adjoining seat, nodded in agreement. 'Ready when you are, skip. Well, we've got an easterly heading, so it could be Australia.'

'You know something, Rogers – I don't damn-well care! Just so long as we get our rubber off this particular runway, I don't give a sweet damn if we spend the rest of this tour circling Mullagalloolibani!'

Behind him, James frowned. 'Where's that, skip?'

'Aw, shut up, Crighton-Padgett . . . and instead of sitting there pretending you're necessary to this tour, why don't you get back there and give Sweetman a hand sorting the animals out?'

'Why, *certainly*, skip,' James agreed readily, believing it was about time he re-made contact with Miss Billy Jo Labinovitch, his in-flight stand-by.

'And leave the dames alone!' snarled Rossiter. 'They've caused me enough grief on the ground ta last eight life-times, I don't want another load in the air!'

Exit James, grinning.

'OK, Rogers . . .' sighed Rossiter, consulting his Check List. 'Here we go, Brisbane or bust . . . radio buses . . .'

Ramjet raised an arm to the roof and manipulated the master switches. 'One and two are . . . on.'

'Flight recorder . . .'

'Tested. Guard closed.'

'Anti-skid . . .'

'Off . . . four black tabs showing.'

'Spoiler by-passes . . .'

'Guard closed.'

'Doppler . . .'

Lord Jim closed the cockpit door behind him and entered the mayhem of Sweetman's world, a pushing, crushed, babbling profusion of humanity, exchanging excited chatter, stowing away their hand-luggage, choosing their seats, changing their minds – and in the midst of it all – Sugar, Babs, and Wilma.

'No, *no*, Miss Wattle, you can *not* sit on a bar-stool while we're taking off. Now, be a good girl and strap yourself in your proper seat . . .'

James came up behind Sugar and chuckled, 'Need any help?'

'Ooh, *honestly*, James, this lot is the absolute end! They've all been at it in the Departure bar . . . and *this* one's as tight as a tick!'

'Cooee, young man!' trilled Minnie, still clutching the bar determinedly. 'Would you be so *very* kind and pour me a brandy . . . for my nerves, you know.'

James grinned. 'Sorry, Miss Wattle, no drinks until we're

up in the air.'

'Oh ... aren't we up yet? I could've sworn I felt the floor tilt just now.'

'See what I mean!' hissed Sugar.

'Steward!' demanded Gloriana Fullbrush. 'I need a pillow!'

'Yes,' muttered Sugar, 'and I know where you need it, too – over your face! Coming, Miss Fullbrush! Now, Miss Wattle, *please* let go of the bar and take your seat...'

'Won't!'

'*Please...!*'

'No!'

'I'll have to tell the captain...'

'Tell him – see if I care.'

'Aw, Miss Wattle...'

James left Sugar to it and pushed his way through the mêlée to Miss Billy Jo Labinovitch of the Tennessee Tatler, momentarily seated alone, the sight of the big, bronzed, brown-haired Amazon stirring him anew and causing him to wonder why he'd bothered with the treacherous Delphinia when this adorable creature had been ready, willing, and available.

'Hi, there!' he smiled, devastating her with his blue eyes and flashing teeth.

'Shove off,' she replied, tossing her chestnut mane.

'Eh? Hey ... what's this, Billy Jo...?'

'What's this, Billy Jo,' she mimicked. 'As if you didn't know. I thought we were getting it together in London, James? Hell, I haven't had so much as a dirty look from you since we landed!'

'Aw, baby, I'm sorry ... but I've been pretty tied up, you know.'

'You deserve to be – then shot! What's with you fly guys? There's Pat Pell over there, eating her heart out. That muscular moron McKenzie promised to take her for a work-out and a sauna and didn't do a damn thing about it ... and Delores Delores – you *know* she's got goosebumps for Rogers...'

'Honey, listen to me – it was the schedule! It was so darned tight we hardly had time to breathe! Aw, I'm sorry, believe me .. d'you think we *wanted* to spend all that time with the press instead of swinging with you girls?'

'Well...' she said hesitantly.

'Of *course*, we didn't. Now, listen...' he lowered his voice secretively, '... we're expecting a pretty long haul this time – maybe twenty four hours. What d'you say you and I get together for a ... tête-à-tête later on tonight – after lights out, hm?'

'Well...'

'Tell you the story of my life – exclusive!'

'You ... think you can make it?' she asked, softening.

'Can I *make* it!'

'OK,' she grinned, eyes twinkling. 'I'll have my ... pencil sharpened – ready and waiting.'

He gave a filthy chuckle. 'Me, too.'

Time: Almost 4 p.m.

Arnold Bottum, deeply ensconced in the Evening Standard, jumped as his telephone rang. Pausing for a steadying intake of breath, he reached with trembling hand for the instrument and brought it to his ear.

'Y .. yes?'

'I have New York on the line,' announced his secretary.

Arnold gulped. 'R .. right, put them through, Miss Monk. Hello ...?'

'That you, Bottum!' Berskin's bark caused Arnold to flinch. 'Berskin here! Whatcha got for me?'

'Colonel...' quavered Arnold, drawing the scattered newspapers towards him, '... a consummate ... unqualified ... success!'

'No kidding!' cried Berskin. 'Then it worked!'

'Like a dream, Colonel, like a dream! We've hit the front page in every southern mid-day paper – huge pics ... banner headlines...!'

'And ... sympathetic?'

'Just as you told it, colonel – almost word for word! Here's the Standard ... "Pranksters Play Cruel Hoax on New Airline – Stolen Uniforms Used in Tasteless Practical Joke"...'

'Beautiful ... beautiful! Go on...'

'The Evening News... "Glamour Airlines Victim Of Student Hoax?" question mark. "Political Envy Not Ruled Out In Mock Suicide Plot"...'

'Fantastic!' bellowed Berskin.

'They're all the same, colonel ... unqualified sympathy for the airline and venomous censure for the unknown perpetrators. No stigma attached to Glamour whatsoever. Colonel, I take my hat off to you, the glory is all yours.'

'Well, that's nice of yuh, Bottum – but a lotta credit goes to you and the girls as well. Tell them there's a bonus of five hundred in it for them – and an extra thousand for yourself.'

'Colonel, I'm overwhelmed ... it really has been the greatest fun setting it up, and...' a laugh, '... I know the *girls* found it no great sacrifice! It was an opportunity to really flex one's PR muscles – and it's certainly done my reputation no harm.'

'You're a good man, Bottum. Send me the cuttings and a full report as fast as you can. Anything else, now?'

'Oh, yes! We got more press mileage out of the photographic session in Trafalgar Square today – a real bonus. Everybody fell in the fountain! I'm afraid ...' Bottum paused until Berskin's uproarious laughter abated.

'Oh, Bottum, you're too damn much.'

'Well, it wasn't strictly my doing, colonel ... Marlon, the parrot, takes credit for that. But I'm afraid the crew's uniforms were ruined – shrank abysmally. I had to fix them up with kitchen whites for the flight. I told them you'd have replacement uniforms waiting for them at the next stop.'

'No sweat there, Bottum, I'll have them run up and shipped out by tonight. Well, I guess *Glamour Puss* is on her way now, huh?'

Bottum consulted his watch. 'Yes, sir, should be taking off just about now.'

'Fine, fine. Well, congratulations again – and a pat on the head for the girls. Tell 'em I'll look them up when I'm in London and thank them kinda personally.'

'I'll do that, colonel ... well, goodbye, now.'

'So long Bottum.'

Grinning gleefully, Arnold replaced the receiver, rubbed his hands together, then leaned to the intercom and prodded a button.

His secretary answered. 'Yes, sir?'

'Miss Monk ... enter with pad and pencil, if you please, there's a covering letter for Colonel Berskin.'

'Certainly, sir.'

A moment later the door opened and in walked a smiling Annabel Bear. 'Was he pleased?'

'Ec-static!' laughed Arnold. 'Oh – *please* be seated, Miss Monk ... I'm sure you're in need of the rest.'

19

And at that precise moment:

'London Tower...' droned Rossiter, 'this is GA 427 requesting clearance for take-off.'

A brief pause.

'Roger, 427, you are clear to go. Bon voyage and happy landings, *Glamour Puss* – and if it's Rome, watch out for the Trevi Fountain!'

'Smartass,' growled Rossiter. He turned his head. 'OK – everybody set?'

'All set, skip.'

'Then let's get the hell outta ...'

'Quite a crowd on the waving bay, skip,' remarked James. 'Quite a touching little send-off. Ha! – let's hope we don't have another ignominious departure – like we had in New York!'

'Crighton-Padgett, shut up! I tell you right now, we're not going through *that* again! Once we start rolling – we go! I don't care if the fucking wheels fall off half-way down the runway, I am not stopping for anything!'

'As you say, skip.'

'Yeh – as I say, skip! Now, if we've all finished with the social pleasantries, I will endeavour to get this candy-striped lunatic asylum inta the air!'

'Certainly, skip – be my guest.'

'Thank you, Crighton-Padgett, OK, here we go ... we are rolling!'

'Hold it, 427!' commanded the tower.

'*What ...!*' gasped Rossiter, slamming on the brakes and bringing the plane to a shuddering halt. '*Now* what's gone wrong?'

'Why, captain...' tutted the tower operator, 'how very remiss. It seems you've gone and left one of your passengers behind.'

'Aaaaggghhhtttfff!' choked Rossiter. 'The *hell* I have!'

'We have a Mister Vincent Martino in Departure expressing a distinct, though somewhat incoherent desire to join you. I wonder if you'd be so kind as to taxi back to us...?'

'Oh ... BOLLOCKS!' bellowed Rossiter.

'Hee hee, here we go again,' chuckled James. 'Oh, what a *great* impression we're making on the world of aviation...'

'Crighton-Padgett ... SHUT UP!' roared Rossiter, shoving the throttle controls forward. 'Just ... bloody SHUT UP!'